For the first time that evening, Beth seemed unguarded. Happy. Hopeful.

And she was definitely one hot and sexy lady. But as much as Daniel wanted to do something about that, he recalled her description of how she hadn't liked the way some men had seduced her in the past.

He wouldn't give her that impression, no matter what he felt. How stirred his body felt by her curves, her newly relaxed demeanor.

Her unintentionally seductive moves.

Sexy? Yes. But he knew what a bad idea it was to give in to those urges—even if she started to encourage him.

Her face looked radiant, as if he had solved all her problems and given her her life back.

Hell, that was his ultimate goal.

His current goal?

To leave and ponder how he might be able to use her to accomplish his task.

But she was looking up at him expectantly. And it wouldn't hurt just to give her an encouraging goodbye kiss....

Dear Reader,

Witness protection programs are generally for witnesses. And, sometimes, their families, too. But under those programs, the person receiving protection and a new identity should be able to provide evidence, which may be eyewitness testimony, at the trial of someone being prosecuted for a crime.

But what if a person knows enough to be certain that the suspect did, in fact, commit a crime—but didn't see it or has no ability other than to point fingers, and cannot provide any evidence to prosecute that suspect? And what if the suspect then threatens that person for coming forward? That person needs protection, too—and the system should also have a way of finding evidence to bring down the bad guy.

That's the background of the ID Division of the U.S. Marshals Service that I created for *Covert Attraction*. In it, the woman whose identity was changed and the undercover operative looking for that evidence both clash—and find their mutual attraction irresistible.

I hope you enjoy *Covert Attraction*. Please come visit me at my website, www.lindaojohnston.com, and at my weekly blog, killerhobbies.blogspot.com. And, yes, I'm on Facebook, too.

Linda O. Johnston

COVERT ATTRACTION

Linda O. Johnston

HARLEQUIN® ROMANTIC SUSPENSE

Recycling programs
for this product may
not exist in your area.

ISBN-13: 978-0-373-27852-7

COVERT ATTRACTION

Printed in U.S.A.

www.Harlequin.com

Books by Linda O. Johnston

Harlequin Romantic Suspense

Undercover Soldier #1714
Covert Attraction #1782

Harlequin Nocturne

Alpha Wolf #56
Back to Life #66
Alaskan Wolf #102
Guardian Wolf #118
Undercover Wolf #154

*Alpha Force

LINDA O. JOHNSTON

loves to write. More than one genre at a time? That's part of the fun. While honing her writing skills, she started working in advertising and public relations, then became a lawyer...and still enjoys writing contracts. Linda's first published fiction novel appeared in *Ellery Queen's Mystery Magazine* and won a Robert L. Fish Memorial Award for Best First Mystery Short Story of the Year. It was the beginning of her versatile fiction-writing career. Linda now spends most of her time creating memorable tales of paranormal romance and mystery.

Linda lives in the Hollywood Hills with her husband and two Cavalier King Charles spaniels. Visit her at her website, www.lindaojohnston.com.

This book is dedicated to those in danger,
and those in love.

And, as always, I dedicate this book to my
wonderful husband, Fred.

Chapter 1

Beth Jones slowly pushed a large heavy cart filled with janitorial equipment and supplies through a second-floor hallway at the Corcoris Pharmaceuticals headquarters. Good thing she'd joined a gym and worked out a lot during her last job as an online magazine and newspaper proofreader in Seattle. Otherwise, this part of her new position as a member of the company's cleaning team would have been a lot harder.

Stopping, she pulled her primary cell phone out of her pocket and glanced at it. She'd put it on silent, so she wasn't surprised that she'd missed another call. That made four. Plus, there were a couple of text messages that said the same thing: Call me.

She intended to call Judge Treena Avalon back. But not till later—or maybe tomorrow.

She'd delay contacting Her Honor—for now. After

their earlier brief conversation, Beth had anticipated the intense response she'd been getting.

But she had work to do. As she'd initially intended when she got out her phone, she moved her gaze toward the time: 8:30 p.m. This floor, filled with labs where they mostly did testing for quality control, should be empty of personnel. So should most of those containing offices, but Beth had no intention of going there, at least not tonight.

Then there was that other building on the company's grounds, where machinery blended and formed the pills that were transported via an automated assembly line to other machines that stuck them into containers. The job she had taken on here didn't give her the ability to check it out, at least not yet.

It didn't matter. She believed she would be able to find what she needed in this building.

She had been instructed on what her cleaning obligations would be when she started work here five days ago. She'd seen it all before—but from a far different perspective. That was when she had worked here to publicly laud Corcoris, its outstanding pharmaceuticals and its incredibly efficient and marvelous procedures.

Before she knew differently.

She'd been another person then. In many ways. The thought made her smile ironically, but not for long. And she didn't stop. She had a lot to accomplish tonight.

She inhaled, smelling both the fresh aromas of the antiseptic products in her cart and the subdued scents of the medicinal ingredients in the labs beyond the closed metal doors around her. The floor where she walked was composed of linoleum that had been washed last night and this morning by others who had her same job. It would be her turn in a little while.

First she had to clean portions of the labs on either side of her. They should yield at least part of what she was looking for. She'd start with the one on her right. She opened that door.

The lights were on in what they called the clean room. She looked around but saw no one. Good.

Even so, she hesitated, but only for an instant. She wouldn't allow nervousness to slow her down. She had a logical reason to be here even if anyone saw her.

Steeling up her determination, she entered, pushed the cart against the wall, then shut the door behind her.

The first room was where everyone who came to this lab had to change into pristine sanitary garb, even the cleaning staff. *Especially* the cleaning staff.

She went to the shelves along the wall and plucked from a pile the aqua smock and slacks that would fit over her beige jeans and T-shirt with the Corcoris Cleaning Staff logo on it. She put them on, then grabbed a matching vinyl cap to put over her raven-black pixie-cut hair, plus covers she donned over her shoes. Last she pulled a pair of sanitary gloves from a box and put them on. At least for what she did, she didn't have to wear a mask.

She then grabbed not the cart she had come in with but a second one with essentially the same equipment. The one kept here was removed periodically by other members of the staff and blasted with sanitizers to ensure its purity, as much as possible. Seemed like an oxymoron to Beth—sanitary cleaning equipment. But that was the way things were done around here.

On the surface, it looked as if the procedures took care of all ills.

She knew better.

Finally, Beth was ready. Using one gloved hand, she

pushed the lever down on the metal door to the inside lab, then got ready to shove the sanitary cart inside.

This one was as heavy as the other cart. She knew that. This was the third time already that she had had the assignment of cleaning the most pristine labs on this floor, which she had volunteered to do. Not that most people on her shift worked this late. But despite being part of the daytime staff, she'd been able to manage it—this once, at least.

She wasn't certain yet what she was looking for, but she knew that whatever she needed to discover was hard evidence of the fraud being committed by Corcoris in the blending and selling of its pharmaceuticals.

Would she find anything at all of use tonight?

Security cameras were posted inside the lab, so she couldn't just snoop around, examine samples, then grab them.

At least she couldn't do it obviously. But people expected the cleaning crew to insert themselves into nearly all parts of an area to scrub them. *Nearly* was the key word. She'd already been warned about the kinds of equipment that were off-limits, cleaned by the techs as they used them.

She was new here, though, and if she happened to make a mistake or two, go too far—

"Hello." A deep male voice from behind her startled Beth. She pivoted, heart pounding, her hand instinctively going to her throat as she gasped.

The man who stood there was tall. Why hadn't she seen him? Heard him? His outfit was white, indicating that he was one of the technicians who worked here, not part of the cleaning staff. His blue eyes stared at her through large black-rimmed glasses. She couldn't see much of his face through the white mask that covered its lower half, but he immediately pulled that down.

Unlike her, he didn't wear a plastic cap, and she could see that his hair was a pale shade of brown that reminded her of amber ale. It was straight and hung a bit over his forehead. His jaw was angular, his smile wide, and his shoulders broad beneath his jacket.

"Hi," Beth managed to say, trying to smile just a little despite her still-quivering nerves—and her dismay. She wouldn't accomplish anything here tonight, at least nothing she wanted to do.

Cleaning, yes.

Snooping, no.

"Sorry I startled you," the man said, still grinning airily as if that was part of his job. It gave the impression he was a friendly geek. He was probably harmless—and definitely good-looking. "I was just finishing up a test. You're here to clean?"

Beth nodded, then made herself look down at the floor as if she were shy.

She'd taken on a whole new personality over the past year, assuming one that appeared quiet and uncomfortable around people. That made her appear well suited to do something that was often solitary, like proofreading—or being a member of the cleaning staff.

"You can start over there, if you'd like." He pointed with his gloved hand toward the far wall, where shelves filled with sealed boxes labeled Beakers and Test Tubes and other items used for testing scaled the walls. Beneath them was a counter with several large metallic microscopes and some testing machinery she couldn't identify.

"Thanks," she whispered, and edged by him.

She felt his eyes boring into her as she passed, and her shoulders cringed.

"I'm Daniel McManus," he said. "Lab tech extraordinaire."

She nodded, but that clearly wasn't enough.

"And you are…?" he pushed.

She turned partway back toward him. "Beth Jones," she said in a raspy voice. "Cleaning crew…ordinary." She hesitated. "I think it would be better if I left and came back later."

"No need to run. I'm finishing up here soon."

"But—"

"Really. It's fine." He turned away from her.

She considered ducking out anyway. But if he really wasn't going to be here long, she could observe some of the procedures he used—and then get to work doing what she really wanted to once he left.

She grabbed the handles of her cart and pushed it along the outer aisle toward the destination he'd pointed out to her. Time to get to work…cleaning.

Pretty lady, Daniel thought. Or so he believed from the little he could see of her. Violet eyes that glistened from beneath that silly, supposedly sanitary, hat she wore. High cheekbones and full lips that she sucked in as if to hide how lovely they were.

He couldn't see her figure beneath the loose clothing but she seemed slender, of medium height.

Beth Jones. He would add her to the list of people here he was investigating, out of an abundance of caution. He didn't really envision cleaning staff as being among those who had banished quality control in exchange for profits at Corcoris Pharmaceuticals. But he'd been in different areas of law enforcement long enough to know he couldn't trust anyone.

He shot another goofy smile toward Beth Jones to

maintain his cover, since she seemed to be watching him out of the corners of those gorgeous eyes as she removed a bucket and paper towels from that unwieldy cart she'd been pushing. Her head turned swiftly as if she was embarrassed at being caught, and she immediately began removing boxes from one of the topmost shelves and placing them on the gleaming metal counter below.

He imagined what might be beneath those unisex clothes as she reached up and began cleaning.

His genuine smile, as he turned back toward the microscope he'd been using, was at his own folly. He'd been here for not quite a month, acting friendly and like a techie nerd. His closest contacts to date were others who conducted quality-control tests in this lab as a backup to the tests run in the manufacturing facility on the Corcoris campus.

His targets included those people, somewhat. But his eyes were more often on the company's muckety-mucks. He'd also had some limited success hacking into their computer files.

Nothing especially useful so far, but he had time.

He smelled the cleaning fluid that Beth Jones was using across the room and glanced toward her. She seemed busy scrubbing that shelf. Not watching him or anything else. Even so, he'd learn more about her. Soon.

Feeling a vibration in his pocket, he took off one glove and yanked out his ultra-smartphone. This was neither the time nor place to talk to his caller, but he'd return the call later—and ask some more questions since he didn't yet have all the answers.

He sent the caller into his voice mail. He took a fresh glove from the box and put it on, then pulled his mask up and got busy working on the formulation he was supposed to be analyzing via the microscope.

Interesting work here.

Too bad it wasn't really what he did.

Except...maybe he could accomplish something. He pulled the slide he was using out and put it aside. Then he crossed the room and approached Beth Jones. "Why don't I help you?" he said, pulling his mask below his chin again.

She stopped scrubbing and stared with a gaze that reminded him of the proverbial deer in the headlights. "Oh. No. I'm fine."

"I said I'd help you." He grabbed another bottle of cleaning solution and pulled paper towels off the roll she had put down on the counter.

"No. Really. I—"

"Don't argue with me. Just take advantage. You'll be able to get out of here sooner." He didn't act like the nice geeky guy he usually did but made his tone curt. He wanted to unnerve her to see what she'd do, how she'd act.

"I'd better just go," she said again.

"And I said no."

She looked almost fearful now, the way she stared at him. He shrugged off the pang of guilt. It was just another method of investigation.

But he hadn't really wanted to scare her.

"I'm a pretty good cleaner when I want to be," he said more winningly. "And I want to be. Let me help."

She said nothing but turned away.

And Daniel got to work scrubbing the far end of the shelf below the one she was working on—keeping his attention more on her than on what he was doing.

He continued silently for about three minutes. Telling himself that he wasn't doing his job by just observing her—as pleasant as that might be—he said, "I don't think I've seen you before. Have you been working here long?"

"No." The briefness of her reply made it even clearer that she didn't want to talk.

"I'm new to this area," he said. "I've only been here about a month, but I think California's Orange County is great, and I love this town—Moravo Beach. Don't you?" No response except the briefest of nods as she scrubbed the shelf even harder. "Are you from around here?" he persisted.

"No," she said. Again, she volunteered nothing extra.

"I didn't set out to go into the pharmaceutical industry," he said, "but I majored in chemistry in college. Even got my master's degree in it, so this is a really good opportunity for me."

As he said this, Daniel realized he might be boxing himself into a corner with his partial lies. What could she respond to that? She was part of the cleaning staff. As attractive and intelligent as she looked, it was possible that she'd never even finished high school, let alone got any higher degree. If he wanted her to relate to him, to divulge information about herself, he was going about it all wrong.

"But I really don't want to talk about myself," he continued. "Like I said, I find this area really great. Do you like to go to the beach?"

"Sometimes," she said.

"Great! We'll have to go there together one of these days."

Her glance at him suggested that she was astounded. "I don't think so. I'm not… I mean, I do as much overtime work as I can. I need the money."

There was something in the way her lips flattened for the briefest moment that suggested she wasn't lying and that she felt ashamed by her situation. Even so, her eyes looked at him almost challengingly—for a short enough time that he could have imagined it.

Or at least he could have if he weren't an operative skilled in investigation and well trained to read people and their body language. Although he could just be looking for signals to give himself a reason to continue to press her.

"Got it." He kept his tone light. "We all do what we gotta do." He paused. "Would you like me to let you know if I hear of any better-paying job opportunities?"

She stopped scrubbing and stood looking at him. "You know, Daniel, if I didn't know better, I'd think you were trying to flirt with me."

He laughed aloud. "I didn't think I was that obvious." No, he was being even *more* obvious. Although not for the reasons she thought. At least not entirely. He didn't want to find this woman, who was dressed in the least sexy outfit he could imagine, at all seductive…and yet she somehow was. "So…how about if we go out for lunch one of these days and you can tell me how a beautiful woman like you wound up cleaning shelves instead of… say, modeling?"

That way, he'd be able to pick her brain even more. He wanted to believe she was what she appeared to be, but his gut told him there was a lot beneath the pretty dark hair of hers that she was hiding.

Would talking to her more help him to gain any of the knowledge he sought at this company?

Unlikely, but someone who could push a cleaning cart around and show up in practically any corner of the large pharmaceuticals company might have observed things that could be useful to him. He'd have to figure out a subtle way to get her to reveal anything she knew.

That seemed as good an excuse to himself as any for getting to know all he could about sexy Beth.

"Oh, but I chose to join the housecleaning staff." She sounded chilly now, as if he had insulted her. Maybe he had. "Now, if you'll excuse me." Her glare told him she was leaving right now, even if he *didn't* choose to excuse her.

Beth followed all the protocols she had been taught in the few days she had worked here to reorganize and sanitize the items she had used on the special cleaning cart, then strip off her sanitary gear and place it in the correct receptacles in the clean room.

She felt she could only start breathing again once she was outside the door with her original cart. It was almost a relief to duck into the ladies' room to fill a pail with water, then pour in the normal kind of cleaning fluid and go back out to start mopping the floor.

Never in her life had she believed she would ever take a job cleaning a building, let alone enjoy it. Sort of. But at least at this moment it was a relief to be out of the presence of that man, Daniel.

Under other circumstances, she might have found him cute, she realized as she pushed the mop back and forth across the floor. More than cute. In fact, he was one good-looking man, which she'd realized as soon as he pulled his face mask down. He had come across as a bit of a geek at first—a techie, scientific sort. And yet his flirtation wasn't geeky at all.

Plus, he had gotten in her way. She'd pondered whether she could flirt back and use his apparent interest in her to extract knowledge.

Instead, she knew it was better that she stay cautious.

Avoid that guy from now on—although she couldn't really know in advance if she'd run into him on the job.

Unless… She paused with the mop handle in her hand and stared at the floor she had dampened.

Maybe it could be a good thing to befriend a lower-echelon member of the lab staff. Without giving herself away, could she use him to help find what she was looking for?

Interesting idea. She needed to ponder whether it could work and how she could use it before attempting to implement it. But for now, she started moving again, even faster than before. She would finish scrubbing this hall as quickly as she could, before Daniel McManus exited the lab.

If she decided to try to exploit him, she was sure she would see him here again.

Chapter 2

It was past 9:30 p.m. when Daniel finally got into his car to drive the few miles on city streets to the small apartment he rented. The place, a few blocks from the beach, was the one perk he allowed himself here.

He was getting paid to be a lab assistant while on this undercover assignment. But he had to turn his wages from Corcoris Pharmaceuticals over to the government to ensure he had no conflict of interest.

No worries, though. He was also being paid by the U.S. Marshals Service as part of its relatively new Covert Investigations Unit within the Identity Division.

He drove under streetlights along four-lane roads in the heart of the Moravo Beach business district, watching his mirrors by habit to ensure he wasn't being followed.

As he neared his rental unit, it was finally time to return the message he'd received while in the lab. Never mind that it would be after midnight on the East Coast, where he'd be calling. There were no fixed working hours in his job, or in the job of the person whose call he needed to return.

He'd considered finding a way to return it sooner. Judge Treena Avalon, who had founded the ID Division as part of the U.S. Marshals Service, a Department of Defense agency, wouldn't have called him here if it hadn't been important.

The phone he used was state-of-the-art and secure. Even so, the judge would have known he could have been with someone who'd notice the call or even eavesdrop if he'd answered before.

Someone like Beth Jones, who might not be exactly what she seemed.

Stopped at a traffic light, Daniel pushed the button to activate the hands-free system within the car, then keyed in the number he had missed.

"Hello, Daniel." The judge's response was immediate, and her low, gravelly voice, which filled the car, confirmed that she was wide awake and waiting for his call.

"Hi, Judge. You're up late."

"No need to state the obvious. I had something to tell you."

"I figured. What's up?"

The light had changed, but Daniel waited a beat, again glancing around to ensure that the other cars in the intersection weren't keyed in to what he was doing. When he accelerated slowly, the car behind him passed.

"There's a potential hiccup there at Corcoris."

"Yeah?" Daniel's attention was immediately captured. "What's that?"

"You remember all I told you about the reasons for investigating the company." It was a statement, not a question, with good reason. His assignment had resulted from a situation that was central to the existence of the ID Division.

"I do," Daniel said. "What's up?"

Among her other functions within the Department of Justice, Judge Treena Avalon heard cases involving individuals who didn't qualify for witness protection but had legal issues that made it prudent for them to obtain new identities.

Once she'd begun functioning in that capacity, she'd made it clear to her superiors that even though there wasn't sufficient evidence to support criminal charges against those who'd put the petitioners in those actions into untenable positions, the situations they described often required further investigation—to allow someone else to collect enough evidence to prosecute.

Someone with the background and skills of Daniel.

His placement here had been the result of one of those ID petitions—one where a former employee of Corcoris had been threatened because of allegedly making claims that the pharmaceutical company was cutting corners and otherwise endangering the public with its medicines.

The whistle-blower's claims had gotten the attention of the U.S. Food and Drug Administration, but the FDA's initial surprise inspection had yielded nothing. Nor was there any other credible evidence against Corcoris...yet.

The whistle-blower had apparently heard from another reliable employee of Corcoris about some pretty horrible stuff—but she hadn't personally seen any of the wrongdoing, so she could not provide any useful eyewitness testimony. Nor had she gathered any physical evidence that could help convict anyone at the company. Nevertheless, the judge had believed her credible enough to help

change her identity—and to have an undercover operative of the CIU check things out here: Daniel.

If such evidence existed anywhere, Daniel would
grab it.

"Well," said the judge, "after I'd approved the case
of the individual involved there at Corcoris, her identity
was changed. She'd started her new life."

That was standard. However— "I hear a *but* in what
you're saying." Daniel turned the corner onto the block
that contained his apartment, only a few doors down. He
pulled up to the curb to avoid losing the call on entering
the underground parking garage.

"Exactly. I heard from her yesterday, and she hasn't
returned my calls since. She claimed that the person
who'd threatened her enough to make her require a new
identity hasn't backed off now that she's disappeared.
He's threatened her family, who lives there in Moravo
Beach. She's kept her new ID but has apparently gone
undercover on her own to gather whatever is necessary
to prosecute Preston Corcoris, the company's CEO, as
well as anyone who's helping him."

"Hell, that's what I'm doing."

"I know. And I'm afraid she'll get in your way. I've
been working on other avenues, but for now I need for
you to locate—and control—her."

Why was it that Daniel had a sinking feeling that he
had already met this woman?

"Wait a sec." He ran a test to confirm that their connection remained secure.

"Are we all right?" the judge asked a moment later.

"Yeah. Okay, now, tell me this person's name."

"As you were told previously, she used to be Andrea
Martinez. Her new identity? She's now known as Beth
Jones."

* * *

Beth sat in the driver's seat of the dark blue economy car she rented by the month here. At least it was small, so it didn't drink a lot of gasoline.

She was only halfway to the tiny efficiency apartment she also rented, in a small town inland from Moravo Beach. She had to make a call before heading to the lodgings she might laughably call home. *As if she had a home.*

She'd parked outside a convenience store with scads of activity going on around her for this time of night. A lot of strangers. No one she recognized and no one who'd likely recognize her even if she wasn't wearing the disguise that was her life these days.

Her mind returned to her "job." If she could fool everyone at Corcoris Pharmaceuticals with her disguise, she wouldn't worry about being found out by anyone else. And so far, so good.

She'd never met that Daniel McManus before, but she had been there for less than a week. He'd claimed to be new, too—only a month. He couldn't possibly know who she really was. He'd acted interested in her, but the guy was probably just flirting.

Under other circumstances, she might have felt more like flirting back. He might be a techie, but he was a good-looking one, and he'd seemed nice. Mostly.

But she couldn't—wouldn't—respond to any flirtation. She didn't dare get close to anyone no matter how lonely she felt. Use him and learn from him? Maybe. But that was all.

She pulled the special phone from the large purse she had bought at a thrift store. For now, she ignored her regular smartphone, the one that contained all the messages from Judge Treena. She wasn't prepared to return them. Not yet. It wasn't time to spend long minutes attempting to explain what she was doing to the kind but domineering woman who'd bent over backward to help her—but only the way Her Honor believed Beth needed help.

No, the call she needed to make would be even harder. Bittersweet. But she had to make it.

The phone she used now was a throwaway, a burner phone with limited minutes and a number that would be difficult, if not impossible, for anyone to trace. She stared at it for a few seconds, gathering her courage. And then she pressed in the number she had known for her entire life.

"Hello?" The familiar voice brought tears to Beth's eyes. No, Andrea's. For these few precious minutes, she would be Andrea again.

"Hi, Mom," she said.

"Oh, honey, I'm so glad to hear from you. Wait just a minute. Stan," she cried, "it's Andrea!"

In moments, her father, too, had joined the call. "Where are you?"

"You know I can't tell you." What would they think if they knew she was only a few miles away from them, from the home where she had grown up?

They didn't know where she had moved after she had changed her identity but were aware it was far away.

For the next few minutes, she exchanged pleasantries with them. Their conversation was mostly superficial, none of them daring to get into what they were all thinking about.

Danger.

But then she had to ask. "Have you made plans yet to go away for a while?"

"Yes, we're both taking some vacation time very soon."

"Don't tell me where you're going, but is it somewhere far from here? Someplace safe?"

"Of course. And we've been talking to those people you told us to, too. They call a lot and sometimes even have police stop by to check on us."

Those were security people who Judge Treena had assured Beth would be communicating with her family, keeping an eye on them, at least for now.

But it wouldn't be forever, Beth was sure. That was why she had to act fast to bring Corcoris down—and keep her family safe.

"And are Ned and his family okay?" She had to ask about her brother. He was involved, too.

"They're fine, Andrea," replied her mother.

Andrea again. It had been such a long time since she had thought of herself by her real name it no longer felt like her. She had truly immersed herself in her new identity. She wouldn't tell her family who she was, though. She couldn't.

"Are they also going away?"

"We think so." But her mother didn't sound convinced.

They talked for a few more minutes about Ned, his wife, Jo, and the kids. Despite her deep concerns about all of them, the conversation made Beth's heart swell, as if her family were safe and she were truly coming home.

But she knew how false that was.

Finally, she could wait no longer. For one thing, she couldn't stay where she was. Time to move on.

But she needed to know. "Mom, Dad, have there been any more calls?"

Neither responded immediately. Then her mother said, "Not calls, honey, but—"

"Letters, texts, whatever," interrupted her father. "Nothing's specific, though we reported it again to the cops and those other security people and they said they tried to trace the sources, but… Anyway, don't you worry about it. You just stay safe. We're being careful. We'll be fine."

She soon ended the call with them, wishing she could just start her car engine and dash the three or so miles to the home where she'd grown up. Hug her parents. Reassure them that she was going to fix things.

But if she simply showed up before they'd retreated to someplace safe, even temporarily, and she hadn't yet accomplished what she needed to do here…well, she wasn't certain whether any of them would survive.

Beth got out of the car quickly before she started crying. Inside the store, she bought a bottle of water and a lottery ticket. Maybe she'd win a dollar or two, and then she would know that her luck had changed.

Or not.

Time to go to the place she had to call home for now. And try to get at least a little sleep.

She managed to drive there in only another half hour. She'd been cautious again. No one seemed to follow her. No one called her. She used a security code to open the front door—one of the things that had attracted her to this place. When she went up the flight of steps to her second-floor unit, she paused. No neighbors were in the hall. And when she went inside, she saw nothing to worry her.

After locking her door, she turned on the TV, wanting to divert her mind from the fear that had brought her back here. Fear not for herself but for her family.

If she could be certain that simply turning herself over to the CEO of Corcoris would keep her parents and her brother and his family from danger, she'd do it.

But she knew better. Preston Corcoris would leave no loose ends.

Tomorrow. Maybe tomorrow she would at last find the evidence she could turn over to authorities to get Preston arrested.

Evidence she hoped to find in or around the lab.

The lab where, tonight, that Daniel had gotten in her way.

Well, she would have to ensure somehow that he wound up helping rather than hindering her. Otherwise, she would need to find a way to stay away from him.

A short while later she stood and pulled the bed out of her convertible sofa. She changed into her nightclothes and got under the covers, leaving the TV news on for a while.

But listening to the woes of everyone else in the world made her feel no better. She used the remote to turn it off.

If only she could turn off her mind as easily.

For a long time she just lay there.

Judge Treena had made promises a month ago when the threats to Beth's family had started. Or at least when Beth had learned about them from her reluctant parents in one of their rare phone calls.

Judge Treena. Beth hated that she pretended to ignore the one person who had genuinely attempted to help her. She would call the judge back. Maybe she would do that tomorrow, too.

Her parents had sounded okay, but how could they feel all right with what had been going on in their lives— thanks to Beth?

She needed to fix things. Fast. But she had doubts about how well things were progressing with her "job" at Corcoris. Was there any way to speed things up? Get help?

Yeah, right. Her notion about figuring out a way to use Daniel—or anyone else, for that matter—was just wishful thinking.

She sighed aloud and tried once more to sleep.

Chapter 3

A new day had begun. About time.

Beth decided to cast her sleepless night behind her and get down to business as soon as she reached the Corcoris offices.

If nothing else, her hours of tossing and turning over troubling thoughts had brought one thing back to her immediate attention.

She had no time to waste.

She got dressed and grabbed an apple from the fridge that she could eat in the car for breakfast. After driving the distance back to the headquarters building in traffic, she looked around the parking garage.

It was early enough that not many cars were there yet, and she saw the backs of only a few people heading for the doors into the office structure.

No sign of Daniel McManus. Not that she'd know

what his car looked like—but she absolutely would recognize him.

His handsome face was one of the thoughts that had haunted her mind all night.

That and her initial indecision about whether she dared to get to know him any better to see if there was some way of utilizing his position and knowledge.

But she had, sometime near dawn, focused on what she had told herself even before she arrived here: *Trust no one.*

No one except herself.

She grabbed her purse and slammed the car door behind her. This was a new day, she reminded herself. She had a lot to accomplish.

She headed straight toward the offices of the head housekeeping coordinator on the floor below the building's lobby. Beside the offices were the vast areas where cleaning carts and the equipment heaped onto them were stored.

Beth was greeted almost as soon as she stepped off the elevator by Mary Cantrera, the cleaning crew's supervisor. Mary had been there a lot longer than Beth's alter ego, Andrea, had worked for Corcoris.

Mary was in her forties, a short, physically fit woman who wore the usual cleaning-staff uniform of logo T-shirt and jeans as proudly as if she were still involved in scrubbing down the facility. Even if she wasn't very friendly to those she supervised.

Instead, she was the boss of that staff, consisting, Beth believed, of about a dozen people of both sexes and all ages. She'd been surprised to meet a couple of male senior citizens who'd apparently taken this on as their retirement jobs.

Not that she knew what they'd done before. Even with

her cleaning coworkers, Beth had kept to herself without engaging much in conversations since she had started here.

She didn't recognize those seniors, or many others on the cleaning staff, from when she—Andrea—had worked here before, either.

Only Mary. Starting to work for her that first day had felt like a major challenge. But the changes to Beth's hair color and style, her different-colored contact lenses, and the special makeup she had learned to apply skillfully to alter her face's skin tone and planes—thanks to the advisers Judge Treena had sent her to—not to mention an entirely different way of dressing, had obviously worked. So had the fact she had lost weight, although even with the workouts she had taken on that had been more from stress than intentional.

Neither Mary nor any others she'd known before and seen since her return knew who she was.

She needed to keep it that way.

"Good morning," she said to Mary in her assumed shy but cheerful persona.

The supervisor stood behind the counter near the storeroom door, checking out the equipment as each staff member collected gear for the day. She hardly looked up as she examined the cart Beth had chosen and ticked off items on her list. Maybe her concentration was one reason Mary hadn't recognized her. If so, Beth wouldn't ruin it by doing or saying anything out of the ordinary.

"I have you listed to start out today in the cafeteria's seating area," Mary said. She had a round face that had puckered with wrinkles since the time Beth had first met her a few years ago. Her curly hair had gone grayer, too, but Mary hadn't started dyeing it, just pushed it back with a bland tortoiseshell-colored headband. "Soon as you and the others have it ready for the breakfast crowd—the early birds are already there—you can head for the storage area on the lab floor."

Given her preference for anonymity, Beth would rather skip the cafeteria. But at least only the company's regular workers started the day there. The executives had their own dining area on the penthouse floor.

Beth hadn't cleaned anything at all upstairs and didn't want to, at least not officially or when anyone might be there. That was where she was most likely to be recognized.

"Thank you," she said to Mary as she started wheeling her cart toward the service elevator.

She wasn't the only one waiting there. Two others on the cleaning staff were ready to begin their days—Gabrielle Maroni and John Jansen. Gabrielle was a vivacious African-American youngster who'd just graduated from high school and said she was working here until she figured out what she really wanted to do with her life. She was new enough at the company that she'd never have met Andrea.

John had been around long enough for Andrea and him to have crossed paths, but she'd heard that the middle-aged man had lost his job in the film industry some time ago and needed this job to help support his wife and three kids. He wasn't the happiest person Beth had ever met, and she was glad for many reasons that he kept to himself.

Fortunately, the two of them were involved in a conversation when Beth pushed her cart toward them. Rather, Gabrielle was chattering away at John, who seemed more interested in scanning what was on his cart than conversing. Both of their carts fit into the service elevator when it arrived, but not a third. Beth got to wait for the next one by herself.

It came fairly soon, and she headed up to the third-floor cafeteria. The place wasn't too crowded, and both John and Gabrielle were already industriously polishing tables still empty of patrons. Beth quickly started to do the same.

She kept her head down as she worked but looked around surreptitiously.

This wasn't where she wanted to be. Nothing here would lead to the evidence she needed.

Neither would any of the personnel. Even so, she eavesdropped on as many conversations as possible without meeting anyone's eyes.

She saw a few familiar faces as people brought coffee and food to tables, ate quickly and left with their coffee cups. The smell of baking pastries and hot beverages was trumped near her by the sweet smells of cleaning fluids she used.

Beth particularly kept watch for Daniel McManus. With his friendliness yesterday, he might start talking to her if he happened to come in—both delaying her and calling attention to her.

Fortunately, he didn't arrive.

Eventually, the three of them had finished all areas of the cafeteria—good timing, since the room started to become more crowded as Corcoris Pharmaceuticals' main group of employees arrived for their midmorning breaks. The early breakfast crowd had come and gone long before.

Time for Beth to leave.

Without saying anything to her counterparts, she shoved her cart back to the service elevator and got on, pushing the button to go down a floor.

She wished she could just insert herself back into the lab where she'd been yesterday. By herself this time. She believed she might locate there at least something that could be used as the evidence she sought, assuming she would be able to recognize it. Samples of medications that contained different ingredients from the ones used for the quality-control tests submitted to the FDA? Maybe, but how would she know? Notes or computer printouts that showed that those medications had been changed somehow? That might be easier for her to recognize, but did people leave those lying around the sterile labs? Maybe not, but there were also labs that contained the workers' cubicles and computers.

Her next official assignment was to start cleaning a room where some experimental drugs and ingredients not yet available to the public were stored in large refrigerators. That was another possible source of evidence—again assuming she could determine what she was looking for.

But she had been back here only less than a week. She would look around, keep her eyes and ears open, and figure out exactly what she needed.

She carefully pushed her cart down the hallway toward the door to that storage room. A few people passed, mostly men and women in white jackets similar to the one Daniel McManus had been wearing yesterday—lab staff.

She kept her eyes averted. But she did manage to check out those around her to ensure Daniel wasn't among them.

When she reached the door, she felt almost disappointed. She hadn't seen the guy who'd gotten into her thoughts way too much.

She moved around the cart just enough to push the

door open. But before she returned to her position behind it, she heard, "Good morning, Beth."

It was that same deep masculine voice that had penetrated her psyche yesterday. Daniel's.

She swallowed, ducked her head a little as if attempting to muster her strength, then turned around. "Good morning," she said softly. She immediately looked away and started pushing the cart through the doorway—but not before getting a glimpse of that handsome, smiling face adorned with those large dorky glasses. Once inside, she turned to close the door—only to find that Daniel had followed her.

He looked serious now, which worried her. Where was that flirtation of yesterday?

Not that she wanted to flirt with him, but it had seemed generally friendly and unchallenging.

This unwavering stare of his blue eyes was a different story.

"We need to talk, Beth," he said. "Join me for an early lunch away from here."

It sounded like an order, not a request. She felt her insides tense up. She hated receiving orders. Prior orders, especially around here, had held a tacit threat behind them.

But she was safe, at least for now. She could say no. And that was exactly what she did.

"Sorry," she said. "I can't. I have to work in here and finish by midafternoon."

"We need to talk," he repeated, and she no longer had the sense that he was just some geeky lab rat. She couldn't help wondering now if he was, in fact, part of what she was here to address.

But talk to him at lunch about it? Alone? No. That couldn't happen.

"Maybe sometime," she said so as not to rile him. "But not now. I need to—"

Her throat closed up suddenly, preventing her from finishing.

Striding down the otherwise empty hall was Preston Corcoris.

She'd known she would see him here eventually, but he almost always stayed on the executive floors, sending his minions down here to ensure that all was occurring the way he intended.

He wouldn't know who she was. He couldn't. But knowing him, if he even noticed this subservient person who was now her and found her in the least attractive, he'd try seducing her.

Attempting not to be obvious, she slid around her cart and farther into the storeroom.

"Hey," Preston called. Was he addressing her?

Surely he couldn't be addressing her. What would she do?

He seemed to be heading toward her. She kept herself from crying out—or just crying. She wasn't Andrea Martinez, public relations star and object of his attempted seduction—and also potentially the person who would reveal to the world exactly who he was and what Corcoris Pharmaceuticals was becoming.

She was Beth Jones, meek and menial member of the cleaning staff. A no one.

"Mr. Corcoris, delighted to see you here, sir." That was Daniel, who stood blocking the doorway. "Were you coming to the lab for us to show you the latest results of our quality-control tests on the CorcoBiotica serum that'll be used in those new antibiotic capsules? I'm too new here to do it on my own, but I've been working with some of the other technicians. It's so cool. Our tests have shown that the upcoming formulation is probably more powerful than anything else on the market, and we've not found the slightest bit of contamination in any of the random vials we've checked out."

"Good work," Preston said, stopping to face Daniel. "Have you guys done any of the additional testing to determine how to avoid contamination occurring?"

"Just starting that, sir. I can show you our report so far on my computer if you'd like."

"No need. I'll send a message for Bert Jackson, our VP of products, to get in touch with you and the others down here when I get back upstairs. In fact, that's why I'm here. Have you seen him today?"

By that time, Beth had slipped even farther into the room and begun wiping the counters down with sterile rags dipped in antiseptic, staying out of the refrigerators that held important chemicals, so she didn't have to don protective gear in a clean room. The place smelled awful.

Shoulders braced, she waited for Preston to come in anyway. But he didn't.

Daniel told Preston he hadn't yet seen Jackson, another executive who might recognize her. She prayed he wasn't on this floor.

For now, she listened carefully to the conversation between the two men. It continued for a few more minutes while Daniel prattled on about another of the new pharmaceuticals that had been developed by some of the company's lead scientists, passed clinical trials with flying colors and was now starting to be available by prescription—supposedly the best and safest weight-loss medication ever.

Soon there was just silence. She listened for a while longer anyway.

Then she heard footsteps and pivoted to see the door. It was still open.

Daniel came in. There was again no dorkiness in his expression, but a serious stare.

"Come with me to lunch, Beth," he said. "We need to get away from here for now."

He again didn't make it sound like an invitation, but an order.

He might not know it, but she owed him.

And he was right. She did need to get away in case Jackson really was around here.

"Okay," she said. "Give me five more minutes to finish, and then I'll be ready."

Daniel had waited for fifteen minutes, since Beth had to return her equipment to the floor where it was stored.

After that he started driving to the restaurant where he had chosen for them to dine. And talk.

Discretion caused him to tell her to meet him there rather than to ride with him. It was some distance from Corcoris—and that was no accident.

Lab assistants here could undoubtedly fraternize with cleaning staff if they really wanted to. It wasn't against any rules he'd been told of, even though it might be frowned on.

But having anyone pay attention to his being with this woman was a bad idea.

She hadn't objected this time. He wasn't sure what her attitude would be when they started talking, but he had learned to read people of all sorts in his years in law enforcement.

She had first acted cool and indifferent and even a little miffed that he was trying to tear her away from her work.

But later, when Corcoris was gone, he had seen relief in her posture and in her lovely violet eyes.

He arrived at the nice-quality deli first and ensured that their table was in a corner.

She got there about five minutes later. He stood and waved, playing his smiley, friendly role as a techie lab guy.

She joined him, and he acted the gentleman, pulling out her chair. She still wore her jeans but had put a flowing blouse of pink-and-red pastel colors over her T-shirt. Not exactly dressy, but somewhat appropriate for an impromptu lunch out.

Or to hide that she wore a shirt with a cleaning-crew logo.

Once she was seated, he sat down, too. She had grabbed the menu, but he could tell she wasn't concentrating on it, not the way her gaze flowed over it.

In a moment, before he said anything to grab her attention, that gaze had rolled above the menu and on to him.

She seemed to breathe heavily. At least her lovely chest was pulsing so much that it made him sexually aware of her. Well, more sexually aware than he'd already been.

Her full lips pursed so enticingly for a moment that he had an urge to kiss them free from their tautness. But that moment passed.

She opened her mouth.

And asked, "Who are you really?"

Chapter 4

Gasping internally, Beth wished she could retract her words.

Not the thought. Oh, no. There was something about this man that didn't feel right. He wasn't the geeky lab guy she'd originally thought—the one that Corcoris apparently believed he was, too.

He had helped her when Corcoris had appeared, almost as if he knew who she really was and intended to keep her safe.

That couldn't be the case, and yet she felt he wasn't what he seemed any more than she was.

His reaction now wasn't what she'd have expected, either. He laughed aloud, but only for a few seconds. "I could ask you the same thing, Beth." He drew out her name as if he knew it wasn't her real one. Despite the mirth that radiated from his blue eyes beyond the confines of his glasses, there was an intensity in them that nearly made her stand and run away. Leave his presence as quickly as possible.

If this had been an actual date with someone she'd just met, she might actually have fled.

Especially since she'd felt a little reluctant to go to a restaurant at all—a public place where she might run into someone who'd known her before. But this one wasn't close to where she'd lived, and she had never been here before. Plus, she trusted her new ID, including how she looked, at least somewhat.

Besides, leaving here wouldn't work. She would see Daniel again at the pharmaceutical company, and she couldn't flee the job that provided at least some camouflage while she sought the evidence to save her family and give her her life back.

She'd imagined using him somehow. Was he instead going to try to use her? And if so, how?

She made herself laugh a little, too, then looked down at her hands in her lap and whispered, "I'm sorry. I'm just a little confused. I—"

"I'd feel a bit confused, too, if I hadn't spoken with Judge Treena before."

Shock radiated through Beth. She was glad that her eyes, now huge, were focused downward. She didn't want to meet his gaze, not until she managed to get control of herself again—the way she had been taught to take control while changing her persona under the aegis of… Judge Treena.

She forced herself to take a deep, calming breath, then looked at him with an assumed expression of confusion on her face. "You spoke with a judge? Are you involved with a lawsuit? Or—"

A server came over and placed the drinks they had ordered on the place mats in front of them. Beth wished she'd ordered something stronger than an iced tea. Maybe a glass of wine. Better yet, straight whiskey. A lot of it. But it was only midday, and she would have to return to the company and continue her cleaning work.

Daniel had ordered black coffee, no cream, no sugar, no latte or mocha. Nothing gooey or effeminate.

Nothing light or effeminate about him, either, no matter how geeky he had first struck her on the job. She moved her gaze up enough to watch his hand as he lifted his coffee cup to his mouth. It was taut. Wiry, with long, agile fingers. It looked strong, strong enough to do a lot more than merely conduct tests on pharmaceuticals and write the requisite reports.

Strong enough to suggest he used those hands for a lot more than the basics a dedicated scientist could do.

She wondered, just for an instant, what that hand would feel like on her bare skin.

She closed her eyes quickly, both to interrupt her train of thought and to keep herself from laughing aloud the way he had done.

She really had nothing to laugh about.

Who was this man? And how did he know about Judge Treena?

Was he one of the security guys Her Honor supposedly sent to check on her family? But if so, what was he doing at Corcoris? And how would he know about her?

His strong lips began to move. "I'm sure you know that Judge Treena doesn't preside over an actual courtroom, or at least not usually," he said. "She's essentially my boss. Yours, too?"

He made the last a question. Even if she wanted to answer, she wasn't sure what her response should be.

Judge Treena did, in fact, give her orders of sorts. But they were to instruct her. Protect her.

And now she was, at least to some extent, ignoring them. Possibly to her own detriment.

But who was Daniel McManus, really?

And did she dare to ask him again?

She bought herself a little more time by taking another sip of her iced tea. Then another.

"So…are we going to have a conversation here?" Daniel's deep voice still sounded calm, yet there was an edge to it.

"Well, sure," she responded, but was glad the server arrived just then with a basket of rolls, distracting them for a minute.

How should she play this? Just because Daniel had mentioned Judge Treena, said he had spoken with her, didn't mean he actually had. He was implying that he was on Beth's side. Had even acted as if he was, back at the labs.

But was he? Or was this some kind of ploy to make her reveal herself?

If nothing else, she again focused on what she had learned over this past year or so: trust no one.

Well, almost no one. She did trust Judge Treena and those few people she had met thanks to the judge's help in setting up a new persona for her. She had to.

And she would always trust Milt Ranich in the slight chance her former ally at Corcoris, who'd hinted at all that was wrong there and then disappeared before she did, was still alive.

Seeing Daniel's curious gaze still fastened on her gave Beth the impetus to act. "Excuse me." She pulled her napkin from her lap and placed it on the table. "I need a pit stop. I'll be right back." That was too much information, but it should buy her a few minutes away from this man.

"Sure," he said, but his smile looked both irritated

and smug somehow. Surely he couldn't read her mind—about the phone call she needed to make immediately.

Or maybe he could.

"Hurry back, though," he added. "Our food will arrive soon."

She considered fleeing, letting him pay for that food and not having to deal with him again.

During this lunchtime. And that was the problem. She would still have to deal with him this afternoon and on an ongoing basis at Corcoris.

She didn't assure him that she would hurry or even that she would return. She felt sure he knew it already. Especially when, after standing, she glanced back and saw him lift his coffee cup toward her in a toast.

Why did she find that smug gesture anything but irritating?

And she hated that it, combined with his gaze at her through smiling, partly closed eyes, struck her as too damned sexy.

She fled toward the ladies' room.

Daniel knew he shouldn't have acted so amused. But at the moment, he enjoyed watching Beth—Andrea?—flee toward the restroom.

She had to wend her way around crowded tables, moving her attractive hips and more to stay out of the way of gesturing patrons and servers with their arms filled with loaded trays. In her colorful shirt and slim pants, Beth's form couldn't have been more fun to watch.

Somehow it seemed sexy. *She* seemed sexy, even fully clothed in that not particularly alluring outfit. Or maybe it was just the way his curiosity was ramped up about this mysterious woman that made him want to know more about her.

Including what she really looked like…

His thoughts were interrupted as the guy who'd been serving them put a plate down in front of him. It held the pastrami sandwich he'd ordered. Smelled good.

His "date" had ordered the house salad, and it appeared delectable, with shredded chicken over a bed of fresh lettuce and other salad veggies.

He hoped she would hurry back to enjoy it, but at least it wasn't anything that would chill or spoil in her absence.

The thought had struck him, as she'd seemed so eager to leave, that she might not return.

But whoever Beth was, she had to have some degree of intelligence, since Judge Treena was helping her.

That intelligence—or at least her common sense— might be limited, since she apparently was also currently ignoring the judge's orders.

Yet so far, Daniel had gotten, and still believed, that there was a lot more to that lovely woman than he had yet seen.

He looked forward to finding out all there was. Not to mention making it very clear that, whatever her reason for being at the Corcoris facility, she had better not interfere with what he was there to do.

He took a bite of his sandwich—even as his eyes continued to stare in the direction Beth had gone.

Fortunately, the restroom was down a fairly secluded hallway. Beth would have preferred going outside or nearly anywhere else, but the only doors beyond the ladies' room were for the men's room, and one that said Employees Only.

She'd get no privacy in either one.

She pulled her phone out of her pocket—not the one for calling her family, but the one that Judge Treena had tried to reach her on. She faced the wall, leaned toward it to try to wrap a small mantle of privacy around herself.

Taking a deep breath to calm herself—and to prepare for what would undoubtedly be a difficult conversation— she pressed first the button to turn it on and then the one that went directly to Judge Treena's number.

As busy as the judge was, Beth didn't expect to reach her immediately…no matter how much she wanted to. She was surprised, therefore, when the phone was answered right away. "Where the hell are you, Jones?"

Almost against her will, Beth felt the corners of her lips twitch into a small smile. No matter how peeved Judge Treena was, no matter how much she might want to kick someone's butt, she apparently never forgot to use the new cover names of the people she helped.

"In the area where I said I might be going." That was another thing that Treena's subordinates had made clear. Never answer anything directly—at least nothing that could make it easy for someone eavesdropping to learn something you didn't want them to know.

Like your location.

"Where you're not supposed to be." The judge's tone was ominous, and when someone passed behind Beth close enough to cause a slight breeze at her back, she startled.

"I understand your feelings about this, Your Honor, but I hope you understand mine, too. My family—"

"I get it." The judge sounded curt, but then she said, "You know my team is approaching this from some other angles, too. We're keeping an eye on your family, for one thing, and also getting cooperation from the local cops. Plus, we understand that your folks are about to leave town for a while. And we're doing something else— something that will eventually resolve the situation."

Beth hesitated. This sounded like a good lead-in for what she wanted to ask. "That's what I wondered. Hoped. But I hope you realize that I also have to do what I think is best. I'll try to stay out of trouble. Out of the way of whatever you're doing—as long as I know what it is."

She hoped the judge would say that nothing at all had been started yet...or, alternatively, that she'd sent a guy named Daniel there to fix everything.

As if he could. Although if anyone could, she wanted to believe that the man who'd appeared to play games with Preston Corcoris and prevail—at least this once—might be able to do anything.

"So that's where we are," the judge said. "You want to be brought into my core group who's told about each operation on a need-to-know basis."

It wasn't a question. In fact, it sounded as if Judge Treena was scoffing at her, letting her know that even if that was what Beth wanted, she could want it forever without achieving it.

But Beth would not let herself be deterred. Not when her family's safety was at stake.

And possibly her own.

"That's right, Your Honor. You can look at it this way, since I do. If it's need-to-know, then if it potentially affects me, I do need to know."

She was surprised when she heard a bark of laughter on the other end of the phone. "For someone who needed to start over in a whole new life, you still have a lot of nerve, Jones."

Beth smiled. "I guess so. And if you could just answer one question for me now, it would really help—so I'll know if I'm in even more trouble at the moment."

"What's that?"

"I take it that this line is secure?" Despite her own

waffling before, she figured the judge would have a better sense of how safe talking to her was. And whatever happened, whatever the answer to her question happened to be, Beth didn't want this conversation to lead to a really bad result.

"It is," Judge Treena responded.

Beth didn't hesitate. She definitely wanted an answer, and she wanted it now. "There's a guy here who seems to be trying to help me, but I don't know whether he's real, whether I should trust him. Is—"

The judge didn't let her finish. "His name?"

"Daniel McManus."

"Trust him," Judge Treena said. "He's one of ours."

They were talking about the same guy. Judge Treena felt certain of it after she talked with Beth a little longer.

At least the woman was astute enough to get more information before trusting just anyone who happened to act as if they were allies. Including how to make sure he was who he said he was.

But that still didn't satisfy Treena.

After hanging up the phone, she leaned back in the tall desk chair in her office at the headquarters of the U.S. Marshals Service in Washington, D.C., and sighed.

Why didn't people obey orders, especially when their own best interests were involved?

But she had come to know the woman who was now Beth Jones well over the months of revamping her identity and giving her a new life. Beth had made it clear how much she cared about and missed her family.

She also clearly gave a damn about the situation that had led her into flight—and it could affect, harm, a whole lot of civilians if not handled right.

Besides, over the course of her legal career, Treena

had met all kinds of people, especially when she was a public defender. A lot of them were vile, but every once in a while someone captured her pity because of the horrid situations they found themselves in with no escape other than possible death.

That was one reason she had fought to help those who couldn't help themselves. Had used family connections to join the U.S. Marshals Service and to found the Identity Division, which was composed of the Transformation Unit and the Covert Investigations Unit.

The Identity Division allowed Treena to help those in need leave their perilous lives despite their inability to produce evidence that would get them into witness protection. Via the TU, Treena gave the successful petitioners each a new identity for their protection. She directed an elite undercover CIU team to find that evidence in their stead.

Real evidence, not the hearsay or circumstantial or logical speculation that the petitioners usually came in with.

Evidence that would lead to the arrest and conviction of the people terrorizing them.

And she had been extremely fortunate in obtaining funding, via official sources, grants, rewards for capture and prosecution of the guilty, and even donations from some of those people the ID Division had saved and who had gone on to better lives. She hadn't had to scrimp on any of the many activities in which the division engaged, including protection and investigation.

Now Treena glanced at the wall to her right, in the direction of the White House. It didn't hurt that her cousin—distant, yes, but family just the same—happened to be POTUS, the president of the United States.

Enough rehashing, she finally told herself. Time to plan.

She stood to look out the window toward Pennsylvania Avenue. She liked Agent Daniel McManus, thought he was more than able to handle his undercover assignment at Corcoris Pharmaceuticals. But when she had selected him and gotten him the training to seamlessly fit in at the company, she hadn't counted on having a distraction possibly get in the way—in the form of Beth Jones.

Things could get even more interesting now. Might even work better. But in case they didn't, she needed a plan.

"So how's your sandwich?" Beth had just sat back down across from Daniel and picked up her fork.

He couldn't say why exactly, but she looked different. Not as tense, maybe. Not as remote.

Which told him, rightly or wrongly, that she'd done as he had anticipated and called Judge Treena about him.

That could be a good thing. Or not.

"Good. I hope you don't mind, but I took a bite of your salad. I think it's better than my sandwich."

He hadn't taken a bite, but he wanted to see her reaction. The former Beth, before whatever she'd done in the past few minutes, wouldn't have yelled at him, but she'd have appeared upset, no matter whether she tried to hide it. Tense. Unsure how to handle the situation.

This new Beth, though?

"You should have asked first. I'd have let you try it, but it's my salad. My decision." There was a belligerence in the way she stuck out her full lower lip ever so slightly. Daniel had never considered belligerence sexy, but he'd not seen it before on Beth Jones's beautiful face.

"You're right. Want any of my sandwich?"

"Yes," she said. "Just a corner to try. One you haven't already taken a bite out of."

He wanted to smile. Even laugh. This conversation wasn't about their lunch, but it was somehow about their relationship.

Hell, they had no relationship, although the thought struck him as provocative. No, what they had was inter- action between two people who were business associates of sorts. Unwilling ones, at least from his perspective.

Unless she proved she could stay out of his way. Or better yet, coordinate what she was doing with him so they could both benefit.

She seemed to want some degree of control. He'd let her think she was achieving it…for now.

Unable to keep a small ironic grin off his face, he hid it by bending his head downward as he used a knife from the table to cut off an unnibbled corner of his sandwich. His look was utterly serious when he gazed back up at Beth and handed her the bite. "Now we're even."

He caught the merest sucking in of her lips as if she clearly wanted to dispute that. But didn't.

"You know," he said in a soft voice as he leaned to- ward her, "I think you and I have a lot in common. Wouldn't you like to explore that?"

"Maybe." She said the word so sexily that he felt his body react—and it reacted even more as she leaned across the table toward him, her lips enticingly apart as if she wanted to kiss him. "But first there's something of yours I want to see."

Okay, that really got to him. He nearly choked as he asked, "What?" She wasn't far from him by then, and he leaned toward her, too.

"Your badge," she whispered.

He blinked at her first, then laughed as he moved

back. "So you did speak to…our mutual acquaintance." He spoke equally softly. "I wondered." He stood and walked around the table. When he was close to her, he bent so it looked as if he were reaching for the bottle of salad dressing on the table in front of her—even as he lifted something that no one else would be able to see from his pants pocket. He nodded toward that hand and let her glimpse his U.S. Marshals badge briefly before tucking it back in. And then, picking up the bottle, he returned to his seat.

"That is good salad dressing," she said with a nod, and her smile then seemed pensive as she returned to eating lunch. She held the bite of sandwich he'd given her, studying it before placing it between her full, enticing lips.

"So are we on the same wavelength now?" he asked.

"I think so." She kept close watch on her fork as she dipped it into her salad, clearly avoiding looking at him. She took a bite. "I like my salad better than your sandwich, too, though. Maybe we do have some tastes in common after all." For a brief moment, her eyes met his searchingly.

He nodded slightly. "So maybe we should talk about those tastes."

"Sure, we can do that. But not here."

"Your place or mine?" he quipped—although he was somewhat serious. The woman turned him on.

But she just laughed. And common sense—not to mention all-too-real experience—said he should forget any sexual innuendos from either of them, concentrate only on getting them together to really talk. Not here where tables near them were starting to fill but someplace secure. And to talk only about what he knew they had in common, the stuff on the surface: compiling evidence against Corcoris Pharmaceuticals to ensure that whatever damage they'd been doing to people who were prescribed their medications and whatever they had done to Beth's alter ego, Andrea Martinez, they'd never do any of it again.

For now, though, he decided to switch subjects. Sure, they needed to talk, but not here. At least not about anything important.

"You know, I'm pretty much a newcomer to Moravo Beach," he said, resuming his undercover character somewhat—for now. "I just got here a few weeks ago to start my job at Corcoris. I'm originally from back East." Which was true. He had grown up in upper New York State and now called the D.C. area home. "I really like this place and also my new job with Corcoris. Tell me something about yourself, Beth. Are you a Moravo Beach native?"

He hadn't caught her off guard. She spun a tale about how she had grown up in Seattle but had decided to move away, and although she had higher aspirations, starting as a cleaning assistant for Corcoris was just fine since she hadn't attended college. At least not yet.

That had to be her cover story. He knew why it was such a good one and why she recounted it so convincingly.

She'd had at least some of it handed to her by Judge Treena and had practiced it as part of her changed identity. But—

"You know," she said as she finished her salad, "it's time for me to get back to work. But I've been enjoying this conversation. Could we get together again later? Say, over dinner? At my place?"

Now, that was unexpected. But definitely welcome. There was a lot more they needed to discuss.

"Sure," he said. "It's a date."

Chapter 5

Beth walked through the back door at Corcoris and downstairs into the basement hallway to the cleaning-gear storage area. The area was empty, and with no distractions—for now—Beth rehashed the lunchtime she had just experienced.

Had she ended it foolishly by inviting the guy to her place to talk? Maybe, but with her discussion with Judge Treena she felt pretty confident about who he was—especially when he had shown his U.S. Marshals badge. And where else could they talk in private?

She could always change her mind. She hadn't yet told him where she lived. But she would before they both left work.

She'd known exactly what was on Daniel McManus's mind some of the time as he'd looked at her. Teased her. Led her on…about their lunch. And hinted, at least a bit, about things sexual. Which had also encouraged her to tease him.

She was surprised to realize she'd enjoyed it.

But it was what neither one of them said—there—that was most important.

Now she had arrived back at Corcoris. She had seen Daniel head to his car but she had driven off first, wanting to arrive alone. Neither had discussed how odd it might look if anyone saw them together, and the restaurant they had frequented was far enough away that it was unlikely they'd be seen by anyone who would recognize either of them.

If anyone did happen to see them and asked why they were hiding, it would be because a geeky tech guy wanting to get ahead at the company shouldn't be going on dates with a lowly member of the cleaning crew. At least that was what Beth would say, and she figured that would also be Daniel's position.

But the reality between them…that was why she had suggested dinner that night at her place.

She hadn't spoken with anyone around there except an officious guy from the apartment building's management company, and there was no manager on-site. She hadn't been living there long, but she had managed to avoid all other tenants.

If she had a guest for the evening, no one would know. No one would care.

But even believing who Daniel was, she would remain cautious. And they really did need to talk.

Reaching the storeroom, Beth eased open the door. She had already removed the shirt she had worn to hide her cleaning-staff T-shirt. It was soft and gauzy and she had been able to stuff it back into her large handbag. She quickly turned to the computer on the table near the door and punched in to show she was back.

"There you are," said a harsh voice off to her right. Beth didn't have to look to see that it was her boss here, Mary Cantrera. The woman scowled at her as if she had taken all afternoon off or worse, but she had been gone only for the permitted hour.

"Hi," Beth said softly, looking down at the room's spotless floor. "Do you have an assignment for me?"

"I definitely do, and you should have started fifteen minutes ago."

Beth didn't bother trying to explain or excuse herself, or even to point out that the time program she had just punched in on showed she had been gone a few minutes less than her allotted hour. It would have done her no good—and she didn't dare get any further on this woman's bad side.

She didn't want to be fired.

"Sorry. I'll go right away." Beth ignored the fact that a couple of other members of the staff—her cafeteria-cleaning buddies from this morning, in fact—were present, too, standing in a corner as if pretending they weren't there.

Why hadn't Mary sent Gabrielle or John on whatever mission this was?

No matter. Beth had to play the game.

"It's lab 6, on the second floor. Apparently someone accidentally swept some collection vials and other things onto the floor. It's already been checked to make sure nothing hazardous was spread around, but the glass is still there. Everyone else has other jobs already assigned to them, so that's where you're to go."

"Right away," Beth said. She collected her cart from along the wall, checked it for sufficient cleaning paraphernalia and solutions, and hurriedly pushed it out the door.

She took an elevator to the second floor.

The hallway there was a lot busier than the one she'd just left. At least six members of the lab staff in their white jackets walked hurriedly along, several heading in each direction. Beth kept her eyes on her cart, steering it carefully as she pushed it so as not to run into anyone.

She had an urge to check out faces. See if Daniel was among those who populated this hallway at the moment. But she didn't want to meet the eyes of anyone.

Despite the complete strategic change in her appearance since she'd taken on her new life, she couldn't help worrying that someone here might see Andrea in a glance, a habitual movement she hadn't been aware of…anything.

Even so, if the person who recognized her happened to be her friend Milt Ranich, because he had returned and was all right, maybe her being identified wouldn't be as bad as she feared—as long as he kept it to himself.

But she doubted that would be an issue. She hadn't seen Milt since her return, or any sign of him.

She reached the door of the lab where she had been assigned, checked the number on the door and pushed it open. Since this wasn't one of the sterile rooms where critical tests and experiments were conducted, she was able to enter without changing clothes, covering her feet or taking on a new cart.

As she pushed her cart inside, she swallowed a gasp. This didn't look like some minor mishap where a container or two had inadvertently gotten pushed off one of the sterile counters.

No, this room looked as if some kind of tornado had swept through it.

This looked like intentionally inflicted damage. Beth wanted to know what had happened. And why.

And, definitely, who.

For now, though, she needed to get to work, even though cleaning this mess looked like a job for more than one person. With a sigh, she scanned the room, deciding on the best approach to take. If she could at least get the layers of glass swept up first—

"What the hell?" A familiar voice interrupted her musings.

She turned to see Daniel standing there, his glasses and white lab jacket turning him into the geeky techie she'd seen here before. But his shoulders were stiff, his expression angry.

"My sentiments exactly," she said. Then more softly, "Any idea what caused this?"

"I heard rumors when I arrived that one of the guys upstairs wasn't pleased with some test results here, but I didn't expect this."

"Corcoris?" Beth mouthed, not wanting anyone else to hear her speculation even though they were alone in here.

Daniel shrugged as he whispered, "Could be." He continued in a louder voice as if expecting what he said to be picked up by a security camera, "It's okay. We'll deal with it."

"But I was sent here to clean it up," Beth contradicted.

"Alone?" He glared at her with his flashing blue eyes as if it were her choice, her fault.

"That's what I was told."

"That's not what I was told. Hold on here."

"No, wait—" she began, but it was too late. He was already outside the door once more.

Damn. Even if she wasn't the one making waves, she

didn't need anyone to make them on her behalf. Call attention to her.

Quelling her initial panic, she decided she would just do as ordered as quickly as she could. She began the initial steps of sweeping up the irregular mounds of jagged glass until she could at least see more of the linoleum.

She began slowly, then got into a rhythm, using a push broom to move some of the shards into a pile, then scooping them into one of the large metal dustpans and finally emptying them into the large garbage can lined with a plastic bag that occupied most of the cart. Fortunately, the liquids that had spilled were not sticky and she was able to use paper towels to mop them up, then cleanse where they had been with cleaning products she'd brought in on the cart. She had to work around the bases of the lab's tables and storage cabinets and its few chairs, but that didn't slow her—much.

She had gotten only perhaps a quarter of the floor cleared when the lab door opened again.

Daniel was there. And so were John and Gabrielle. "These guys offered to help you," Daniel said in a cheery voice. "I told them how awful this looked and that I really needed to work in here by the end of the day. I explained what a great job you're doing, but there's just so much to do that you needed help."

She wanted to object, but in some ways she was glad to see them. Only— "I had it under control. Mary said you had other projects you're scheduled for this afternoon." Her eyes were on her two cleaning coworkers. Fortunately, neither appeared angry—just overwhelmed by what this room looked like, as she had been.

"It's okay, Beth," Gabrielle said. "We just had our usual scheduled stuff—the downstairs halls and labs up on the third floor. But when one of the lab guys like

Daniel begs Mary for help…well, that's important. She asked if we were okay with working here, and we were."

Beth glanced at John for confirmation. His quick nod told her he wasn't complaining, either.

"Thanks to both of you," she said. "All of you." This time she encompassed Daniel in her gaze.

After the others went back into the hall for their own carts, Beth said softly to Daniel, "Should I be yelling at you instead of thanking you?"

"I think we'll both have a better idea of that after dinner tonight. Oh, and do me a favor and mark the garbage bags from here with these." He handed her a sheet of stickers with smiley faces on them, winked at her beneath his black-rimmed glasses, and then he was gone.

Damn, Daniel thought as he headed for the lab where he was currently assigned—on the third floor, not the second. He wanted to stay there with Beth. Not just to help her, although the thought had crossed his mind despite having recruited those other cleaning-staff members. But now he wouldn't be able to collect whatever had been in those destroyed vials.

They might have been exactly what he was seeking: potential evidence proving that Corcoris was cutting corners and endangering those who took their pharmaceutical products by using inferior-quality ingredients. It was unlikely, though, that those vials' contents would have been useful. The damaged stuff had been in a lab in this building, where the quality-control tests provided to the FDA were conducted, so the materials here were undoubtedly first-rate. Right?

That seemed to be what he was learning by rumor, at least, since his arrival here, but so far he hadn't discovered any proof.

Just in case, he would ask Beth later where any garbage bags the cleaners filled were discarded, including
the ones he had asked her to mark, but he was fairly sure
they'd go in the Dumpsters with all the other nonhazard-
ous detritus from this business, as designated. Would it
be worth having them picked up and sorted through by
someone hired by the CIU?

Unfortunately, the answer was most likely no.

Finally back in her small apartment for the evening,
Beth felt exhausted. Under other circumstances, she
would have called whoever she'd invited over for dinner that night and offered a rain check.

Not Daniel, though. They needed to talk. And the
number of topics to discuss had been raised a notch or
two that afternoon.

Besides, around here—now—she wouldn't be inviting
anyone home for dinner or anything else unless there was
a really good reason. As there was with Daniel.

She had stopped at a nearby supermarket on her way
and picked up the fixings for a nice but not ostentatious
chicken dinner.

It had been a while since she had done any serious
cooking. Not when she was feeding only herself. And
she still wasn't ready to assume her outgoing Andrea
persona in front of Daniel.

Neither did she have to be all shy and quiet, as Beth
had been taught, rightfully so, by Judge Treena and her
crew.

Judge Treena. Beth had quizzed her for a while to
make sure that the man she had met was the same one
Her Honor had mentioned, and the judge had mentioned
that the undercover guy she'd sent there would be car-
rying his badge.

Even so, was it foolish anyway to invite him here? Maybe—but she would remain on guard.

Now, in her tiny but functional kitchen, Beth wished she had an apron. She always used to keep fashionable ones around, a different design for every kind of meal. Not any longer.

But then again, keeping her bland yellow T-shirt and jeans clean shouldn't be too difficult, and if she slipped and dropped something on herself, her clothing could just be tossed in the building's downstairs pay-laundry facilities.

She finished seasoning the chicken breasts with onions and honey-mustard sauce and popped the casserole dish into the heated oven. Then it was time to start working on the rice.

A buzzer rang, indicating that someone outside the building wanted to get in. Beth's eyes widened in momentary fear until she remembered she shouldn't feel startled. She knew who was there.

She put down the box of rice she'd been holding and smoothed her hands over her clothes. Then laughed at herself. That gesture had been habitual but totally unnecessary. She turned and maneuvered her way out of the kitchen and toward the intercom box at the apartment's front door.

"Who's there?" she said.

"I think you can guess," said a familiar male voice.

"I think you can tell me," she countered.

"Daniel McManus."

"Okay. Come on upstairs to apartment 2B." Beth smiled as she pushed the button that would open the front door. She liked pushing Daniel's buttons that way, too. But she had selected this apartment partly because of its security system, and she intended to use it.

A knock soon sounded at her door. Sure, she knew who it was, but even so, she looked through the peep-hole just in case. It was habit, yes. It was also self-preservation.

The person standing outside was, unsurprisingly, exactly who she'd anticipated. Even so, she took a deep breath before pulling the door open.

He smiled at her, and she felt herself smile back—an unusual reaction these days—as she saw that he carried a small bouquet of daisies, which he held out to her. He didn't wear his geeky glasses, and there was no slouch at all to his posture. He was even taller than she recalled, and he was clad much nicer than she, in a blue-striped shirt tucked into dressy navy slacks.

As if he considered this not an air-clearing and strategy session but a date.

"Come in." She hated that her voice sounded hoarse. She hated even more how his blue eyes seemed to flash in amusement. She didn't take the flowers from him, but after she closed the door behind him, he thrust them into her hands.

"Here," he said. "Put them in some water."

She opened her mouth to protest, although she didn't know what to say that wouldn't sound petty, but he interrupted her. "Yes, I know this isn't a social engagement, but I figured it wouldn't hurt to make it look that way in case any of your neighbors happened to notice that you have company."

She didn't bother to say that her neighbors didn't pay any more attention to her than she did to them. That might have been wishful thinking on her part. She had often considered the awful possibility that her cover here wasn't as solid as she'd hoped, which was all the more reason to act like subdued Beth—while remaining as alert as Andrea had become.

"Good thinking." She took the flowers from him. Her fingers accidentally touched his hand and she pulled away as if he had shocked her.

She didn't want to be conscious of him as a man. He was just a person she needed to understand, to get along with. And work with, at least on some level, since they apparently had a mutual goal.

She turned her back and walked the three steps toward the narrow tile walkway that constituted the kitchen floor. She owned no vases. She barely had the basics of plates, cooking paraphernalia and flatware.

She opened one of the narrow cupboards over the counter, pulled out a glass, poured water into it from the faucet and stuck the flowers into it. "There," she said. And then, belatedly, she remembered her manners. "Thanks."

Daniel had followed her into what passed as a kitchen. "Smells good," he said.

"Nothing fancy," she responded, then could have kicked herself. She didn't have to apologize for dinner. She didn't have to apologize for anything. "So," she said, "I can open a bottle of Chianti if you're interested. I also have beer."

"Beer sounds good."

It did to her, too. She pulled two bottles from the fridge, some light domestic stuff that she'd bought in case she wanted something cold and alcoholic.

Tonight that sounded good.

She used the end of a can opener to open the bottles and handed one to Daniel. "I need to finish up some stuff," she told him. "Why don't you wait in the living room? I'll be there shortly."

"Nope. You can just put me to work in here."

"But there's no room."

"I'll improvise."

She wanted to yell at him to get out of her space—in more ways than one. But when she looked up into his eyes, she felt an almost magnetic charge pulling her into their depths.

He wasn't smiling. Neither was she.

What was going on between them?

Nothing, she told herself. Sexual attraction? Well, yeah. But that was all.

She couldn't afford to care about anyone. Not now, not until she had her life back.

Maybe not ever.

"Fine," she retorted. "Help yourself. Want to make the salad?"

"I'm great at chopping stuff." This time he smiled. It was one damnably sexy smile. Challenging.

She made an exasperated face. "I'll just bet you are." She turned her back on him to open the refrigerator and extract a head of lettuce, tomato and green pepper. Nothing extraordinary. Just as the rest of her life was supposed to appear here.

She reached under her sink and pulled out a plastic cutting board, then got a serrated knife from her silverware drawer. She set the board at the edge of her tiny granite counter. Not much room, but he didn't complain.

"Here," she told him. "They're already washed."

She tried not to be conscious of his rhythmic movements as he cut the veggies while she put rice, water and seasonings into a pot to put onto the stove.

Rhythmic? Heck, that just underscored the guy's sexiness, and that was something she didn't dare to focus on.

Finally, he was done. The chicken and rice were cooking. She thanked him, put the salad he'd fixed into two small bowls, and carried them around the corner to the tiny table against the wall at the entry to her apartment's single, all-purpose room. Fortunately, the table had come with two chairs. She wouldn't have bought them separately.

She hadn't believed she would ever have a guest.

She returned to the kitchen, stirred the rice and turned the stove down to a simmer, then checked on the chicken casserole in the oven. It appeared to be progressing well.

"Let's eat our salads first," she said. She picked up the bottle of Italian dressing she'd left on the counter along with her beer, walked back into the other room and sat down at the table.

The apartment was pretty much as Daniel had expected, a generic locale for someone on the run to hang out temporarily.

Beth, though, wasn't what he'd expected of a subject being helped by the ID Division.

But he needed more information to determine whether that judgment would stick. He took his place at the opposite end of the small oblong table from her and put his beer bottle down. She'd already set the table, so he politely stuck his napkin on his lap and picked up his fork.

She was watching him, and as he moved, she repeated his gestures, as if she followed his lead even in her home environment. Why was that?

Her gaze was wary, her violet eyes shadowed, and she quickly looked down at her salad as she took her first forkful.

He wanted to leap up and shake her. Better yet, kiss those luscious-looking full lips so they stopped curving into a nervous line.

Instead, he decided it was time to begin with what he'd come here to do.

"So, Beth," he said. "Or whatever your real name is. Why don't you tell me who you are and why you're actually here?"

"I asked you first." She'd stopped chewing and her lovely face had gone pale. He wanted to reassure her that all was well, that he wouldn't hurt her, but he couldn't guarantee that. Not if he wanted to fulfill his own assignment.

He'd do his damnedest to protect her, though.

Unless she got in his way.

"Yeah, I guess you did," he agreed. "But I think we're at a stalemate here."

"What did Judge Treena really say about me?" she countered.

"Not much."

"Then, yes, I guess we are at a stalemate." She stared him straight in the eyes again, then calmly stood and started walking toward the kitchen. "I'd better check on the rest of dinner—although I suspect we're going to be eating it in a pretty chilly atmosphere." She stopped and looked down at him, a grim smile lighting her face. "Unless, of course, you want to start talking first after all."

Daniel had a sense that they were about to embark on some very interesting communication. He would definitely enjoy their verbal jousting.

"Well, sure," he said. "Why not? Want me to help you bring in the rest of dinner? I suspect we're both going to lose our appetites soon, but we'll have a very interesting conversation."

Chapter 6

Beth kept her back toward Daniel as much as possible as they maneuvered around each other once more in her tiny kitchen. She'd placed the empty salad bowls in the sink and set plates onto the table.

Now she had to maneuver a bit more to open the oven door and extract the casserole dish filled with the seasoned chicken—and Daniel was much too close to her then, ostensibly digging out the serving bowl she had asked him to extract.

If she had backed up just a few inches as she bent over, her butt would have touched his. And that might only spur her disloyal mind to think about what else of hers could rub against his....

Heck, she wasn't really attracted to him. Not much anyway. That would be sheer folly, and she was not a foolish person.

Besides, she didn't like playing games, either physical or mental ones. She hadn't liked them as Andrea, and she certainly didn't like them now—especially when she had to mistrust everyone…even, to some extent, Daniel.

Sure, he appeared to be undercover here, sent by Judge Treena. And he had helped her when Corcoris was around. That meant he was more than a potential tool to help her find evidence in the labs, as she had imagined before.

He might actually be an ally.

With her hands in protective mitts, she lifted the casserole dish from the oven, inhaled its savory scent and shut the door. Daniel had finished scooping rice into the bowl. Chicken and rice after salad. This was a very simple dinner, Beth thought.

For a not-so-simple meeting. But she didn't feel like eating much anyway.

"All set?" She inclined her head toward the door to the living room.

"Sure am."

In another minute, they were both seated at the table, scooping the remaining elements of their meals onto their plates. They stayed silent.

Beth wanted to kick Daniel to get him to start speaking. His shin, under the table? Better yet, a more vulnerable part of him.

The thought made her flush with uneasiness…and, yes, curiosity.

Why did the guy cause such sexual interest in her? Because she hadn't even thought of sex now for…what was it? More than a year. And her thoughts back then had been woven around a really scary situation, not being turned on by a hot guy.

Daniel regarded her with what looked like both interest and curiosity in his smiling blue eyes. Darn the man.

It was as if he knew at least part of what she was thinking. The slight stubble on his angular face this late in the day only added to his appeal, and she looked back at her food…for a moment.

"So I thought you said you would tell me something about your background first," she finally said.

"Yep, I guess that's the plan." He looked so blasé, taking in another bite of chicken. Why had she done this to herself? Why had she invited him? "First, though, even though I think you know who I am, I need to make sure you're really who I think you are."

She pasted a "you've got to be kidding" look on her face. "Okay, then, who do you think I am?"

"Judge Treena said there was someone working at Corcoris who was one of her group's…protégés, for want of a better word. Someone who was supposed to be far away from here. She gave me both of her names. You're Beth Jones, right?"

"That's right." She had already told him that.

But she knew what his next question would be. "If you're really her, she also has another name. The name she used all of her life till she became Beth. Is that you? And if so, what's your real name?"

Even if she were someone else playing a game, she would probably know the real name of the person she was pretending to be.

But if he was fishing, trying to learn her real identity? Well, Judge Treena had already told her to trust Daniel.

"My real name is Andrea Martinez," she said.

So far, so good, Daniel thought.

He'd figured right, and so had Judge Treena. But he needed to learn more about why Beth had come back here to the place where she'd been put in danger in the first place.

First things first, though.

He took a drink of beer, watching her attractive yet worried face the entire time.

He wondered what she would look like with hair longer than the short black do she wore. He suspected that was a new style for her new persona.

So, probably, was the violet shade of her eyes. Contact lenses. They looked great on her—but what were her eyes really like?

Maybe he would find out someday.

For now, he needed to gain her trust. "Here's my story, Beth. I assume you'd rather I call you that to help ensure that neither of us slips up while around other people?"

She nodded. "That's who I am now."

"Okay, then, Beth. My name really is Daniel McManus. I'm an agent of the Covert Investigations Unit, which is part of the Identity Division of the U.S. Marshals Service. As you probably know better than anyone, we have an important mission. I'm aware that you're one of the folks that Judge Treena has helped who aren't qualified for any witness protection program since you don't have enough evidence or personal knowledge to allow you to testify against your enemies who want you dead, right?"

Her face turned ashen. "Right," she whispered.

"Okay, then. We're on the same side. I'm here to gather the evidence you need so we can put your enemies away for good."

"Really?" The look on her face somehow melded hope and doubt and fear.

"Yeah. So I'm working on figuring out what Corcoris Pharmaceuticals, or at least some of its execs, are up to. And before you ask about my credentials, here they are. My parents are both cops, so I grew up wanting to be a good guy. I joined the Marines as soon as I was old enough and realized that combat training was good for a little while, but I wanted a different direction. When my tour of duty was up, I joined the FBI and became a special agent. But..."

Okay, while wanting both to impress and reassure Beth, he had strayed too close to revealing something about himself, his background, that he didn't talk about. Not unless he absolutely had to.

Judge Treena knew. So did a few other trusted people. But Beth didn't need that extra information.

"But?" she encouraged, her voice still low and raspy. As if she sensed he held something back.

So what if he did? "But I was looking for more, and when I heard about the newly forming CIU, I jumped at it. I liked the idea of the ID Division, and that its Transformation Unit not only helped to change the identities of deserving people, but it also advised CIU operatives going undercover on how to change our looks and personalities. Now I take great pleasure in going undercover whenever and wherever to help people who deserve answers. Like someone named Andrea Martinez."

The expression on Beth's face suddenly morphed into unabashed hope. Her mouth opened, and her lips parted. Much too enticingly. It was as if she wanted to run to his side of the table and kiss him.

Hell, he wouldn't mind that. In fact, he would welcome it.

Instead, she said, "Thank you. Thank you so much, Daniel. I'd heard a little about that aspect of Judge Treena and the CIU part of the ID Division but no one completely confirmed it. If I'd been sure...well, I'd have had to come back here anyway. But I'm so relieved to have someone I can work with." Her expression suddenly hardened. "I'm not just being a fool here, am I? I mean, you could tell me anything to make me let down my guard."

"And if I tell you you're not a fool to believe me? Looks like we have another stalemate forming. I'll understand if you stay wary of me. But I've told you the truth, Beth. Whether or not you fully believe it, you can trust me." As long as she didn't make his job harder.

He had an unwelcome urge to seal that thought with a kiss. But he believed that any sudden motion on his part, anything other than acting professionally, would only scare her all the more. He instead finished his beer, then took another bite of rice. "Beth Jones is a good cook," he said. "But I'm a better one. I'll have to invite her over to my place for dinner one of these evenings."

Beth laughed. The sound surprised her. So did her sudden relief.

She knew better than to fully let down her guard, but she'd check again with Judge Treena to try to confirm what Daniel had said. But it did at least comport with what Her Honor had said to her, which eased Beth's concerns even more.

He hadn't told her everything, though. He'd hesitated in the middle of his story and his expression had gone completely blank for a few seconds. As if he had swallowed something back inside.

It might be irrelevant, even if it made her curious.

For now, though, she didn't hesitate—much—when he asked her to do her part in this conversation.

"You can undoubtedly get the necessary details about me from Judge Treena," she said lightly, then took a sip of her remaining beer. "And you probably know at least some of it since she sent you here to go after Preston Corcoris. But here's the gist of what happened. I was in public relations here at Corcoris Pharmaceuticals for a couple of years. Enjoyed my job helping to tell the world about our wonderful products. But then, as I was researching some of the newest things to determine how to promote them in the best light, I was told things about perfect quality-control reports being fudged somehow. Hidden flaws despite how glowing the reports were. Maybe even bribes to the outside labs that were starting clinical trials on people. I started asking questions. As I became more visible in the PR department, Preston Corcoris started coming on to me. In my naïveté, I thought I'd go along with him in a limited way—not have sex with him, of course, but see if I could get some more information from him."

She stopped and swallowed hard, hating all the memories but that one most of all. Corcoris and the way he had attacked her physically. She had gotten away before he could really assault her, but there were no witnesses, no way to prove that any more than she'd been able to find any proof about the rumors she'd been hearing about the pharmaceuticals.

"Are you okay?" Daniel had stood and come over to her and was kneeling, with one arm supporting her shoulders.

She considered turning in her seat and throwing herself into his arms, but that would be a bad move.

"I'm fine," she assured him. "Really. But I'd like some more beer. How about you?"

"Sure."

She went into the kitchen and got them each another bottle. "Just leave all that." She waved at the table of dirty dishes, inviting him onto the beige plush sofa in the living room. "I'll clean it up later. Let's sit more comfortably while I finish this, okay?"

"Whatever you'd like," he said.

Surprisingly, what she'd have liked at the moment was to throw herself into his arms. And cry? Probably not. But the guy looked so damned caring. So sexy. She might be able to get a moment of amnesia about all the horrible stuff if she could drag him into bed for a minute.

And here, sitting on her convertible sofa was like dragging him onto her bed, if not into it for sex. But she wouldn't tell him that.

Nor would she act on her lust. Too foolish to even think that way.

She remained tempted nonetheless. Good thing he seemed more inclined to tease in the moments he departed from protective or planning mode—but she even found that too sexy.

She settled down on one side of the couch and he took the other. "Okay." She placed her beer bottle on the coffee table in front of them. "I can finish now. I'd been so thrilled to start working for Corcoris in the first place that I didn't want to believe what I heard. My mom has a rare blood disorder that has been kept under control for years by a Corcoris product. I wanted to be part of the company. Give back to it. And yet…well, I didn't know whether things had changed or what, but I started to get horrified about the rumors I was told—stuff I tried to look into but could never prove. I tried going to the authorities, and the FDA did conduct an unannounced 'for cause' inspection but found nothing. I couldn't prove it, since I'd been told by someone else, and anything I could claim in court would only be hearsay. But this supposedly mistaken whistle-blower—me—started receiving verbal, unprovable threats and having what looked like, but weren't, accidents. I had to leave, but, with no ability to testify in court against anyone, I couldn't get into witness protection."

"And Judge Treena heard about you." It wasn't a question but a statement from Daniel.

"That's right. She saved my life—and I guess she sent you to find all the evidence I couldn't before other people, ill people who are relying on Corcoris, are killed. Or more are killed. Some of the rumors indicated there'd already been deaths."

"That's right." His tone was gentle.

She sat up excitedly. "Have you found anything yet? Oh, I'd be so happy—"

"Not yet, but I will." There was no hesitation in his voice, and his craggy, handsome face looked so certain that she again wanted to kiss him. "I've been here for about a month already, have been collecting information and working into being accepted so people will talk more around me. I've ideas about what kinds of meds and their ingredients I'll want to sneak out of there, as well as some computer files, but I haven't gotten much yet. And you?"

"This is such a different perspective from how I looked at the company before. I've only been here five days so far, so I'm mostly just trying to figure out what I need and how to look for it. But I intend to discover whatever evidence there is and get it out of here."

Did she sound too optimistic? Hell, she had to be optimistic.

"Sounds like at least one of us had better do that," Daniel said, lifting his brows as if just humoring her.

She stopped herself from snapping at him, keeping her voice calm as she continued, "You have to understand. My family has been receiving threats, and even though they're supposedly under some protection, that's why I'm here—to find the necessary evidence to stop Corcoris once and for all."

"All right. Here's the reality. In case you haven't figured it out by now, finding that evidence is my job." His expression had turned stern, but she ignored it.

"It's *our* job," she corrected. "And there's something else, too. Have you met Milt Ranich or heard anything about him? He's my former immediate boss, and he's apparently not here any longer. I can't ask questions about him but I have looked around and put out some feelers about his position. Someone else has it now. He's the one who told me about the fraud being committed here and probably could have proven it. He also tried to protect me. But he disappeared, and I've still not learned what happened to him."

The name was familiar to Daniel. Judge Treena had passed it along to him along with other matters he was to investigate. But—

"No. I've heard of him but not since I arrived here. I'll follow up on it even more, since it's definitely important to find him. Was he trying to get the word out, too?" He hadn't testified against the company, so he wasn't in WitSec—the Witness Security Program administered by the U.S. Marshals Service—any more than Andrea Martinez was.

"Maybe, but I doubt it. He was ambivalent about spilling everything, even though he wanted to protect me."

"Well, I'll see what I can find out." Daniel felt oddly gratified to see a huge smile appear on Beth's face. And she obviously wasn't going to back off, no matter what he said. So he'd go along with her, at least temporarily. "And it won't hurt for us to work together on this for now."

But unless she started coming up with evidence soon or in some manner otherwise helped him, he would side with Judge Treena and encourage Beth to leave before she got hurt.

For the first time that evening, though, Beth seemed unguarded. Happy. Hopeful.

And she was definitely one hot and sexy lady. But as much as he wanted to do something about that, he recalled her description of how Preston Corcoris had tried to seduce her—or worse.

He wouldn't give her that impression, no matter what he felt. How stirred his body felt by her curves, her newly relaxed demeanor.

Her unintentionally seductive moves.

Sexy? Yes. But he knew what a bad idea it was to give in to those urges—even if she started to encourage him.

"Thank you so much, Daniel," she said. Then, after a moment's hesitation, she asked, "What do you really think of Moravo Beach? I can't do as much around here as I'd like, despite my disguise, since I don't want to run into my family or anyone I know, but I loved growing up here."

For the next few minutes, they talked about nothing, just having a friendly conversation. Daniel let it continue. The other information he wanted from her could wait for another time.

But it was getting late. "Why don't we clean up the dishes?" he asked. "I should be going soon."

"I'll take care of them," she said, but he insisted.

It didn't take long to bus the few items they'd taken out to the table. They had to engage in minor choreography so they could both work in the kitchen together, but in a short while all the plates and cooking containers had been rinsed and placed into the dishwasher.

"Thanks," Beth said when they were done. Her face looked radiant, as if he had solved all her problems and given her her life back.

Hell, that was his ultimate goal.

His current goal?

To leave and ponder how he might be able to use her to accomplish his task.

But she was looking up at him expectantly. And it wouldn't hurt just to give her an encouraging goodbye kiss.

He took the lovely, sexy Beth into his arms and, bending down, placed his lips on hers.

He was kissing her. Gently.

Beth found herself kissing him back. And enjoying it.

She pressed closer. It had been forever since she had even considered making love. Never at all, not even once, since becoming Beth. She had never wanted—dared—to get close to anyone, not even just physically.

And while she was still Andrea, Preston Corcoris's horrible power-assertion attempts over her—his attempted seduction coupled with threats—had turned her off completely from getting close to any man.

But now, with Daniel...

Her conscious thoughts seemed to evaporate as she found herself even more engulfed by his intensifying kiss. His mouth was hot, demanding, as he thrust his tongue against hers as if daring it to play sexy games. His scent so close was tangy. All masculine.

Control. She needed to keep control. Of herself. Of her surroundings. Wasn't that what had been drummed into her with her instructions on how to change her identity, her personality?

But at the moment, all she could do was concentrate

on that kiss. And Daniel, his body against hers, hot and strong and hard, so hard, in all the right places.

She felt utterly aware of his erection pressing against her middle, and she felt herself strain against him even more.

Even as her arms held him even closer, her mouth teasing, kissing him as lustfully as he did her.

"Beth," he muttered against her. "This isn't—"

"No," she responded. "It isn't." But as he started to pull back, she felt his hands go between them. To push her away? But she found herself leaning her upper body toward him even more.

His hands were suddenly beneath her T-shirt, touching her bare skin, creating a path of heat that moved upward, beneath the strap of her bra. She realized a moment later that he had unhooked it.

Now was the time to stop…if she was going to. But she didn't stop him. Didn't want to. Hadn't she already encouraged him? It wasn't past the point of no return, but…

He knew who she was. She knew who he was. Even so, they barely knew each other at all, and yet she somehow wanted to know everything about him.

Including his body and how it reacted with hers.

Her knees suddenly felt like buckling—or was it her libido telling her to lead him to the sofa behind them? The couch that pulled out into a bed…

Foolish. Foolish. This was no way to react simply to feeling relieved that she was no longer completely alone.

Assuming he'd told her the truth about who he was and why he was here.

But she knew her moment of mistrust was disappearing into the hot insistence of his touch. Her open bra was now pushed up above her breasts, and his hand had come between their bodies to caress her gently, teasingly, as her nipples reacted by tensing at his touch.

She heard her own soft moan, even as she thrust her hips forward against him. It wasn't fair that his skin, his hands, were playing so magically on her while she wasn't touching him that way. She lowered her hands, realizing that she would have a more difficult time than he had. His shirt was tucked in. Hers hadn't been.

It was a hurdle she could easily conquer. In moments, she had pulled the tail of his shirt from the back of his pants, then ran her fingers up the heated, smooth skin of his back.

This time it was his turn to moan. The sound was low and sexy and motivated her to inch slowly backward, one step, another, until her calf touched the sofa.

Bad move. She knew that, even as she let herself go limp enough to sink onto it.

Daniel bent forward toward her, and in moments they were both stretched out on the couch. It was narrow, so her body remained close against his. Both were still mostly clothed.

What a shame.

He must have had the same thought, for her T-shirt was suddenly being pulled up over her face, and immediately after that her bra was fully removed.

His head bent, and his mouth closed gently over one of her breasts, even as his hand reached downward to unfasten the button on the front of her jeans.

No fair that this be so one-sided. Even as she arched her back so his tongue, now playing with her nipple, could continue its games, she unbuttoned his shirt. But the angle was too difficult for her to do much more.

"Take your clothes off," she murmured against him.

"I will if you will."

Even as she laughed gently, she carefully moved back and stood, tearing off what was left of her clothing. He remained on the sofa, and she watched lustfully, all of her need suddenly billowing to a crescendo, as he removed what was left of his own attire, baring his toned, muscular chest with its skiff of light brown hair and his long hard erection.

He reached up toward her. "Come here," he said.

She quickly, delightedly, obeyed.

Chapter 7

Daniel was a government agent, a professional. With a conscience. And experience that taught him what a bad idea physicality could be.

But he cast those thoughts aside even as he looked at the slim, gorgeous figure of Beth Jones.

And that was exactly who she was to him—every tantalizing inch of her. Her breasts were taut and full and enticing. And below she was so damned sexy that he didn't want to wait to have her.

He held out his arms, noting that she was taking in every inch of him, as well. Looking longingly toward his stiff arousal, and that only made him grow all the more.

"Come here," he said gruffly, and suddenly she was back on the couch beside him. Against him.

Making him nuts with his need for her.

He moved. Touched her where it mattered. She was wet, and her legs opened as he caressed her.

She, at the same time, began gently pumping his shaft with her hand. Making him even harder, readier to thrust inside her.

But despite his disinclination to stop, his lust didn't make him completely a lunatic. "Wait," he growled, then moved again to grab the trousers he'd tossed on the floor near his feet. He managed somehow to get into his wallet, where he kept condoms in case of emergencies—like this one.

He ripped one open, then looked at her, right into those glazed, lustful violet eyes.

"Care to help?" he asked.

She took the condom from him. He bent over her, and she rose slightly and attempted to slip it on his aching penis. But whether it was the angle or her lack of experience or her shakiness because of need…who cared? She didn't fit it on immediately.

He took it from her, slipped it on and without waiting another moment laid her down and plunged inside her.

Beth gasped with need and delight. Thank heavens he, at least, was maintaining some degree of sanity.

She felt herself rock upward with his every thrust, gasping and moving and concentrating completely on what his body was doing to hers.

His pace quickened, and so did hers.

In moments, she felt herself flying over the precipice into her orgasm, even as she quietly screamed, "Daniel!"

Foolish. She knew how foolish she had been as she remained on the soft plush upholstery of the sofa, lying there facing Daniel, his body warm against hers as it flexed from his heavy breathing.

But it had been so long since she had felt a shred of

trust in anyone she had been in contact with—except those she had met as a result of Judge Treena's coaching. Her instructors in changing her identity had been tools, nice enough people she'd believed she could rely on, but she hadn't allowed herself to feel anything at all for any of them, male or female, except gratitude.

Even at that, she realized they were just doing their jobs. Giving her orders and advice based on their prior experience with other people—people who weren't her, who hadn't been in her situation, at least not exactly.

Now, though, she had made love with the one person here who might actually be able to help her reach her goal.

Had she blown that by her indiscretion this night?

Or…was it possible that she had increased her chances by giving him a reason beyond his job to help her?

"You okay?" His voice, rough from his still-heavy breathing, startled her.

"More than okay," she heard herself admit. So much for protecting her feelings. Although maybe complimenting him on his lovemaking prowess might encourage him to work with her.

Especially when her enjoyment had been so real…

"Yeah," he said, drawing the word out. "Me, too." He paused, and she felt his whole body grow rigid, as if he'd tried to pull away from her on the narrow surface. "But—"

"Yes, I know," she interrupted, anticipating what he was going to say. "This wasn't a good idea."

His brief laugh brought him up close to her again, and his arms went around her. "You could say that. But, hell, I'm glad we did it. Just this once."

"Just this once," she echoed, even as she felt a deep

pang of sorrow pulse through her. They'd gotten any sexual attraction out of their system.

Now they had to figure out how they could work together to achieve the goals they both were here to accomplish.

"So," she said brightly. "How about if I get dressed and make us some coffee?"

"Good idea," he said. "We still need to talk."

Daniel watched with appreciation as Beth slid off the couch in front of him, still gloriously naked as she knelt to retrieve her clothes from where they'd ended up on the floor.

As she rose again, her eyes scanned him before locking on to his. Her smile appeared both happily aware of him and his continued nudity, too—as well as rueful.

She pulled her clothes up to block her breasts and lower points of interest from his view, but only momentarily. With a tiny snort of laughter, she moved her garments again and began donning them as he watched.

When she was fully dressed once more, she said, "Your turn." But as he got up and retrieved his own clothing, she, too, looked him over first, nodded with what appeared to be an appreciative grin, then turned her back and headed into the kitchen.

He heard the sounds of the refrigerator door opening and something being moved on the counter as well as water running in the sink and figured she was well on her way to brewing their coffee.

That gave him time to think. No regrets. That was fruitless. And besides, he'd enjoyed it. A lot. The bigger regret was that they couldn't do it again.

Too many things—like his job and, of paramount importance, too, her safety—stood in their way.

He had watched the death of a lovely, scared confidential informant when he had worked for the FBI, after allowing their mutual attraction to distract him.

Edie.

That would not happen again. No more sex. And definitely no deeper feelings.

What he needed to figure out now was how he should approach his upcoming conversation with Beth that also had to be a strategy session.

Especially when wherever they sat to talk he would be aware, really aware, of the delights that lay below the surface of what she wore—and how those enticing parts of her body were once again way off-limits to him, as they should have been before.

When Beth popped her head through the doorway again, he was fully dressed. "It's brewing," she said. "Let's sit down and wait for it, okay?"

"Sure," he agreed. He resumed his spot at the same place at her small table where he'd sat before. "So," he began—all business, making certain not to add even a hint of what they'd done in his tone, "the background description you gave me before was really helpful, but I want to dig into it more, okay?" If it wasn't okay, he'd have to figure out a way to make her talk, or he'd waste a lot of time trying to extract information she had that he needed.

"Sure," she said in a soft tone that was a lot more friendly than his. "What do you want to know?"

"Why don't you just tell me what you heard back then that made you worry and who you heard it from. And why it was that you didn't have enough information to be considered a legitimate witness who'd be able to testify and get into WitSec."

The satiated glow he'd seen on her face suddenly

morphed into sorrow—and pain. He regretted that, but this was a conversation they had to have, the sooner the better. They had to move on, immediately.

And as much as he wanted to take her back into his arms to soothe her, he wouldn't do that. Instead, he forced himself to sit still. And wait.

She looked down at the table as if it were covered in chocolate or some delectable food so exciting that she couldn't take her eyes off it. But he understood that was both to hide the moistness that now threatened to spill down her cheeks and to allow herself to focus on what was now filling her mind.

"I'm not sure where it started," she said in a low, husky whisper. "I was so excited to be part of Corcoris, to be able to give back to the company that had saved my mother's life—and to be paid for it, too. It felt amazing. Of course, the medications she's still on were developed when Preston Corcoris's father was in charge, not now. But I didn't realize things had changed when I began working there."

"That's what I was told when I started this assignment," Daniel said. "The quality of the medications apparently hasn't been fully maintained since Preston took over—only the profitability. Right?"

"Exactly." Beth shook her head. "But I didn't know that, not then. I was just so pleased to be working here. I started by helping more senior members of the marketing staff write and edit television spots and magazine ads. We could say lots of good stuff about the products, but we also had to add the applicable warnings so people who were interested in asking their doctors to prescribe certain medications would also be aware of possible side effects."

"Right." Daniel, like everyone else who watched TV

these days, was aware of the minute-long ads where thirty seconds were taken up with telling people why they shouldn't take the medications being promoted. He always found that odd. So was telling people what they supposedly needed but that they had to convince their physicians to prescribe it for them. He mentioned that to Beth.

"Most doctors are happy to prescribe the pharmaceuticals that are being advertised as long as they fit a patient's diagnosed conditions," she said. "Companies like Corcoris make sure of that by giving out lots of free samples as well as swag to the doctors, even tickets to shows or ball games or whatever. They expect the doctors to act ethically, of course. Or that's what my new bosses at Corcoris always told me. Until…"

"Until what?" Daniel prompted.

"Just a minute." She rose and headed into the kitchen, for the coffee, Daniel figured. He followed her, and they spent a few minutes pouring their java into brown pottery mugs. She took a dash of milk in hers. He again took his black.

She offered him some cookies from a package in her narrow pantry, but he declined, leading her back into the other room and the table where they'd been sitting.

"You were saying?" he prompted.

She shut her eyes for a moment, once more indicating pain. But then she said, "I don't know how much you know about pharmaceuticals." She regarded him quizzically.

"I did a lot of research and worked with some experts before coming here undercover," he said. "But am I an expert? No."

She nodded. "Well, you probably learned that the patents on medications last for a certain number of years, and then generics pop up all over for the good, effective ones."

He nodded. "That's why the companies are always busy developing more. Or trying to. Not all their attempts are successful."

"Right." She took a sip of coffee, her lovely full lips touching her cup in a way that made him want to kiss her again.

Heck, it had been long enough that the idea of making love with her passed through his mind once more. But that couldn't happen, not tonight or ever again.

"When I started working at Corcoris, the medication that had saved my mother was then available as a generic. It was cheaper and just as effective. I was fascinated by the number of other drugs they were working on then, all in different stages of development. Being a public relations assistant, I helped to promote the company and its products that had recently gone through the FDA's approval process and were then on the market. I reported to Milt Ranich."

Daniel was aware of that—and had known even before Beth mentioned it that the man had disappeared. Where was he? And was he still alive?

"I still don't know exactly what happened." Beth was still talking, as if she needed to get everything on the table in front of him. Maybe it was cathartic to her to disclose it to him. She'd undoubtedly told Judge Treena everything before, too. "But Milt—well, one day we were best buddies, even though he was my boss. And then he seemed to withdraw into himself. Just started telling me what to do, without any friendliness between us. I kept pressing him gently, but I felt hurt. And worried. I didn't know what was going on."

"But he eventually told you?" Daniel asked.

"Well…yes. And no." Beth sighed. "If only he had really let me in on it. It might have been better for both of us."

The coffee was bitter at the back of Beth's throat as she took her next sip. It was cooler, too. She quickly rose and took her mug and Daniel's back into the kitchen to pour in a little more to heat it up.

That gave her a minute to think about what to say next.

Daniel hadn't moved. When she placed his mug back on the table in front of him, he regarded her with what appeared to be sympathy with those handsome blue eyes of his—much more apparent and expressive now that he wasn't wearing those geeky glasses that were part of his undercover garb. *Remote* sympathy, from one stranger aimed toward another with issues.

It was as if their lovemaking had never happened. They were instead all business.

She was fine with that. She had to be.

"Better now?" he asked gently.

"Nothing's better now." Her focus was all on their discussion now, not on him. She knew she sounded upset and bitter, but he was forcing her to delve into memories she had purposely tried to suppress—before. But since she was again working here, in her own form of being undercover at Corcoris, they were back in her conscious mind anyway.

Better to share them with someone who might be able to use those memories to achieve what she wanted: justice at Corcoris and a way to bring Preston Corcoris down before he had her family harmed.

"Okay," she finally said with a sigh. "Here it all is in a nutshell. I acted completely friendly with Milt—well, it wasn't an act, he *was* my friend—until he finally broke down. He was so upset…and what he told me involved some of the newest designer drugs that Corcoris was getting ready to put on the market. He said that he'd learned that the formulations weren't exactly as being disclosed to the FDA—a little more of this ingredient, a little less of another. The quality of those ingredients depended a lot on where they'd originated, and what was being used in the actual medications wasn't always what was used for the tests that were reported to the FDA. And then there were also questions about how the clinical trials were conducted. Supposedly all the information was being doctored, so to speak. The drugs themselves were being altered for testing, using better quality ingredients—maybe. Maybe there were payoffs to certain employees or to outside labs conducting the trials…but Milt wasn't specific."

She looked into Daniel's face and saw more interest than sympathy there, or so she thought. But, hey, this was exactly the information he needed from her, wasn't it?

She understood his attitude—really. The fact they'd made love didn't change the fact he had a job to do. And maybe he'd even had sex with her to open her up to him—in more ways than one.

Cynical? Yes, but she'd learned the hard way that cynicism wasn't always far from the truth.

"So Corcoris, or at least some of its personnel, were involved in a fraudulent attempt to get drugs on the market quickly to make them more money?" Daniel asked.

"Exactly," she said. "And cheaper than the quality they were represented to be. Milt had heard about it. The fact crushed him. And then he told me. And…"

"And?" Daniel prompted when she stopped.

"Things got so out of control after I learned about it," she said, feeling as if her heart were constricting inside her chest. "Milt shut down after that, didn't talk to me. And then he disappeared—supposedly on a business trip, but I kept trying to call him on his cell phone and got no answer. People said he'd just up and quit because he couldn't handle the stress, but I didn't believe that. He had no family, either, so I couldn't try to find him that way. At the same time, I was suddenly Preston Corcoris's golden child. He kept calling me into meetings as if I were the head of the company's PR department, but there were others with a lot more seniority than me. And then—"

She felt her eyes close but that didn't keep out the vision of the horrible man appearing in her office late one night when no one else was around.

"What happened, Beth?" That was Daniel's voice, its deepness low and sympathetic yet pushing her somehow to respond.

She tried to make her own tone light and amused, knowing she fell woefully short of that. "Oh, he visited me in my office one night when I was working late and told me how gorgeous I was and how he had been yearning to make me his. All that ridiculous seductive stuff that if I were really naive I might really have eaten up."

"So he came on to you?" Daniel prompted when she grew quiet again.

"Yeah." Her eyes closed yet again. "He tried to seduce me, and when I told him where to go as gently as I could since I wanted to keep my job, he started talking about Milt and demanded to know what that disloyal SOB might have told me. I tried to laugh that off, too. But he didn't buy it—and he started threatening me. I…I acted scared. I *was* scared. And then I heard a noise in the hall and screamed. He grabbed me, but one of the nighttime security team broke into my office. I was so upset, but I still thought I might want to keep my job—until I had a moment to think. I just smiled, grabbed my purse and went home."

"So when did you try calling the cops?" Daniel asked gently.

"I had a friend who was in law school," she said. "The sister of one of my high school classmates. I called her and told her the whole story. She said I should go ahead and contact the local cops about the attack on me, which I did, a couple of days after it happened. But they didn't arrest Preston. I was advised not only by her but also by those cops that I could try suing him or whatever but I had no proof."

Daniel's gaze appeared sympathetic as he continued, "And what about your accusations against Corcoris Pharmaceuticals?"

The frustration she had felt back then resurfaced, but she responded. "I told the local authorities about them at the same time but wasn't too concerned when they didn't get involved since I had no direct proof of that, either. I needed the attention of the FDA, which I ultimately got after a face-to-face meeting a few weeks later. Their surprise inspection maybe a month after the attack on me only bolstered the company's claim that I was a disgruntled fired employee making false accusations—yes, I was let go almost immediately after Preston's assault because of my supposedly false accusations. I couldn't testify as to anything regarding the fraud except that some guy who'd left town had made some allegations that, to me, were all hearsay. And apparently there was some correspondence from Milt that I didn't see, so no one thought anything bad had happened to him. But I doubt that any of it was real."

She knew that tears were flowing down her cheeks

by then. She wanted to throw the coffee mug against the floor, shatter it to distract her from the horror and sorrow and despair that flooded her mind all over again, as they had so many times since all that had happened nearly a year ago.

She anticipated that Daniel would do his job and push her for suggestions of where to look for evidence of what Milt had told her—evidence that she hadn't been able to provide when she'd needed it so desperately.

Instead he rose, took her by the shoulders and brought her to a stand, too.

And then he took her into his arms. Held her tightly while she broke down sobbing.

"It was all so—so horrible," she said. "I couldn't find another job, and when I swallowed my pride and tried to rescind what I'd said at Corcoris to get my job back, everybody had been told about all the lies I'd supposedly made up because our beloved boss, Preston Corcoris, had gently tried to avoid my attempts at seducing *him*." She laughed bitterly through her tears. "As if," she finished.

Daniel hugged her against him. Once more she was aware of his hard body—and the growing erection that pressed into her.

She almost tried to encourage him to make love to her again. That, at least, would get her mind on something a lot more enjoyable than the fear and grief that engulfed it now.

Instead, he pushed her away gently and looked into her eyes. His seemed full of sympathy—or was she just reading that out of hope?

"It's getting late, Beth," he said. "If you'd like, I can stay here. Sleep on the floor if necessary. But even though I think we still have a lot of strategy to talk about, we'd better save it for another time."

She drew her breath in raggedly, forcing herself to cease crying and smile at him.

"I agree," she said. "I'm just so glad that Judge Treena sent someone here to help me bring that bastard down. Thank you, Daniel. It's fine for you to leave. I'll be okay now."

"You're sure?" He sounded dubious.

"Of course. I'm too tired now to continue discussing this anyway." She gave an exaggerated yawn. "I'll be able to talk to you more about it another time, and we can plan what comes next together. Right now I think I just need a good night's sleep."

And time to watch TV or read a book or anything at all to distract herself from all he had brought back to her frazzled mind with his questions.

Distract herself? Heck, she could just go over their delightful lovemaking in her mind. Remember every moment of it—when it had been the result of her own decision, not the horribly frightening attempt at seduction by Preston Corcoris.

Cementing it all in her mind would be a good thing anyway since it was strictly a one-time occurrence.

"Okay," Daniel said, murmuring against her hair. "I agree I'd better leave, since if I stay, I know I'm going to have to fight wanting to make love with you again."

Her entire body reacted with a sudden need for him to do just that.

Which forced her to laugh out loud and say, "Better go ahead and fight it, then—at your own place. It was fun. But now—good night, Daniel. I need some alone time, and I'm sure you do, too."

Chapter 8

He felt damned bad. A real louse for leaving Beth when she seemed at the end of her emotional tether.

Especially after shifting gears so adamantly from where they'd been back to where they should be.

But what he had told her was right. If he stayed, he would want to continue holding her. Touching her. And after that bout of incredible sex, one thing would undoubtedly lead to another once more. Or at least he'd wind up attempting to seduce her again, for the physical experience only. But anything like that was a bad idea.

She had to cooperate with him as long as she was here.

He remained outside her apartment building for a while, sitting in his small well-used car, which was part of his undercover disguise.

It wasn't likely that Preston Corcoris or anyone else had followed her home that night—not any more than he might have any other night. On the other hand, there'd been that minor interaction when he'd been there to re-direct it.

Could Corcoris have recognized Beth?

He hadn't seemed to. Plus, Daniel had kept his eyes open as he'd driven here before. There'd been no indication that Beth was being followed.

Of course, the company would have her home address on file. That was one good reason for Daniel to check for strangers driving in this area now. But the street was quiet. He was the only one around, watching things.

Even so, he sat for maybe half an hour. A couple of cars drove by. Another one stopped and parked, and its driver, a woman, went into a similar-looking apartment building across the street.

Another woman parked and got a kid out of the back-seat, then entered Beth's building.

Everything seemed fine. He was overreacting.

Maybe because he had an urge to see Beth one more time that night, and...

He gave a snort as he turned the key in the ignition. He had way overstayed his welcome around here.

He drove off, steering his car toward the Moravo Beach apartment he rented while pretending to be a lab rat at Corcoris. It was only about five miles from her apartment. Even so, it might have been across the state. He couldn't cross that distance again—at least not until he felt certain that he could control his own body from pouncing on her while they were alone.

Unless, of course, he had a genuine reason to believe she was in danger, and his being near her wasn't the result of his sexual interest in her.

When they were both at the Corcoris headquarters, their minds would be occupied enough to sublimate any physical attraction between them. At least his mind would be, and he trusted Beth and her intent to work to put Corcoris down to do the same.

As he drove, he thought about his presence here. He had been working with CIU for a couple of years. He liked Judge Treena and her attitude. Enjoyed working with her, so far, at least.

But he had initially wondered about the value of CIU.

Why protect people who couldn't contribute anything other than disclosing that there might be a problem of great interest to the government or its agencies—like, in this case, the Food and Drug Administration—without being able to prove it?

People like Beth, who might really have been threatened but had only heard rumors about what was wrong with an outfit like Corcoris.

On the other hand, if what she claimed was right, and Corcoris was cutting a lot of corners and doing such a good job of hiding it that the FDA had initially been fooled, many people who took their medications could be in danger.

It didn't hurt to check things out and look for proof.

Besides, going undercover like this was fun—and now, he admitted to himself, the job was even better since he had met the person who'd made the claims and was now being protected.

Would he have decided he liked what he was doing as much as he did at the moment if that person under protection was someone other than the sexy Beth Jones?

Didn't matter. He would do his job anyway. And add to the protection in any manner that was needed.

No one else was going to die under his watch.

He soon turned onto the side alley that led to the entrance of his building's parking lot. He saw no one out and about. A good thing. He needed time and solitude to digest what Beth had told him—and to ensure that his body stopped reacting just because he thought about her.

He pulled his car into his designated space, parked and headed up the stairs.

To her surprise, Beth had slept reasonably well last night.

Maybe it was because she knew someone was not only aware of her real identity but willing to protect it and, perhaps, her.

Maybe it was because of happy exhaustion after her temporary but utterly enjoyable physical interlude with Daniel.

In any event, she'd had sweet dreams and smiled a lot to herself—until she reached the Corcoris Pharmaceuticals campus that morning.

She parked in the employees' lot, pulled her bland Corcoris Cleaning Staff T-shirt down over her jeans and at the same time turned her expression into something just as bland.

She was back. Here, where she had work to do—two kinds of work. And she didn't dare get them confused.

That was enough to stick a nail into any balloon of cheerfulness.

Would she see Daniel today? She suspected they would both find a way to be sure of it. That gave her a warm feeling inside, but she quickly shoved it off.

She approached the rear of the main office and lab building as usual, via the rear door. She swiped her ID card, then headed downstairs to the basement and its cleaning-gear storage area.

Once again she punched in at the computer to show that Beth Jones had reported for work this Wednesday right on time.

Would she wind up with another miserable assignment today like the awful one she had wound up with yesterday—cleaning up after someone had trashed a lab area?

She still wondered who had done that—and why.

Mary Cantrera approached from where she'd been talking to another member of the cleaning crew beside a cart.

"Good morning," Beth said brightly, then looked down at the floor in shock. She had sounded chipper, happy, not the shy little thing she was supposed to be here.

Just because yesterday—and its evening—had held surprises, including some that were more than pleasant, didn't mean she could dare to break her cover.

But Mary gave a return "Good morning" in her usual snide tone, which made Beth feel a little better.

"What would you like me to do today, Mary?" Beth kept her head down, her voice barely more than a whisper.

"You can start out in the cafeteria again," Mary ordered. "Gabrielle and John are already there but we need to finish cleaning it fast today. There's some kind of lunch being thrown there by the execs." Her tone sounded almost accusatory, as if Beth somehow held up finishing the cleaning by arriving not early but on time.

"Of course." Beth hurried to the nearest cart, where she started inventorying the equipment and supplies. She was joined immediately by Mary, who began moving things around to fit more liquid cleaners on the shelves below.

Slowing Beth down. But of course she didn't complain about it. All she did was murmur, "Thank you." And hurriedly push the cart out the door as soon as her boss completed her interference.

Although it wasn't as bad as cleaning the trashed lab,

this wasn't an assignment Beth particularly wanted, either. Working in the cafeteria was repetitious. There was virtually no possibility of snooping into formulations, computer data or lab notes for something that could eventually be used as evidence against the company or its executives.

And there was more possibility of running into some of those executives again—thereby increasing her risk of being recognized as Andrea.

But objecting wasn't in her job description. Nor did it fit with Beth Jones's personality.

She headed for the service elevator and pushed the button. The door opened in just a few seconds. The car wasn't empty, which didn't surprise Beth.

Nor should she have been completely surprised to see that one of the three people on it was Daniel, even though he could have just as easily taken one of the regular elevators here. Or the stairway.

He wasn't on the cleaning staff, so why use the service elevator?

Maybe it was part of the role he played here in his undercover capacity.

Besides, this wasn't the Daniel she had spent time with late yesterday. No, this was the man she'd first met. The nerdy, slouched guy with the white lab jacket and black-rimmed glasses who smiled endlessly and geekily.

Her mind immediately shot back to the previous day here. She'd interacted with this guy then, particularly when he had diverted Preston Corcoris's attention from her and on to other lab-related things.

The fact she'd run into him before meant it was okay to acknowledge him.

"Good morning," she said, not quite meeting his eyes as she bent her head in her shiest persona.

"Hi," came the loud, happy response. "Need any help with all that stuff?"

Was that his way of saying they needed to get together and talk? If so, why?

In case it was important, she wouldn't negate the possibility. "No, I'm fine," she said. "I won't have to push it far anyway. The cafeteria is near the elevator."

That told him where she was going. And if he did happen to show up there, she'd know she needed to take a restroom break or otherwise figure out a benign way to leave her fellow janitorial-staff members.

She got into the elevator and pushed the button for the third floor. She squeezed herself behind the cart and turned.

Through the still-open door, she saw that Daniel the geek was still in the hallway. He was talking to the two guys he'd ridden in the elevator with. Both wore suits. Were they executives? Then what were they doing on that floor?

Or could they be security? Beth felt uneasy seeing them there, too.

But sometime, preferably later today, she'd find a way to quiz him about who those guys were—and what they'd been talking about.

Interesting, Daniel thought as he stood in the downstairs hallway, forcing himself not to look toward the departed elevator.

Not to think about Beth and last night, let alone why they both were here…

He quickly faced the guys he was showing around. They were doctors, here for a lunchtime meeting in the Corcoris Pharmaceuticals cafeteria. They'd asked for a tour of the headquarters building, and Ivan Rissinger, right-hand man to Preston Corcoris, had given Daniel the honor.

Did Rissinger even know who Daniel supposedly was, what he ostensibly did here? Why give a lab rat like he was supposed to be the duty of giving people the company hoped to impress an exciting tour?

Obviously these guys didn't rate highly with the company execs.

Or maybe there was more to it. Maybe they had the execs' ears and he was on trial.

Which made him regret that he'd offered to help Beth and thereby put her, even for an instant, on their radar.

"Not much to show you down here," he told his charges, Dr. Kresge from Riverside and Dr. Adams from Bakersfield. He shrugged and smiled. "I don't get here often myself. The labs where I work are mostly on the second floor. There's just support stuff around here, as far as I know—storage, cleaning equipment, offices for the janitorial and maintenance staff, that kind of thing. Now, if you're ready to go up to the second floor, where I hang out, it's a lot sexier than this." His gesture took in the wide hallway with its clean but well-worn floors and the door-riddled walls that also could use some updating.

No people were around at the moment, a good thing. No distractions as Beth had been a few minutes ago.

"Sounds good," Dr. Adams said. What was his first name? Rissinger had mumbled it when he'd introduced Daniel to these guys. Kresge's, too. But obviously Daniel wasn't their equal, so he was just to call them each "Doctor."

"No need to use the service elevator this time," Daniel said. "Fun to ride it now and then for the experience, but the regular elevators are much nicer, and two come down to this level."

He had been surprised when Rissinger had pointed to it while sending Daniel on his way with these two. But other people had been walking around then near the other elevator bank, so maybe he'd figured they'd be able to use the service elevator more quickly.

A short while later Daniel took the doctors in one of the nicer elevators to the second floor. Once again he showed them around. He wasn't surprised to see a few of his fellow lab assistants doing the same thing with other suited people—women and men—who must be there for the luncheon, too. The low buzz of voices permeated everywhere. People wandered in and out of a lot of the labs.

Hardly sanitary, Daniel thought. But no one seemed to be going through the doors into the most secured and highly clean areas.

He had a feeling that Beth and her fellow cleaning staff would be busy here later in the day, or even tonight.

And in the labs, too? Beth had enough on her mind around here, and he hadn't wanted to add to her angst by talking about yesterday's mess she'd had to clean, but he suspected there'd been more to it than some kind of weird accident. He'd started putting out feelers to some of the guys who'd been there awhile and had two impressions so far. One: that wasn't the first time it had happened. And two: no one wanted—or dared—to talk about it.

But he'd listen and nudge and find out more about it.

For now, though, he wasn't pleased that he and his fellow lab geeks weren't important enough to get notice of the lunch meeting, let alone hear what it was all about. Which didn't mean that he couldn't find this out, too. Maybe even finagle some kind of invitation.

One way or another, he would watch, and listen to, what was going on.

* * *

With only one set of steps to get these guys up to the third-floor cafeteria, Daniel led them to a close-by stairwell as it neared eleven o'clock.

The doctors had seemed particularly interested in one of the labs that Daniel had told them was primarily used for quality control.

"What kinds of medications are being tested there right now?" Adams asked.

"It varies," Daniel parried. "I was working on an existing antibiotic and also assisting a bit on our new diet med. I think it's okay to mention that to you as long as I don't go into any detail. You know that our company, as well as most others, is pretty proprietary about what we're doing."

"But that's exactly why we're here," Kresge said, smiling. "We're both weight-loss specialists and we were told that the meeting today is to get our input about what we'd like to see more of in assistive medications." He was maybe Daniel's age, early thirties, and looked bright eyed and excited about the possibilities, as if he were a kid who'd been handed some new technological gadget to try.

His counterpart, Adams, was probably twenty years older and tried to look jaded, although Daniel had seen some interest as he pointed out some of the newest testing devices.

Interesting news about the lunch meeting, Daniel thought. Even though he hadn't been officially invited, he decided he would become best friends to these two guys so he could hear what was going on.

"That's right," he said to Kresge, smiling as if he knew what he was talking about. "We're all interested in what you physicians who'll be in a position to prescribe our latest formulations want to see. And I'll just bet our new diet drug that just came on the market will fit your needs." No one could say that Daniel was anything but a company guy if they overheard that.

If they only knew.

Both doctors nodded noncommittally, and Daniel showed them around just a little more before ushering them to the stairwell to walk up one flight to the cafeteria floor.

The two doctors were chattering then about what they both would be saying at the meeting. Daniel tuned them out, at least partially. That wasn't what he was here for.

But maybe something that occurred during or after the meeting would prove useful.

When he opened the door to the hallway, he saw that farther down it Beth was standing beside her cart, waiting for a service elevator. He had an urge to go offer his help again but knew she wouldn't appreciate it. It would only call attention to her once more.

And he'd be doing it more for himself than for her.

Instead, he ignored her and led his charges down the hallway in the other direction, which was fairly crowded. He stayed with them as they entered the cafeteria and noticed that there was an executive at each of the dozens of tables, apparently holding a guest list or seating chart.

That didn't bode well for his ability to stay and listen.

But what if this assembly led into a discussion about things the doctors' patients had experienced that indicated problems with prior Corcoris medications?

He needed to at least hear that, just in case.

He decided to take another approach. After helping Drs. Kresge and Adams find their seats, he said goodbye to them and wended his way back through the noisy and apparently exuberant crowd.

He suddenly had an urge to help the kitchen crew.

They could always use another pair of hands, couldn't they?

It turned out they couldn't. But Daniel happened to be in the right place at the right time. As he maneuvered his way back among the tables, one of the executives he hadn't met before, a woman dressed in a black business suit, stood up and blocked his way.

"We had a cancellation at my table," she said softly but urgently. "You're one of the quality-control test guys, aren't you?"

"That's right." The description was close enough to what he was purportedly doing here.

"Then join us for lunch. And get ready to answer a bunch of questions."

Daniel wanted to collect answers, not give them.

But this at least gave him a reason to stick around.

Chapter 9

Beth had burned with curiosity as the first visitors had begun to arrive at the cafeteria while she finished her cleaning detail.

By the time she'd left, she had ached with a desire to stay there somehow and listen to the people, who she'd gathered were mostly doctors being primed to love and prescribe Corcoris Pharmaceuticals products, especially the highly hyped new weight-loss medication that had only recently passed its clinical trials and first gone to market.

How did they really feel about the drugs before the lure of a fancy meal—and the totes filled with all kinds of swag that were stacked at each table?

Did any have patients who'd had bad experiences with Corcoris Pharmaceuticals, the way Andrea had heard before fleeing?

While she had worked here in PR, she had been involved in downplaying the few lawsuits against the company that were made public. All pharmaceuticals companies had claims against them, but, she'd been told, those that were filed against Corcoris were because of individual bad reactions not described in their warnings, not because there was anything wrong with—or unsafe about—their products.

But she had come to suspect otherwise. Since then, she had watched the news for lawsuits against Corcoris, but still no major claims had arisen—or at least been publicized. Even so, she didn't doubt what Milt had hinted to her. Was Preston paying off those who'd been harmed, both for their injuries and also to keep quiet?

She wouldn't put it past him.

He could be saving a lot of money by using inferior ingredients and fudging test results. And she would, somehow, find the evidence to prove it.

Beth had seen Daniel with those two men downstairs, then walking into the cafeteria with them. That was a good thing. Maybe he would be able to listen to what was said and extrapolate any bad stuff. Maybe he could even get any doctors who'd seen bad results to send him information that they could use against Corcoris.

He'd have to be careful, but that was Daniel's job. And Beth had no doubt he could do whatever was necessary to accomplish it.

But she needed to acquire more information on her own.

And she had an idea how a mere member of the cleaning crew might be able to at least listen in on some conversations.

Fortunately, Mary Cantrera wasn't there when Beth parked her cart inside the storage area, and neither were any of her fellow cleaning staff. She picked up some rags, brushes and bottles of liquid cleaning supplies, stuck them into a storage basket from one of the carts, and headed out.

She did see fellow cleaner Gabrielle approaching from down the hall and managed to duck into the stairwell before she was noticed. She definitely didn't need any questions or conversation about what she was up to.

Although she did have more questions for Gabrielle about the kind of mess that they'd cleaned in the lab yesterday. But there had been no appropriate downtime for her to ask anything yesterday, and this certainly wasn't the time, either.

Fortunately, no one else was in the stairwell. The basket wasn't too heavy, and Beth walked up to the third floor with no interruptions.

When she arrived there, she opened the door slowly and carefully, looking to see if there was anyone to notice her.

Not that it really mattered. Her planned cover should work just fine here.

The hallway was empty, and as she walked toward the ladies' room she heard a voice amplified by a loudspeaker projecting from the cafeteria.

She nearly froze. It was Preston Corcoris.

She would never forget his voice.

She stood still for just a moment, listening. He was talking about all the planning and testing that went into each new pharmaceutical developed by Corcoris. A standard spiel.

Before, when she'd been Andrea and had been working here in public relations—before it all went south— she might even have written a speech like that for him.

Grimacing, Beth ducked into the restroom. There, she

set the basket on the floor and began slowly working on cleaning the sinks.

Eventually, some women would venture in here from the luncheon. Would they say anything useful? She could only hope so.

She wondered where Daniel was at the moment. Probably inside the room, sitting at one of the tables, enjoying his lunch.

It would be much easier for him to pick up something said by one of the people attending the lunch.

But was this day a waste of time for both of them?

It was late now, past normal working hours. While in the restroom, Beth had heard some interesting conversations between visiting doctors as they'd washed their hands, sometimes criticizing Corcoris and its products. She'd made a mental note of what they'd talked about. There had been other times when the guests had asked questions of some Corcoris female executives. Without more, all she had eavesdropped on was just hearsay and couldn't be used as evidence, but Beth had hopes that at least one of the topics would lead to something helpful.

Once she had walked back out of the restroom, practically invisible as one of the cleaning staff, and headed downstairs, she had taken her own lunch break. Later Mary had sent her and most of the other cleaning-crew members back to the cafeteria to clean up. But that was after everyone had left. And she'd still had no good opportunity to try to elicit a discussion about yesterday's laboratory mess, let alone something more useful.

Now the rest of the cleaning staff had gone home, even Mary. Beth felt somewhat frustrated after believing there could be a breakthrough today with all the conversations around—yet finding nothing.

She decided to return to the lab floor and do some "cleaning." If no one was around, she could try once more to get into the computers.

At least now, after hearing a little criticism of Corcoris's new weight-loss medication, she would have a better starting point of where to look.

And on one of the lab floors…well, there was always the possibility of running into Daniel again. If he had heard something helpful he, too, might be following up on it.

For this effort, looking official was more important than invisibility. She wheeled her cart down the hall and pushed the button for the service elevator. It came almost immediately, and Beth pushed the button for the second floor.

Before deciding which lab area to use for her undercover efforts, she began peeking inside the doors to see if any were occupied.

The third one was. And not just by any lab rat conducting tests or working on reports.

Daniel was there, sitting at a desk in a cubicle and working on a computer.

He looked up as she entered, appearing startled behind his dark-rimmed glasses. And then he smiled at her.

Despite their phenomenal lovemaking, she didn't know him that well, but she thought she read relief on his face.

"Cleaning crew," she piped up, partly in case there was someone else around whom she hadn't noticed and partly just to be funny. Were there security cameras in this lab? She glanced around but saw none. Not that she could trust that.

"I've got a mess over here for you to clean up," Daniel said, then made a come-here motion with his head that

made her smile. She obeyed, leaving the cart by the door
and moving over to join him. As always while on his job
here, he wore his white lab jacket—even as he had done
while showing those doctors around.

"Where's your mess?" she inquired, pretending stern-
ness as she stopped behind him and looked over his
shoulder.

"I'm working on it." But he stood slightly, just enough
to give her a small kiss on the mouth.

There had better not be any security cameras around,
she thought. But Daniel, who'd spent more time in these
labs and was better trained to observe such equipment,
would be aware of where any were located.

And how that little touch sent such streams of fire
through her she wasn't sure. Anticipation, she supposed.
But that was ridiculous here, let alone anywhere else
with Daniel. Been there, done that, and there was to be
no more.

"Let me know when you're ready for me to clean up,"
she said. "I'll—"

"Look," he said quietly. "Don't know if it'll lead anywhere, but I'm into a different part of the computer system than that I'd been able to look into before. I heard
some stuff today at the lunch, but more important, I got
to help one of the execs, a woman seated at my table.
Poor thing lost her cell phone for a few minutes, too. I
happened to find and return it—but not before I uncovered a couple of key passwords."

"Is that why you're on the computer this late?" Beth
knew she sounded excited. "Have you found anything
that could lead to some tangible evidence?"

"Working on it, but nothing yet." He turned up toward
her again. "I'd like to get together with you later. I heard

some things that might ultimately be useful and want to run them by you."

"Me, too." When he looked at her quizzically, she said, "Women sometimes chat in restrooms, and the one near the cafeteria was really dirty today. I thought it a reasonable time to clean it up."

He laughed. "Good girl. Look, give me about half an hour here. If I haven't found anything by then, I'll still need to get off-line. We can go out for a quick dinner and conversation, if that's okay with you."

Feeling a little cocky, Beth said, "Fine. But one of these days I expect you to cook me dinner at your place."

His light brown eyebrows rose. "Deal," he said, "but not tonight." He glanced at the computer screen. "It's seven-thirty now. I'll call you on your cell at eight."

"Fine. Meantime, I'll see if there's anything I can get into on this floor for the next twenty minutes or so."

She met his eyes, smiled sexily, then shook her head as she left. No use flirting with the guy.

But if they could share information that turned useful… Yeah. That was why she was here.

She pushed the cart back into the hallway—and froze. Preston Corcoris was just exiting the main elevator.

It was her turn this time to protect Daniel. She wished she could duck inside the lab, tell him to log off and disappear.

That wouldn't happen. Corcoris had already seen her. Where was he heading? Maybe he wouldn't come too close, wouldn't get near this door at all.

But she couldn't count on that. Instead, she began fussing over items on her cart, as if looking for some piece of cleaning equipment. As Corcoris approached, she prayed that she didn't resemble her former persona, Andrea, in any way he would recognize.

She ran through the checklist in her mind.

First she bent her knees to look shorter and splayed her upper lip just a little to appear as if she had a mild case of buck teeth.

She now always wore her Beth makeup—deeper complexioned than Andrea had been, eyebrows darkened and at a sharper angle. Her violet contact lenses were in. Her hair was black, in a pixie haircut, instead of the light brown highlighted locks Andrea had always worn long.

Edginess and working out made her thinner than Andrea.

And she'd keep her voice low, subservient. Her gaze down at the floor.

It could work. Should work.

Despite Daniel's help the last time, Beth always knew she would run into Preston Corcoris. Now was as good a time as any to test her new persona.

He approached where she stood, and she examined him with her fleeting glance. He seemed taller than his nearly six-foot height now, but that was undoubtedly because of her assumed shrinkage. He wore a white shirt, red-striped tie, black trousers and shining dress shoes. All executive, but of course, he'd been entertaining people earlier.

His mouth was a thin, irritated line. She'd seen that before. In fact, it was his usual expression except when he had leered at her as Andrea. His face held a hint of pudginess accentuated by the straight brown lines that were his brows. Fortunately, he apparently accepted the fact that she was a nobody janitress and barely looked at her despite her being somewhat in his way.

She forced herself not to quiver. "Hello, sir," she said loudly, wanting to be sure that Daniel could hear her.

"Have a good evening, sir." And then she began pushing the cart away.

"Good evening," he repeated.

She felt relieved that he didn't appear to pay much attention to her. Her disguise was working.

Plus, he seemed determined to get into the lab where Daniel now worked.

Had Daniel heard her? Had he gotten off the computer or at least logged off the sites he wasn't supposed to have entered? By using someone else's password, he should be safe from being identified via the computer—she hoped. But she had a feeling that Daniel McManus knew his way around stuff like that and could protect himself.

Given enough time.

Just in case, she frantically combed her mind for something else to do or say that wouldn't give her away but would nevertheless again give warning as well as buy Daniel more time. Push the cart in Corcoris's direction, as if by accident?

Too obvious.

Shout out some other kind of greeting? Like what?

Ask him a question—the time, perhaps? But she was wearing an obvious cheap watch. Even if he didn't recognize her, he would wonder what she was up to.

Okay, then. She could—

She nearly gasped as the door opened just as Corcoris reached for the knob.

Instead, Daniel was the one to gasp as he stood there staring. A false gasp, she figured, but it made sense. "Oh, hi, Mr. Corcoris," he said. "I didn't expect to see anyone here."

Did that ring false? After all, she'd spoken loud enough to be heard.

But then she noticed that Daniel had earbuds in his

ears, wires running down toward the breast pocket of his white lab jacket. As if he'd been listening to music on some device and couldn't have heard her.

Smart man.

She turned away and began pushing her cart down the hall. She didn't need to eavesdrop now. But she would want to touch base with Daniel later, make sure he hadn't been found out. Hear what Corcoris had wanted.

And learn if Daniel had, in fact, found anything that could help them reach their goal.

"I didn't expect to see you here, either, er..." Corcoris looked at Daniel expectantly.

"Daniel, sir. McManus. I was just so excited about some of the ideas those doctors mentioned at the lunch today that I wanted to get right to work on jotting down a couple of blending ideas I had." He didn't want to lay it on too thick, though, so Daniel made himself appear chagrined. "I guess I tried too fast, or without enough time thinking them through. But I'll brainstorm with some of the other lab guys tomorrow so we can all come up with the best approach together." He smiled once again, a big dorky grin that he hoped looked like a guy who never gave up—even when outclassed.

Like by the company's head honcho.

"Good idea," Corcoris said.

Daniel wanted to get by him into the hallway, get a glimpse of where Beth had gone without being too obvious about it. She'd given him enough warning that he'd gone off-line and done his magic to delete the history of what he'd done on that computer.

He wanted to thank her, but definitely not here or now. There'd be time for that later.

For now... "Is there something I can help you with,

sir?" he asked Corcoris in a voice intended to sound hopeful, as if he wanted to impress his ultimate boss.

"No. Thanks." Corcoris nodded curtly as if to end their conversation, then edged past Daniel into the lab.

Why was he there? Daniel didn't get why Corcoris had shown up on this floor as much as he had during the past few days. His dad might have started this company, and Preston might have some knowledge of chemistry and blending of drugs, but he wasn't a Ph.D. He was more likely to be savvy about the pharmaceuticals industry—development, sales and all that. He could and did hire the folks who did the hands-on work.

Did he want to oversee every aspect of the work?

Was he ensuring that no one else was breaking glassware in the labs as had been done the other day apparently out of anger?

Or had he come here himself to break something?

Daniel felt as if his curiosity could cause an eruption inside him, but he had to bolt down the lid. Maybe someday he would be able to ask Corcoris his rationales for everything, if ever they became buddies.

And *that* was as likely to happen as Daniel's finding a way to take over the leadership of Corcoris Pharmaceuticals.

The door closed behind him. He was now alone in the hallway. Beth must have taken her cart and headed back to its storage area in the basement.

He glanced at his watch. Ten till eight, a few more minutes until the time he'd said he would call her.

Time to head for his car. And look forward to his discussion with Beth that night.

Before he left, though, he stood very still, listening. Was there anything Corcoris was doing, like talking on his phone, that Daniel might be able to hear?

Nope. He wasn't going to get any further information here tonight.

But maybe Beth would be able to clue him in on something of interest. He, at least, had a little to tell her.

Beth was in the company parking garage, walking briskly along the concrete floor toward her car, when her cell phone rang. She pulled it from her purse and recognized Daniel's number.

She glanced at the time. Exactly eight o'clock, when he'd said he would call.

The guy seemed reliable, at least when it came to the little stuff. The big stuff, like finding something useful? That remained to be seen.

She answered, "Hello?"

"Hello, Beth." She heard the words echo and turned.

He was right behind her, near the tail of a car she had just passed. The smile on his face seemed smug, and even though he still wore his geeky dark-framed glasses, she could see the handsome undercover agent beneath the disguise.

She pulled the phone from her ear, pushed the button to end the call and slid it back into her purse.

Nervously, she looked around. They were still on Corcoris Pharmaceuticals property. She saw no one else around, but she had no idea if someone could be sitting in his car watching.

As he reached her, Daniel stayed in character, modifying his smile to look even more dorky. "I saw you a couple of times cleaning today. How did it go?"

"Fine, sir," she said, looking meekly down toward the floor. "Busy. There was a lunch meeting, you know."

"Yes," he said, "I know." And then in more muted tones, he said, "Randalf's Restaurant in Redondo?"

Redondo Beach was a town about fifteen miles from Moravo Beach. Randalf's was a family-style chain restaurant. It wouldn't be hard for her to find, but it wasn't a likely venue for anyone who could possibly recognize her.

She nodded once. "Have a nice evening, sir," she said loudly. She stepped up her pace toward her car—both to end their conversation…and because she really looked forward to their next one.

At Randalf's.

Chapter 10

This probably wasn't a good idea, Beth thought as they followed the hostess through the family restaurant to one of the farthest tables from the door. She was still relieved that it was so distant from what had once been her usual environment, but it had taken some time to drive there, especially in traffic.

The walk through the half-filled place gave her even more time to think, and she'd already had a lot of think time in her car.

Getting together with Daniel to talk? That was fine. *He* was fine, and that was part of the problem.

They definitely needed to find a way to compare notes. Would it be better to do it by phone when they weren't together? Probably not. As with lunch yesterday, someplace like this was preferable, and at least this far from the Corcoris facility they could be more relaxed. Sort of. Even so, they stayed in character, in the remote possibility they ran into someone they knew.

Daniel still wore his glasses. She had buttoned another nice blouse over her cleaning T-shirt for now, as she'd been doing while off the job.

In case they were spotted, it might not be so bad for a geeky techie to look brave enough to date an introverted member of the cleaning crew and appear reluctant to have anyone else know about it.

In fact, she was mulling over the possibilities of allowing their alliance to be noticed since it appeared that they were going to spend more time together and it was always possible that somehow, somewhere, they'd be seen.

But she hadn't fully thought out the ramifications yet. And even if she decided it was a good idea, maybe tonight they should have gone to Daniel's place or hers, considering what they intended to discuss. Who needed anyone eavesdropping?

And yet she couldn't fully buy into that, either. After the last time they'd been alone at one of their residences, they'd made a big mistake: engaging in sex. And not just any sex. The mind-blowing kind. The kind that—

"Here we are." The hostess gestured toward a small secluded table in a corner. She handed them each a menu.

Beth hoped she wasn't blushing, though her face felt hot.

"Thanks," she said as Daniel held her chair out for her.

"You okay?" he asked in her ear, so close that she could feel his breath on her cheek. Instead of cooling her off, that only made her flush more.

"Fine." She immediately started studying the menu as if she had been looking forward to reading it, watching over its top as Daniel sat down across from her. He held his menu, too, but he looked not at it but at her.

And smiled that sexy, smug, nongeeky grin again, as if he knew what she was thinking.

Beth remained silent while she scanned the menu, decided what to order and calmed herself. No matter how sexy Daniel was, this, like their other meetings, wasn't a date. They were, in effect, business associates dedicated to the same goal. That was all.

Business associates who'd engaged in sex...

Business associates who would separate forever once their mutual goals were met.

"I think I'll have their pot roast dinner," she finally told Daniel, as if he had asked. She looked up to see him still reading his menu.

"Steak," he finally said. "I've had grilled steaks at other Randalf's before, and they're not bad."

"What would you like to drink this evening?" That was a server, a friendly young woman whose blond hair was pulled back into a bun.

Beth decided on a wine. Some kind of alcohol to try to relax a bit seemed like a good idea. Daniel tacitly agreed by ordering a beer. They ordered their meals, too.

Then it was time to talk.

Daniel regarded her with his intense blue eyes behind those glasses. "I heard some interesting things at lunch today. I gather you did, too, while cleaning the ladies' restroom." He smiled. "Too bad I wasn't there."

"Yeah, you could have hidden in a stall and no one would have known it was you." Beth allowed her sarcasm to show. "But it was definitely too bad that I couldn't sit in on the lunch. That could have been more appropriate."

"Right. A member of the cleaning crew joining the esteemed Corcoris execs and their guests." He wasn't bad with sarcasm, either.

She laughed. "Okay, enough. How about a bit of realism? And sharing."

"And sharing," he agreed.

But before saying anything else, she glanced around. Fortunately, the few tables nearest theirs weren't occupied. Maybe it was a good thing that they were eating this late.

"We're okay," Daniel said. "We can talk."

"Yes, but we've got some sensitive things to discuss, and I don't like being out in public."

"Me neither. Wanna come to my place?" He leered, and she laughed.

"Yes, actually, I do." She realized that, after all, it would have been a better decision. "Or my place. Somewhere private. But—"

"But the last time we didn't only talk," he said. "And that's the problem."

She felt her heart sink. He considered that amazing sex a problem? Well, actually, she did, too, under the circumstances. But that didn't matter. In fact, she had a sense that Daniel McManus, undercover agent of the CIU, must enjoy a challenge. So she would challenge him.

"It is," she agreed. "And we can discuss things here tonight as long as no one's too close. But I think we need to schedule regular meetings at your place or mine—as long as we're careful. In fact, plan on my place tomorrow evening, okay? We can bring in pizza or whatever if you want to eat there. But we'll just talk." She had intended to challenge him but saw his return dare in the way he raised his brows and shot her a suggestive grin. "Just talk," she reiterated.

"Fine." The word came out casually, and he took a slow swig of beer, still staring into her eyes in a way that made her insides start to simmer.

Just who was challenging whom?

Well, no matter. Maybe this way they'd both feel more like competing to stay cool than engaging in sex.

As their server placed food in front of them, that moment was lost—which suited Beth just fine. Her pot roast, flavored just right and with an appetite-tweaking aroma, had been served with delicious-looking steamed vegetables and a dollop of mashed potatoes, and she tried to dig in.

But she wasn't really hungry. Nerves—and sensual awareness of Daniel—outweighed her need for food.

Nothing appeared to be in Daniel's way, though. His steak had similar side dishes, and it smelled even better than her dinner. "So," he said after taking a couple of bites. "First things first. How's your meal?"

"Good," she said. "Yours?"

He nodded. "Fine. Now tell me what you learned in the ladies' room."

She had been expecting that, but she almost snorted with laughter at the way he'd phrased it. "Nothing I didn't already know," she managed to say. "I've been— Never mind." But then she grew serious.

She'd actually wanted him to start their conversation by telling her what he had found on the computer, if anything. But they'd get there. She would be the one to start.

"The most interesting thing was a couple of lady physicians who seemed to almost storm into the bathroom," she told him.

Daniel's expression immediately grew interested.

"Did they say anything?"

"Yes. I'm not sure if they'd been sitting at the same table, but I got the impression that they both needed immediate potty breaks because of the way the discussion at the luncheon was going. I gathered from the bit of conversation I heard that some Corcoris exec had been praising CorcoTrim, apparently calling it one of the company's newer medications and saying how wonderful it was that it was now on the market and that it would soon become the country's foremost diet drug. If I understood what they said, and didn't say, they'd both already prescribed the stuff to some of their patients, and several of them suffered some pretty bad side effects not listed in the company's warnings."

"The same kinds of problems?"

Beth realized how much difference that might make. If each patient had different issues, that wouldn't necessarily indicate that the company's testing could result in any of the problems becoming anticipated risks that would need to be added to warning labels, let alone suggest that the medicine shouldn't be sold at all. The issues could have been related more to the individual patients' quirks than the product.

"I'm not sure, but they both indicated their patients had been hospitalized."

"Okay, then. My next step, when I get on the computer, will be to dig even deeper to see what I can find on internal reports and emails on CorcoTrim."

"Then that's not one of the products that you were investigating when you checked the computer today?"

"Unfortunately, no, although I'd hoped to. The passwords I…found…led me to some interesting stuff, though."

She looked at him as he took a bite of his steak, waiting for him to continue.

And there was that teasing, sexy look on his face again. The guy obviously wanted her to push him for answers.

"Hey, I thought this was a game of 'you show me yours, I'll show you mine,'" she grumbled, then realized the dual connotation of that phrase. She felt herself reddening again, especially when he once more shot her that damnably sexy smile. "You know what I mean."

"Yes," he said softly. "I do." He swigged some beer, then straightened. "Okay, let's get serious. Here's what I found when I 'accidentally' plugged in Georgine Droman's password—some email correspondence from the boss that didn't exactly order her to modify some reports on quality-control test results for CorcoBiotica before sending them to the FDA but told her to recheck the test logs to verify what she found."

"The boss meaning my pal Preston Corcoris?"

"Exactly."

"I remember Georgine's name from when I worked there before," Beth said. "I'm not exactly sure what she does at Corcoris, though."

"That I found out easily enough—and in fact, as a techie dabbling in combining chemicals to figure out new products, I'd heard of her, too. She's now the director of quality control."

"Interesting," Beth said slowly. "I gather that the reference was to the handwritten notes I heard about when I worked here before that are jotted down in a prescribed format in the manufacturing building by date, time and results and initialed by whoever did the review. Could you tell from the emails if she did indeed 'recheck' those logs and make sure the reports jibed with them?"

"Good thinking. That's what I suspect, too—that the notes, once scanned into the computer, are somehow doctored before being used in the reports. But unfortunately, that was what I was looking for when I heard you greeting our great and powerful boss out in the hallway. I had to work fast to get out of the email and do the magic I know that hides that it had been compromised."

"Then you do know how to do that?" Beth felt her

shoulders relax. Not that she'd kept them tense from the time she tried to let Daniel know that Corcoris was headed his way, but there'd been a part of her inside that had been worried.

"Of course. Do you think Judge Treena would have let me go undercover anywhere without cyber protection as well as other kinds?"

"Not our Judge Treena," Beth acknowledged with a smile.

They ate silently then for a couple of minutes. They had both gotten hints of directions in which they could go to look for evidence that would let the world know what at least some people at Corcoris Pharmaceuticals did so the company would turn a profit: ignore safety issues and somehow hide questionable—or worse—test results from the FDA.

Beth was determined to find out more—more that was provable. And she was glad she now had an ally who was not only on the same wavelength but who also had skills and access that she couldn't easily achieve.

"What are you thinking?" Daniel finally asked.

"I could ask you the same thing," she responded, "but, okay, I'll answer you first. I'm just thinking I'm really glad we're working together on this. But even so, we need to make plans about how to proceed. We both have our roles at Corcoris that we've been using, but I wonder if there isn't a more efficient way to handle what we're doing."

"That's pretty much what I was considering." Despite his glasses, Daniel had a businesslike and challenging expression on his face now. Not especially sexy, and yet it attracted her.

Did she really go for guys who seemed driven to utter

success on a project? Or just this guy, and this project? After all, it was, at the moment, her life.

Maybe her family's lives, too.

That thought shot a dart of fear through her. She was making some progress. But was it fast enough to ensure their safety?

How could she know without being in closer contact with them?

But closer contact could harm her—and them.

"What are you thinking?" Daniel's sharp question brought her back to the moment.

She bit her lip. "I'm really proud of how much we're achieving, but—"

"But what?"

"Is it enough? Is it fast enough? Is—"

"You're worried about your family." His voice was soft, and he reached his hand across the table palm up, inviting her to place hers in it.

She did. "Yes," she answered. "I am."

"And Beth Jones can't call them as often as Andrea Martinez would like to."

She nodded sadly. "I know from them and from Judge Treena that there's at least some security around them, but they haven't left town the way I'd hoped."

"Well, next time I report to Judge Treena, I'll ask her to find a way to give them further incentive. That's something that CIU can help with—maybe making reservations for them, paying for some of their expenses, whatever."

"Really?"

"Really," Daniel responded. "Moving them for a while might cost less than providing some protection where they are."

Tears of relief filled Beth's eyes but she blinked them

away. Relief was premature. But at least knowing she wouldn't be the only one urging her family to go someplace safer, at least for now...well, that was good.

Even so, she had an urge to go around the table and give Daniel a big grateful kiss. But she restrained herself.

"And you'll tell me her response and what's being done to encourage them to leave faster?"

He nodded. "Of course. And it should be okay for you to continue to contact them now and then in the same way Judge Treena and her identity-changing gang worked out for you before." He tilted his head slightly as he observed her with those inquisitive blue eyes. "The team did provide a way for you to get in touch occasionally, didn't they?"

She nodded. "Yes, a prepaid phone. That's how I knew they were being threatened in the first place."

And why she had chosen to disobey Judge Treena's orders and return here.

"Right. Okay, then. I'll check with the judge first thing when I get up tomorrow. And you've got to realize that her quid pro quo may mean that you'll need to leave and let me do my job."

Beth glared at Daniel. "Is that what you want, too? I thought we were helping each other."

The gaze he leveled on her in response was unreadable. "I'll tell her that so far at least, you've seemed more of an asset than a liability."

"Gee, thanks." Beth's sarcasm poured out once more, disguising the hurt she felt that he wasn't expressing more satisfaction with what she'd hoped was turning into a mutually beneficial effort.

"You're welcome," he said easily, apparently deciding to ignore her snipe at him. "There's probably no easy way to pass along at work tomorrow what Judge Treena says, though."

Almost as if a whole wave of new diners had just entered the restaurant, the tables around them suddenly filled.

Beth knew that the best way to continue for now was to act as though they really had chosen to remain as teammates—which, in a way, they had, at least for the moment. That meant they should discuss what their next moves, respectively, should be. But here and now wasn't a good place to get into that. Not while it would be so easy for them to be overheard.

"All right, then," she said, "tomorrow night we'll start meeting at our respective apartments to recap what each of us has done and to plan what comes next." That should be vague enough so that even if they were overheard, no one would know what she was talking about.

"Yeah," he said. "Sure you can keep your hands off me?" He aimed that now-familiar sexy smirk at her.

"And what'll you do if I don't?" she demanded, forcing herself to smile back.

"Wouldn't you like to find out?"

Oh, wouldn't she? Yeah, especially if it helped to convince him to stay on her side. But this kind of sensual banter was okay only while they couldn't do anything about it. When they were together alone again, needing to plan their respective actions, they had to do just that: plan. Stay focused. Talk.

And staying away from each other physically? Was that possible?

"Look, Daniel, maybe this isn't such a good idea. Can we figure out another way to coordinate what we're doing? Maybe there's someplace else where we could meet that's neutral but not as public as a restaurant. Or just talk over secure phone lines."

His smirk was gone. His handsome features beneath his spectacles were serious once more. "No need. You're right. Under other circumstances, all this teasing and fooling around might be fun, but not now. We'll keep our minds focused and our hands to ourselves, no matter where we are. Deal?"

"Deal."

Beth felt relief wash over her. There was a hint of disappointment, too. But she would live with it.

"All right," Daniel said. He looked around, then leaned toward her. "Since we have an agreement and some strategizing to do—and we can't really talk much here—let's start those private meetings tonight."

She stared at him. He was challenging her again? Well, she would meet that challenge, hands down. "Sure," she said. "Let's do it."

His place was slightly closer, so that was where they headed. As before, they drove their own cars. He had given Beth his address, but she didn't know this area well and was following him.

That gave Daniel time to remind himself of the potentially volatile nature of their relationship. And to consider what this meeting would be like.

Informational. Maybe even instructional, he figured as he drove along surface streets toward his apartment. There were no convenient freeways, and besides, it wasn't far.

He checked the rearview mirror of his clunker often to make sure he saw the headlights of the economy car that Beth drove. She'd said she had rented it for the month—

and hoped to accomplish what she needed by the time she needed to turn it in again.

He hoped so, too. Maybe with the two of them focused on the same goal, it would happen.

He had recognized her pain when he'd reminded her she shouldn't be here. He wouldn't pursue that further for now, though. Not as long as they continued to complement each other's actions. And as long as she didn't forget that he was the one with the job to do here.

He usually kept the local news station on, but at the moment he wanted to concentrate on the drive and on planning their upcoming discussion.

Beth kept up with him despite the hour. At least he stayed on major streets that were lit fairly well.

It didn't take long to get there. He had told Beth to park on the street in front of his place, and he motioned her to an empty space. Then he pulled around back to the entrance to the underground garage.

The most interesting part of the evening was about to begin. But as much as he kept reminding himself not even to think about the steamy sex they had shared before—and as much as the reminder made his body stand up and take notice—he would do the right thing from now on.

Their time together was limited. It was important that they just talk and strategize so their efforts could remain in sync. They could not get any more involved, not on any level. He wasn't about to engage his emotions again in a dangerous work-related situation, even though he had no intention of allowing anyone to harm Beth.

Even him.

And so he would keep his hands off her.

Chapter 11

"Nice place," Beth said as she entered Daniel's apartment. It was on the upper floor in a small development consisting of a block of three-story buildings, some connected and some that appeared like narrow attached town houses. They were all granite-colored stucco with matching multipaned windows and attractive landscaping.

Daniel's unit apparently had at least one bedroom, unlike her own tiny efficiency apartment. A hallway with several doors led to the right of the small tiled entry area.

The living room lay straight ahead. She glanced that way and saw its sofa in plush tawny upholstery with three fluffy pillows. It matched two armchairs set at angles nearby. They all looked comfortable but as impersonal as hers. She suspected the furniture had been rented for Daniel's time here, too.

At least the sofa looked far different from her convertible bed. That was a good thing. Daniel's couch would be used only for them to sit and discuss plans for finding evidence at Corcoris.

The whole way here, she'd mentally kicked herself for agreeing to come despite her needing to ensure that they continued to strategize together. Sure, they hadn't come up with any better way to hold their discussions. But stay professional and focused while all alone with this guy in his apartment?

She could do it. Would do it. It didn't matter that she was attracted to him. She wasn't attracted at all to his cavalier attitude about their working together.

Even so, staying physically away from the guy would require effort. That was okay. She was used to meeting challenges, no matter how hard.

Hard…like his body? Like his erection?

She laughed internally without cracking a smile. No way did she want him to suspect what she was thinking.

Daniel followed her in and shut the door. An overhead light illuminated the living room but he flicked on a surprisingly ornate lamp on an end table between the sofa and one of the chairs. "Have a seat." He gestured toward the couch. "Would you like anything to drink?"

Being alone here with Daniel gave her an urge to have another alcoholic drink to boost her bravado, but she said, "A glass of water would be great."

Taking her seat, she watched him go down the hall, presumably to the kitchen. He returned soon with two glasses of water.

Good. He would remain in control of his urges, too.

Too? She really wasn't sure that avoiding another drink would ensure that she stayed in control. She was alone with the hottest man she had met in a long time. Maybe ever.

One she had shared a phenomenal sexual encounter with just last night.

One she ached to have sex with again—if only that weren't the most foolish thing imaginable. She had to make sure he was convinced about her professionalism.

"Here you are." He neared where she was seated and held out one of the glasses to her, apparently misinterpreting her momentary stare at his strong and agile hands. "The water's safe. I have a new filter on my sink. But if you'd rather, I can give you a fresh bottle."

She laughed. "No, I'm fine with tap water, particularly if it's filtered." She accepted the glass and took a nice long sip, again contemplating something stronger. She inhaled deeply and met his gaze. "Okay, let's get down to it. Where do we begin our discussion and strategizing tonight?"

He sat down on the far end of the sofa from her, put his glass down on the glass-topped table in front of them and crossed his muscular jeans-clad legs. The movements were casual, yet they still managed to increase her awareness of being so close to this man who got her juices flowing by just being nearby.

She sipped some more water. Good thing it was cold.

"Just preliminarily," he began, "I want more information from you. We talked a bit about it before, but tell me more now about what happened when you first decided to become a whistle-blower."

Beth felt her mood change immediately from sexual awareness to sorrow and frustration. Maybe that was a good thing.

"Before I ran away from Corcoris and Moravo Beach," she said, "I'd thought by just letting the authorities know what I'd heard and the threats I'd received that I'd be able to bring down at least Preston, and maybe more.

We talked before about my going to the local cops. As I said, I wasn't surprised that they didn't follow up on my suspicions about games being played with drug testing and quality control—that was a federal thing. But the threats, after the attack on me—"

"You had no proof." Daniel's mouth was puckered in a thin line. "No emails or phone messages or anything except allegations. Your word against Corcoris's."

She bent her head in sadness. "Right," she whispered. But then she forced herself to rally. "But I knew enough after working for a pharmaceutical company for a while to recognize that what I'd learned about the meds issues had to be reported to the FDA. It was my obligation, since people's lives were at stake. When I left this area, I flew to D.C. on my own nickel and set up a meeting there. But by then, having been brushed off by the local authorities, I suspected that the feds would want more than just my reporting what I'd heard. That's why I didn't try a local district office first. I was wrong. The FDA took me seriously enough to conduct an inspection—and found nothing." Tears rushed to her eyes, damn it. She sloughed them away, not looking at Daniel.

"Frustrating," he suggested gently.

"Yeah. But I made enough noise and must have sounded like I spoke with some reason for my suspicions—and fear—since I got a call from Judge Treena before I could slink my way out of D.C."

"And the rest was history."

"Unfinished history," she contradicted. "So, yeah, in addition to getting my new identity thanks to Judge Treena's granting my petition, I received some facts on what would have constituted genuine evidence. Just for informational purposes, she and her peeps told me. No way was I ever to get near Corcoris or his pharmaceuticals enterprise again." She snorted. "I wish that was true. But I was damned if I'd let him harm my family."

"Just make sure you stay damned alive." His expression had turned hard. Cold.

"I will." But she sensed there was a lot more that he wasn't saying. "You don't need to worry about me."

"Yeah. I do. You're my responsibility as long as we're working together."

She wasn't going to let that stand. Besides, she wanted to know what he was thinking. Was that why he kept reminding her of Judge Treena's opinion that she shouldn't be here? But she wasn't asking for his protection. There had to be something more that he wasn't saying.

"Forget that," she said insistently. "I'm my own responsibility. If you think otherwise, you'd better tell me why. I don't think it's CIU policy, since the recipients of new IDs and CIU agents aren't really supposed to meet."

He stood, his fists clenched as if he wanted to strike something. Not her. She knew he was still in protective mode and wanted to understand it.

"No, it's my choice," he finally said. "I lost a confidential informant once when I was with the FBI. It's not going to happen again."

Oh. Interesting, but not really relevant. Even so—"Tell me about it," she said softly, patting the couch to encourage him to sit down again.

He complied but scowled at her. "Not much to tell. She was my CI. She didn't follow my instructions. And she died." The pain on his face was unmistakable.

Beth couldn't help asking, "And you cared about her, didn't you?"

"Yeah, I did." His voice was low, and his words pierced her. "But you don't have to worry about me, either. As long as you're around, I'll protect you, you'll be okay, and that'll be it."

She took another long swig of nice cold water despite the chill she already felt. "Of course," she finally said. "I'll be fine." She hesitated. "Can we get back to our discussion?"

"Good idea." He looked at her, his expression easing. "So why don't you just tell me what your plans were when you came here besides finding a way inside the headquarters' walls?"

That was a definite return to their conversation. No emotion. As if they hadn't even mentioned what was really on his mind.

It was better that way. Unless it made sense otherwise, she would pretend, too, that he hadn't said anything personal.

She needed to digest what he'd said…later.

For now, she just gave a shrug. "Preston had threatened my family," she said. "I figured I'd determine a way to get some kind of real evidence once I was here."

"And I gather that you're still working on it." His expression was now encouraging, but his tone sounded skeptical. Which wasn't surprising. He had been here a few weeks longer than she had, he knew more of what to look for…and he, too, hadn't yet had much success.

"Of course I am. And I'll succeed." She felt her lower lip jut out obstinately, as if daring him to tell her what a fool she was.

Sure, she knew it. But that didn't stop her from trying.

"What about you?" she countered then. "You're here officially and you got some guidance. You must have come with a good idea of what you're after and how to get it."

"A good idea? Yes. And I wouldn't have come if all I had was a cloudy notion of what's needed."

Beth was suddenly angry. First he acted overprotective, and now he was criticizing her? She stood, ready to either throw the rest of her water in his face or leave. Or both.

"Calm down, Beth," he said gently. "We really are on the same side, you know."

"Then why are you—"

"Ribbing you? Because I want to make sure you realize that in that respect I agree with Judge Treena. It's not a good idea that you came here on your own, especially without a plan. Now, sit back down and we'll discuss possibilities, okay?"

He was right. Might even be saving her eagerly anticipated case against Corcoris…and maybe her life. "Okay," she agreed quietly, and resumed her seat.

At least now, despite their location, she had no urge to drag Daniel off to bed. He had turned her off but good. In more ways than one.

Her pride was wounded. Her self-confidence, too.

And whatever had happened the other night, he clearly didn't care about her other than as someone he had to work with—unlike that confidential informant he'd lost.

Well, he was the professional here. The undercover CIU member had knowledge and traction, and backup would be sent here if he needed it.

The only backup she had was him. Maybe.

"Here's where I think we are," he said. "First, do you know much about the feds' real witness protection program?"

"A little." She had looked into it some when she had hoped to be able to participate, before she had been informed that she wasn't really a witness.

Daniel, still seated, leaned forward, his hands clasped between his jeans-clad knees. Why did that gesture appear sexy?

Maybe it was because the muscles in his arms rippled as he moved.

But Beth ignored how her insides tensed at the observation, forcing herself to just listen to him.

"Since the beginning of the program," he said, "a lot of the actual witnesses were members of the mob who decided, for their own longevity, to testify against their former cohorts. They could describe in court what they had actually seen and heard and experienced, even what crimes they themselves had committed."

"And all I could testify about was what I'd heard from Milt." Beth sat back. She curled her arms around herself protectively. "Or that Preston Corcoris had come on to me, then threatened me. But he was so discreet about it no one else ever saw or heard anything, and he left no evidence."

"That's what I was told when I was brought into this case. Not that I was informed about who you were now, but that the crimes I was to look into here involved unproven allegations by a former employee named Andrea Martinez. If any of the allegations were true, those connected with drugs being manufactured here could lead to illness, or even death, of innocent patients being prescribed those meds."

"So…well, we've talked about this in generalities before, but specifically, your mission is to find tangible proof that can be used in court to prove that the test data recorded here was falsified and that the company's quality control has been compromised. The stuff I heard rumors of but had no evidence about before I left."

"Exactly."

That was his official job. Watching over her was the personal mission he had taken on—but not if she could help it. Not now. But working together was fine. Necessary.

At least the conversation was calm now. Beth felt relieved. Daniel wasn't criticizing her for not collecting evidence before she'd left. That never happened— exactly—with Judge Treena and her subordinates, either, but what was left unsaid sometimes sounded as loudly in her mind as what her ears actually heard.

"That's what I hoped to do here, too," she said. "I'd figured that if I worked in the labs, preferably when no one else was there, I'd at least pick up on something but I haven't gotten much so far."

"Same here, but I'm thinking more and more about those log sheets and how they can be fudged to look good in reports, at least on the computer. What do you know about them?"

"I'd heard about them before, when I worked here, and I also heard some speculation after the FDA's unannounced inspection as a result of my claims. The logs are kept all the time in the manufacturing facility across the way, handwritten and initialed with names, dates, information about ingredients and their origin, and test results. The log sheets are then scanned into computers here—and nearly all the information, even regarding the drugs that I'd heard from my friend Milt Ranich were trash, apparently looked perfect. But as a member of the cleaning staff, I haven't had much opportunity to try to find those reports and check them somehow against the quality-control tests being performed here by the lab techs like you."

"That's why I'm trying to 'borrow' passwords," Daniel said, "and find out what might be buried in the executives' private files."

Beth nodded. "Great. I hope you'll keep me informed. And that's not all I hoped to accomplish. I keep a phone in my pocket with recording ability so I can capture any conversations like the ones I could only say I'd heard before…although so far no one has talked to me like that except those doctors in the ladies' room. I did record all that, by the way."

"Good, although their allegations don't prove anything any more than yours. But the CIU will be able to interview them and check out their claims by also talking to their patients—as long as we can work around patient-physician confidentiality. And to protect those patients, I have a feeling we'll get everyone's cooperation." He paused.

"What?" she prompted.

"There's another thing you can do while you're there cleaning and no one's around. Some of our suspicions involve the possibility that what's brought into the labs for testing aren't the same medications that are sold as prescriptions. If the situation arises where you can pick up some samples and get them out easily—and safely— then do it. I've been working on that angle myself but a woman who first pushes a cart, then leaves the facility with her purse may be able to succeed more easily than a geek who's not permitted even to bring his own computer or anything in a bag except maybe his lunch onto the premises."

"I've wondered about that. Sure, I'll start collecting samples when I can." Beth smiled. "Sounds like we're on the right track."

"We're on the right track," Daniel acknowledged. "But we still have a long way to go."

"I get it. But, oh, Daniel, I can't tell you how relieved and even happy I am to hear that. Not only because we've made some progress but because *I've* made some progress. Toward my own vindication. And even more important, to finding a way to protect my family not just in the short run but forever—at least if we get that evidence. And with your help, I really think we will."

She didn't plan it, but she was suddenly standing. So was he. And it seemed inevitable and right when they each took a step toward the other.

Into one another's arms.

His mouth came down on hers as if they had both planned it. His kiss was hot and insistent and somehow even reassuring.

And sexy. Oh, yes, it was sexy, especially with the strength of his well-toned body against hers. She felt his erection pushing against her middle. It was a familiar feeling. The last time, it had led to their tearing off each other's clothes. Making love with such heat and passion that she knew she would never regret it, would only want it again and again if she let herself.

But that couldn't be. Not now or later or ever.

He wouldn't ever really care for her. She couldn't care for him.

Even so, she was kissing him back, though, taunting his tongue with hers even as she strained against him, holding him tightly with her arms.

But as his hand began inserting itself between them, as her nipples started hardening in anticipation of his touch, she stopped.

And pulled back.

"We can't do this," she said against him.

"We can," he contradicted, but he allowed her to move

away. "But you're right. We've already decided how bad an idea it is."

Despite its rightness, his statement hurt her.

She looked him squarely in his sensual and provocative blue eyes and repeated, "Yes, it's a bad idea. Let's just talk now, okay? And really collaborate about gathering evidence."

Daniel had been impressed—and turned on—by Beth's lovely appearance, her sexuality and her determination to achieve her goal.

And angered by her goading him until he wound up mentioning how he had lost Edie. But he'd been able to turn that off. It did him no good to focus on it, now or ever.

So afterward he'd been able to sit calmly on his own living room sofa listening and sharing ideas and watching Beth for more than an hour, until it became quite late.

She had some good thoughts about what to look for in executive Georgine Droman's company account and collect on a memory stick.

Computer stuff was more up his alley than Beth's, but he appreciated bouncing ideas off her. For one thing, she might find a way to clean Georgine's desk sometime, too, and potentially pick up other helpful information.

He also gave Beth some ideas on how to approach various lab areas for cleaning when no one else was around and she could manage some extra time there—and seeing what kind of chemical compounds were stored there, perhaps bottling small samples and hiding them so he, later, could remove them as if he had collected them himself. She told him she had considered doing that previously but had been unsure how to achieve the necessary chain of custody to prove where the samples came from—or where to take them to be tested since the FDA had already ruled all was well at Corcoris.

But the CIU was different—and it could handle those samples.

They hadn't quite figured out how, but one or both of them also needed to find a way that appeared logical to not only visit the main manufacturing building on the campus but determine what was there that could be useful in their search for evidence. But the place already had its own cleaning staff, and lab geeks who performed quality-control tests did not really have a reason to go there.

Except maybe, Daniel thought, to satisfy a geek's unending curiosity about technical things that went on around him.

By the time they were finally done with their discussion—or at least ready to break for the night—he'd become even more impressed by Beth's quickness. She had not only caught on to all he'd said but also helped to turn it into potentially workable ideas.

The differences in their respective undercover personas would allow them to delve into even more aspects of hunting evidence than either of them had originally considered. The similarities in their goals would allow them to work together well—and get what they needed fast.

Now Beth stretched her arms and legs out while still they traded intense conversation.

Daniel wanted to muse over their respective suggestions that night on his own before he went to bed.

Alone, of course. Neither of them would encourage or act upon their apparent mutual attraction. Not again.

"Thanks for all this," he finally told her, "but I think we'd better call it a night."

She nodded without even a hint of protest—or interest

in going to bed with him. That was a good thing, since he would have had to gently decline.

Wouldn't he?

Of course, he told himself as he walked Beth outside to her car.

By habit, he found himself scanning their environment, making sure no one else was around. He saw no one, although one car and then a second drove past them down the street.

In one, a man drove with a woman in the passenger seat. They appeared engrossed in a conversation.

The other was driven by a woman he recognized from the neighborhood.

"You're sure you know your way back to your place okay?" he asked Beth. He didn't call it her home. Her home was in Seattle now, with the new identity she'd absorbed. That was where she would return after all this was over, at least until the evidence they collected was used to prosecute Corcoris—and he was certain now that they would gather enough good stuff to lead to a successful prosecution—and that would be the end of things between them.

"I'm fine—even though this little car doesn't have GPS, I've got it on my phone. And I'm pretty sure I can find it on my own anyway."

They were talking like business associates. That was as it should be.

Even though he really wanted to take her again into his arms. To celebrate their camaraderie, that was all. With a nice nonintimate good-night kiss. But that wasn't to be.

The lock on the door of her little car popped up. She'd taken her key out of her purse and pushed the button. He pulled the door open.

She stood there on the sidewalk for a moment longer. Her slim body, in its jeans and button-down shirt, seemed lithe and carefree and magnetic.

Good thing he'd made up his mind to stay far away.

Only…well, as she got closer to slip into the car, she reached up and cupped his face in one hand and brushed his lips with hers in a nonsuggestive yet oh-so-enticing kiss.

"Good night, Daniel," she said. "See you tomorrow during the day. We should find a way to each let the other know if we need to get together in the evening to discuss progress—or lack thereof."

"Sounds good," he said. "Good night, Beth." He closed her door.

He had an urge to poke his head through the window and give her another brief good-night kiss. But he stayed still.

"Good night, then, Daniel," she said. She closed her window. He stepped back as she began to drive off.

As soon as she did, an SUV he hadn't noticed before, one that was parked across the street, pulled out behind her.

Surely it was just a coincidence.

But when that SUV also made a right turn at the second corner, right behind Beth, it set off alarms throughout Daniel's head and gut.

Chapter 12

Daniel grabbed his phone from his pocket. Did Beth have hands-free in her car? Didn't matter. Talking on cell phones was a ticketable offense in California, but it might be a good thing if a cop was actually around and pulled her over.

But no cops were likely to be there when you needed one. He pushed in Beth's number and waited.

It rang once. Twice. Damn. Wasn't she going to answer?

"I'm driving, Daniel," she finally said into his ear. She sounded peeved. "I'll call you when—"

"Listen. I may be overreacting but I think someone followed you from here. Are you anywhere near the Ralphs' shopping center?" That supermarket was along the road she'd turned onto and was open twenty-four hours a day, although other nearby shops were probably closed. Even so, it wasn't yet ten o'clock. There would probably be people in the parking lot.

"Yes, I'm right beside it, but—"

"Pull into the lot and find an area with lots of cars and as many people as possible. Park there and wait. I'll be there right away."

He had been running toward his building and the parking lot beneath his apartment complex as he talked, heading for his car. With the phone still at his ear, he reached into his pocket with the other hand, pulled out his key and pushed the button to unlock his vehicle. Despite its age and condition, it still had automatic locks that worked.

"Daniel…what does it look like? I'll watch for it." She sounded scared. That was probably a good thing. Maybe she would be more cautious.

He described the SUV generally, even though once he was behind the wheel of his car he reached into the glove compartment and pulled out a small pad of paper, where he jotted down the license number he'd seen. Didn't intend to forget it, but just in case…

"See you in a minute," he said, exaggerating the time a little. But it would be no more than five minutes. He'd make sure of it.

Then he hung up, turned the key in the ignition and raced off, following the direction where Beth had gone.

Followed? From Daniel's? The idea creeped Beth out, but she didn't buy it.

After all, in an abundance of caution, she'd been checking her surroundings and her rearview mirror as had become her habit over many months and especially since returning here.

And she was already very aware that the guy thought

he had to protect her. Maybe he was just being over-zealous.

Even so, she put on her turn signal, carefully pulled over and drove into the parking lot. It was well lit, and there were people here and there, mostly hurrying to or from their own cars.

She glanced into her rearview mirror. No indication of anyone zooming over to stay behind her. No SUV there, either—just a couple of cars.

Surely Daniel was mistaken.

She hoped.

She pulled into a parking spot directly under one of the lights on a tall pole and just sat there, feeling the erratic thumping of her heart in her chest.

Of course Daniel was wrong. Who would even have known she was at his place?

Or, in the off chance he was right, was it someone who wanted to convey a message to Daniel, not her?

But if so, how would they know that he and she were together that evening?

Unless they'd also followed them from the restaurant. And that could mean they'd also followed Daniel or her *to* the restaurant.

From Corcoris?

But why?

She prayed that neither of their covers had been blown. She had seen Preston Corcoris before she had left the offices, but there'd been no indication he considered her as anything other than one of his lowly cleaning-staff members.

Even so, she would do even more now to avoid him and not tempt fate into giving her away.

This was more than worrisome. It was scary.

A few minutes later she felt relieved to see Daniel's

clunky old car drive by behind her. He was going slowly, and as she watched she saw him drive up one row of cars and spaces and down the next.

Probably looking for the vehicle he'd thought he had seen chasing her.

Well, she had kept an eye out for the SUV he had described. It had sounded like many others—common type, silver color and all—but she hadn't noticed any like it around.

Soon Daniel pulled into a nearby parking spot. She watched expectantly, but he didn't get out of his car. In moments, though, her cell phone rang.

"You okay?" he asked.

"Except for being a nervous wreck, yes. I didn't see anyone following me."

"Good. Here's what we'll do."

What he described made sense. She would pull out of her space and continue toward her apartment. He would be her wingman, waiting here for a short while and watching her leave, then taking the same route as she did at some distance behind her.

If anyone was following her, then Daniel would be following him.

Beth didn't like obeying orders—or at least Andrea hadn't. She had an urge to tell him fine, but she wanted to go inside the store first and buy…what? She really didn't need anything.

But he would be able to see if anyone got out of a vehicle and followed her inside. If so, he'd be able to catch the guy. Wouldn't he?

Daniel had seemed to appreciate her coming up with ways to improve his plan before, so she suggested this one now.

"No!" he practically shouted in her ear.

"But if there is anyone—"

"It could be more dangerous."

Her chest muscles tightened as she prepared to argue with him. She could do as she wanted, and he could protect her or not, his decision.

But she knew what that decision would be. And why. Which was why she backed down, if only a little. "I'm willing to try it," she said, "if it'll help us figure out who it is." She hated that her tone sounded so pleading.

"It's a good idea, Beth," he said—most likely just trying to make her feel better. "It would work fine if we had a team behind us to grab anyone who came after you. Since it's just me, though, I want to be more cautious."

"All right," she said. "But…well, what should I do if you see someone following me as I continue driving?"

"I'll call you again with a plan."

"But—"

"It'll work. You'll see. If someone's following, I'll direct you to the nearest police station and you'll pull into their lot. I'll block the guy, and that'll be that."

That sounded like a plan—but one that could work? "Okay," she agreed reluctantly. "And if you don't see anyone following?"

"You'll still see someone behind you—me. So…are you ready to go?"

She suddenly felt okay, as if all of this was part of her plan. Maybe that was again because she had someone watching her back.

And not just someone, but Daniel—trained in law enforcement and confident about what he was doing.

"I'm ready," she told him, and turned her key in the ignition.

* * *

She might feel braver—but as she approached the block where her apartment building was located, Beth slowed down.

And she hadn't been driving fast in the first place.

She'd looked in her rearview mirror a lot but had not seen any car that appeared to be chasing her—not even Daniel's.

On the other hand, he was probably savvy enough about pursuit techniques not to be obvious about it, either to her or to anyone who might actually be following her.

Even so, as she pulled into her designated parking spot at the side of her building, she sat for a minute without turning off the engine. She kept the lights off inside her car, although there was a dim glow from the back of the apartment building.

Mostly, she just wanted to watch and make sure she didn't see anyone's vehicles pass by—except perhaps Daniel's.

Her phone rang. She pulled it from where she had rested it on the passenger's seat, glanced at the number and answered. "So, is all well? Did anyone follow me?"

"Not anyone I saw." Daniel's expressionless tone scared her almost as much as if he'd said she'd been followed by a whole caravan of cars. If he'd simply said no, she would have felt a lot better.

But maybe that was the idea. He wanted her to remain wary.

She supposed she should have felt relieved that she was in Daniel's sights and under his protection. But she'd rather have been the invisible nobody she'd felt like before they met.

"That's good," she returned brightly, ready to say good-night to him. "Thanks for checking it out."

"Wait where you are," he said. "I've just parked and I'm coming to walk you up to your apartment. You're in your assigned parking space?"

Don't bother, she wanted to say to him. Yet what if there really was someone after her? Someone who knew where she lived, who hadn't followed her home, because he had driven ahead to wait for her.

She despised this direction of her thoughts. But she realized she couldn't be too careful.

"That's right." She also hated how raspy she sounded. "Come ahead. We can laugh about your overcautiousness over some wine, if you'd like."

But would she like it—having him in her apartment after such an emotional time?

Well, he wouldn't stay long. She could make sure of that.

She could pretend to try to seduce him. That would scare him off.

"Fine." There was a hint of an echo and, startled, she looked out the window on her side of the car.

There he was, looking in. Unnerved, she nearly jumped.

What if there really had been someone following her—and he had crept up on her that way?

Okay, she would allow Daniel to walk her to her place and make sure it was safe, and then she would rescind her offer of a glass of wine.

He was frightening her, and she didn't like it.

Daniel was on full alert as he walked briskly beside Beth to the front door of her apartment building, holding her close, one arm around her. She was on his left side just in case he had to grab his gun from his pocket with his right hand.

Yes, he had come armed. He always kept a semiautomatic pistol in his car, and he'd grabbed it before hustling over here to be with Beth.

He could have been mistaken about that SUV following her, but he doubted it. He'd been working for the government in law enforcement positions too long to doubt his instincts.

And on this assignment, he'd latched on to the feeling that there was no such thing as being too cautious.

The atmosphere at Corcoris just didn't feel right, even after today, when he'd felt as if he had made a little bit of progress—both in finding something to hold against the company and its executives and in coming up with a plan to work better with Beth for now.

Work better with her? Yes. And keep her safe without letting himself get so seduced, so involved, that he'd let anything happen to her.

Like Edie.

"Excuse me," Beth said formally, and pulled her arm away. She dug inside her purse for her key.

That gave him an opportunity to look around, to their side, around the high oleander bushes that grew near the building's door. Behind them, toward the dimly lit and currently traffic-free street.

Where his car was parked now.

There weren't a lot of spaces left, and he'd checked the curb for a block either way before joining Beth. None of the parked vehicles was a silver SUV with the license plate number he had memorized.

That didn't mean the driver wasn't around here somewhere, although Daniel hoped he wasn't. Daniel preferred not having a confrontation while he was here undercover.

He would do everything he had to, though, to protect Beth and himself, even give away his good geek cover and take on a physical fight. And he was damned good at fighting when necessary.

But what he really wanted was simply to collect the necessary evidence against Corcoris, then get out of there. Get them *both* out of there.

Beth pushed a code onto the keys of the building's security system and then opened the door. He followed her inside, then closed the door and made sure it was locked.

"Thanks," she said. "It was nice of you to make sure everything was okay, but I'm home now. Or at least my home for the moment." Her smile toward him was both brave and bittersweet.

It made him want to take her into his arms, but he wouldn't do that. Even so, he wasn't through with her this evening.

"Let me make sure your apartment's okay, too, and then I'll leave," he told her.

She looked ready to protest.

"Yes, I know your building has good locks and a security system and all that," he said, "but you might as well not argue and let me check. Then I'll be on my way."

Her smile looked frustrated, but that was all right. He followed her up the stairs to the second floor and waited while she again carefully unlocked the door.

"Let me go first." He slipped by before she had a chance to argue with him.

Holding his firearm out and swinging it from one target point to another, he looked around the tiny unit. It would be hard for anyone to hide here, but he checked everywhere, including even the bathroom and between the narrowly spaced kitchen counters.

"Looks fine," he said. He hesitated. "Would you like me to come by in the morning and make sure you aren't followed to work?" Maybe that was overkill, but he knew what he had seen, and he was worried for her.

"No. I'll be fine." She smiled up at him, her violet eyes luminous and sparkling and seeming to dare him to contradict her.

"I'm sure you will," he said huskily, wishing he meant it. Damn, but her stubbornness seemed to make him want to protect her even more.

Her acting so brave and ornery shouldn't turn him on, but it did.

Hell, he wanted to tease her. Make her feel even a fraction of the sexual need that, now that the danger seemed past, had begun flexing through him.

"I don't suppose you'd want to give me a good-night kiss to send me on my way." He made it a statement but caught the sudden heated awareness that seemed to pass across the smooth contours of her beautiful face.

Did she intend for her full lips to edge out in a pout like that? Intentional or not, she was challenging him.

He had an unrestrainable urge to kiss her.

And so he lowered his mouth to hers, even as he bent to take her into his arms.

Okay. Maybe she had wordlessly agreed that he could kiss her by not responding to his dare.

But she knew what she was doing—didn't she? Sure, she was attracted to this man. She admitted it—to herself, at least.

That was all, though. She was not looking for any relationship any more than he was, didn't want to seem as if she were paying him back for his help, his protectiveness, his working with her instead of trying to send her away, whatever.

Yet another kiss? Sure.

It didn't mean anything.

She threw herself into it, adoring the feel of his heated mouth on hers, even as he pulled her closer yet.

She also adored how hard his body felt against her. Again.

Oh, yes, his touch along her back and side made her feel so aware of her sexual needs all over again. Needs she'd thought she had tucked inside once more, to be awakened someday only when she intentionally decided it was the right time and the right man.

This was definitely the wrong time and the wrong man, and yet she heard her soft moan as she again pressed herself against him.

His voice was husky as he murmured against her lips, "You'd better throw me out right now, Beth. Otherwise, I'm going to touch you all over. All over." As if in illustration, one of his hands went from her side upward and forward and gently grasped her breast, teasing her nipple with his thumb.

"Time for you to leave, Daniel." She attempted to sound firm, to pull back, but instead she gasped as that hand traveled down the front of her body, stopping at her aching hidden feminine hot spot below. He grasped her there, outside her jeans, and she suddenly wanted nothing more than to yank them off, let him touch her skin to skin.

Had all those threats, those descriptions of someone following her, been a ploy to get her back in bed with him?

But if so, why not just try to seduce her at his apartment?

"Okay, I'll leave," he finally said, but he hadn't removed either his mouth or his hands from her.

"Good." But she had slid her hands down his back

and now gripped his buttocks, pulling him more tightly against her so she held not even the tiniest doubt that he was as turned on as she. Not with that hard erection pushing against her so erotically and insistently. She wanted, even more than pulling off her own clothes, to undress him and touch him there. Stroke him.

And more.

Bad idea, she told herself, even as she felt him unbutton her shirt and pull it off. Then he reached down for the closures of her jeans.

"No," she said firmly. She was breathing hard, definitely eager for more but finally coming to her senses. Wasn't she?

She took a step back before he could completely undo her jeans. Looked at him and saw the enticing bulge in his pants that she had felt moments before.

She wanted him.

But all they were was collaborators in a plan to save lives—including, perhaps, their own.

This kind of attraction, this need, was foolish.

Yet did it really matter in the scheme of things if they took advantage of this additional time to bond, to make love, to relieve a little of the pressure they'd been under?

No, it didn't matter. And in fact, didn't it make sense to be allies in as many ways as possible?

"Come here, Daniel," she said, grasping his jeans at the waist.

And then she steered him, ignoring his sexy, smug and oh-so-magnetic smile, toward her couch.

"Okay, you're the big strong man," she told him, cocking her head slightly as she attempted to mirror his hot and inviting smile. "You can pull this to convert my sofa into a bed."

He obliged immediately.

That was when his phone rang.

Chapter 13

Daniel froze. He had just lowered the base of the pull-out bed to the floor and glanced at the neatly tucked-in floral blanket on top of it. Much better for making love than the narrow surface of the couch. And the last time had been great even so.

But now the continuous ringtone of his phone grated at his ears, jabbing at the anticipation that had hardened his body.

Hell. He might as well answer. The sensual mood that had enthralled them was already toast.

He glanced toward Beth. She regarded him expectantly. Of course she figured he would answer. Was that a hint of regret shadowing those gorgeous violet eyes?

He yanked his phone from his pocket and looked at the caller ID number.

It was one of the CIU internal staff, the guy he had contacted before to run the license plate of the SUV that had followed Beth.

This was a call he should have expected, particularly since he'd made it clear that the information sought could be critical to helping his search for evidence—and, perhaps, to saving the life of one of the people whose identity the ID Division had helped to bury.

He should have turned off the damned phone.

On the other hand, if the information was critical, he'd have kicked himself for not grabbing it immediately. He pushed the button to answer. "Hi, Greg. Whatcha got?" He slowly lowered himself onto the nearest surface of the pullout bed, realizing he'd be a lot better off if he had more than one free hand to reposition his now-shrinking erection, not to mention his messed-up clothes. He'd take care of both later.

"I found the info on that plate," was the response. "I'll text it to you, too, but figured you'd want to hear."

"So who's the SOB who owns that SUV?" Daniel tried to keep his tone and words light to ease the fear that suddenly appeared on Beth's face. He reached out his free arm and gestured for her to join him on the bed. Just to sit.

"It's registered to a guy in Malibu, name of John Waterson. He reported the thing stolen yesterday morning."

Daniel made himself continue to breathe evenly to avoid scaring Beth even more. But the fact the vehicle was stolen vindicated him.

The driver had at minimum been a thief. Had he stolen it to try to obscure his identity when he used the SUV for something heinous?

Like following and harming someone in his sights… Beth?

Did the thief work at Corcoris Pharmaceuticals or otherwise for Preston in some other capacity? He doubted it was Preston himself, but he'd reserve judgment till he learned the ID of the culprit for sure.

Hell, someone needed to find the stolen vehicle and check it for prints. Not to mention arrest the thief before he could do any further harm.

"I wondered about that," Daniel responded. "And I'll look forward to your texting the info. Has the vehicle been located?" He felt Beth stir beside him and glanced her way. *Stolen,* he mouthed.

Her eyes widened. She might not have believed him before about the vehicle following her. She might not now, either. The fact it was stolen didn't mean the driver had any interest in her. But it certainly gave more credibility to his concerns, and she clearly got that.

He spoke with Greg a little longer. No, the SUV had not yet been located but its information had been added to the various official lists of stolen vehicles. Yes, as a member of a federal task force with interest in that particular SUV, he would be notified if and when the thing showed up.

"Thanks, Greg," Daniel finally said, and hung up. He turned to face Beth, who still sat beside him, unmoving. The torrid, sensuous expression that she'd worn before when he'd pulled out the bed had been replaced by what appeared to be a studied blankness. No emotion at all radiated from it.

Which made him want to take her into his arms anyway to comfort her.

Instead, he said, "I gather you got the gist of all that."

She nodded. "Then you were right about my being followed."

"Could be." He didn't need to rub it in, especially when there was, in fact, a little bit of doubt.

"And it's still missing?"

He nodded.

"So what do we do now?" She turned slightly as if assessing where they were—on her bed.

"We do as we'd already planned." At the sudden shock and negativity in her expression, he laughed. "Not that. But even though we shouldn't have gone so far anyway, too bad we were stopped by something like this." He paused, waiting for her to invite him to start again. He wanted to. But he also knew how much of a mistake it would be, especially now.

"You're right," she said. "Let's forget about that. But tell me more about that SUV."

Was she forgetting about how they had started to have sex again—how hot they'd been? How attracted?

Somehow, considering the sad expression on her lovely face, he doubted it. But he wouldn't press it. "What I meant," he continued, "was that I'll double-check your premises, then go home. Tomorrow we report for work as usual at Corcoris, continue our respective searches there for evidence and report to one another as needed. A couple of changes, though."

"What?" Her voice was throaty, as if she had tried to swallow her fear. He forbore from taking her back into his arms. Her body had withdrawn from him, and he suspected her mind had, too.

"I'll be checking on you often," he said, "and you won't take any chances. Not that you're likely to see that particular vehicle again, but watch for cars following you, be careful when exiting your own car to be sure there are plenty of people around when you're not home and keep alert around here for anything—*anything*—that strikes you as off. If something does, you just drive off and call me. Got that?"

She nodded. "Yes. And Daniel?"

"What?"

"Thank you."

When Daniel left ten minutes later, Beth followed his instructions and made sure the door locked behind him. As if she wouldn't have done that without being told.

Then she went into her kitchen and poured herself a glass of red wine—a little something to try to take the edge off her emotions.

Now that she was alone, she felt as if she had been stabbed and emptied of everything inside her.

She hadn't believed Daniel had been joking about that SUV following her, but she had assumed he was a trained federal agent just being overly cautious, partly as a result of his prior experience.

Or he was a man who wanted to find a way to get some close-up time in again with a woman he'd had sex with before.

It turned out he might have been both.

When he left, she didn't convert her bed back into a sofa—even though looking at it that way, she couldn't help thinking about what might have been: steamy, memorable sex yet again that night with a man who was incredibly hot.

Instead, she sat on it against the backrest and sipped wine as she watched the TV across the room. Her legs were stretched out, one crossed over the other.

This was fine, she told herself. She was fine.

But who had followed her…and why?

Damn! She couldn't obsess about this. She was here for a reason.

She got up, retrieved her laptop computer and began making notes on what she intended to do—particularly after the planning session she'd had with Daniel.

* * *

Daniel did not sleep well. He kept chiding himself for not insisting on staying with Beth.

Not for sex, despite how his body ached when he even considered resuming the activity they'd started.

No, to make sure she stayed safe.

Especially since he knew she wasn't too pleased that he was telling her what to do.

He hadn't simply left, of course, when he had departed from her apartment. He had slowly walked the hallways of her building, watching and listening. Then he had done the same thing on the street.

But there was no indication that she was in danger. No hint that whoever had been following was anywhere around.

He nevertheless hung out in his car as he had done before for less reason, watching, for maybe an hour. Waiting for his phone to ring in case Beth called to tell him she was scared and wanted him to come back.

But she didn't.

He eventually headed back to his place and dropped off to sleep in his own lonely bed, his phone near him. No more sounds of his ringtone that night.

When his alarm went off, he sat straight up and looked around. He knew exactly where he was. His first urge was to call Beth to reassure himself that she was all right.

But he made sure that reason prevailed. Instead, he first got up, dressed and made coffee in his kitchen, which was small but more functional than Beth's. Then, a mug in his hand, he called Judge Treena to give her an update. At least now it was nine-thirty in the morning in D.C. rather than the middle of the night.

She answered right away. "About time you reported in, McManus."

"I'm always available for you to call, Judge," he said. "Unless, of course, I'm at Corcoris playing tech monkey and can't talk."

"Too early for that at the moment," she observed. "Okay, tell all. Especially about that SUV. Greg informed me that you had him run some plates on a vehicle that turned out to be stolen."

"That's right, but I'll get to it in a minute." He wouldn't tell everything, of course—at least not about how he and Beth were getting along. But he had plenty to tell the judge about yesterday's events at the Corcoris offices, including the lunch and his "borrowing" of the password of one of the execs. "I saw some stuff that might have been interesting but couldn't save it or study it more. Not then. I heard noise outside—Beth Jones warning me that Corcoris himself was walking toward the lab I was in."

Daniel poured more coffee into his mug and sat down in the kitchen. He leaned his forehead onto one of his hands as his elbow rested on the table.

"Then she's still there and you and she are actually working together?"

"In a way." He then told the judge about what Beth had said about eavesdropping in the ladies' room.

"Smart lady, even if she is in way over her head," the judge said.

"I can get the list of all attendees at yesterday's brunch for physicians," Daniel said, "and I'll also confirm with Beth which ones she heard talking. I think it'd be worthwhile for CIU to contact them about their experiences after prescribing Corcoris drugs to their patients."

"I'll do that," Judge Treena said. "Okay, continue."

Daniel related how Beth and he had gone out for dinner far from the Corcoris headquarters, then decided they needed more privacy and met at his apartment to strategize.

"When she was ready to leave—that's when I saw that SUV start after her."

He then described how he'd called Beth, then met up with her—with no further sign of the SUV.

"I followed her home myself and made sure she got in safely and locked her doors," he finished.

"And that's all?" Judge Treena asked.

"Everything except details about how we're going to try to work together more in gathering evidence," he said. The judge sounded as if she had accepted Beth's presence there at last—or at least she wasn't arguing about it now. He wasn't about to even hint at their amazing attraction that nearly drove them into her bed for hot sex… for the second time. The judge didn't need to know that.

Even so, Daniel had the uncomfortable feeling that she was reading between the lines.

He took a long drink of coffee, decided it was getting cold and stood to heat it again in his microwave.

"That's it, then?" the judge asked.

"So far, but with us working in concert that way, I'm hoping that the concrete evidence that's eluded both of us so far will finally flow into our hands. Despite now having an exec's password, I didn't have much success before hacking into anything beyond what a lab technician was allowed to see, let alone checking out other parts of the company server for useful information. Instead of doing anything that can be traced, I'll download to a thumb drive rather than printing or forwarding, then hiding what I did…just in case there's someone even more savvy than me who looks into it."

"Fair enough. And Beth? Has she found anything while cleaning that can help?"

"Other than eavesdropping and recording some of what she's heard, no, but we're working on other things she can do. One thing I'm suggesting is that she bring samples of drugs or their ingredients out of the labs for CIU to get tested independently against the contents of what's on the market. She carries a purse, so that's a possibility, at least—but of course, she'll still need to be careful. There'll still be a chain-of-custody angle to work out, but if we find anything useful, that can be dealt with. I know she's eager to find something really spot-on that she can pass along for you to use in prosecuting anyone."

"Good. Keep at it…and you can tell her the same, from me. She might be surprised to hear that."

"I suspect she will be."

"By the way, Daniel. Here's a heads-up for you. I'm working on another angle. The FDA is always checking on all pharmaceutical companies and their required periodic reports. That includes Corcoris, of course. I've worked out a new contact there, one who's a grumpy old fool who always suspects fraud when he gets a new report and doesn't trust the pristine results of the last Corcoris inspection. He sounded absolutely over the moon when I told him his suspicions are right about Corcoris even though we don't have proof of it yet. He's going to send another team in soon to perform another inspection. I don't know when or anything else but I'll keep you informed."

"Great," Daniel said without completely meaning it. "But…well, since the last time the feds were there they found nothing, why will this one be any different?"

"Because you're there now. And if you can find at least preliminary evidence before and show them where else to look when they get there, it'll be all the better."

Daniel felt dubious—but also determined to work even harder.

"And you'll let me know if you figure out who stole that SUV and chased our Beth," the judge said. Not a question but a statement.

"Sure, Judge. And I will find out. Count on it."

Beth hadn't been asleep when her alarm went off that morning. She had lain awake a lot of the night rehashing everything that had happened the day before.

Including the apparent fact that she had been followed by someone driving a stolen vehicle—but why?

Now she was up and dressed and eating her morning fruit ration for breakfast. She wished she had a watch-dog who could have barked if any of the sounds she had heard while lying in bed overnight had been from some-one trying to break in rather than normal apartment-building noises.

But a dog might bark at those, too, and scare her all the more.

Too bad she hadn't begged Daniel to stay last night. She suspected it wouldn't have taken much to convince him. Only...well, here the only place he could have slept would have been in bed with her, so maybe sleep would not have been on the agenda.

Mindless, wonderful sex that could take her mind off her worries would have, though.

She shook her head as she put her dirty bowl in the dishwasher and prepared to grab her purse and leave for Corcoris.

Her ringtone sounded from her purse. She gener-ally kept it turned on when not at Corcoris—or avoid-ing calls. Even so, the unexpected sound startled her, and she nearly dropped her bag as she reached inside to find the phone.

She saw right away that her caller was Daniel and started to relax.

But why would he be calling at this hour? Was something else going wrong?

"Hello?" She tried to make her voice sound unshaky and carefree.

"Your escort awaits, my lady," he said in a formal voice.

"What?" She had no idea what he was talking about.

"Come on out to your car, Beth." His tone sounded amused. "I'm outside. Oh, and if you're checking out your windows and rearview mirrors, as I told you to do, and you see a vehicle following you, it's fine—as long as it's my dilapidated clunker and not a stolen SUV. I'm accompanying you to the office."

Beth did as ordered…this time, at least.

She was careful as she left her apartment, checking the hallway before heading out. None of her neighbors were there, but neither were any strangers.

She carefully locked her door, then headed downstairs, where she did the same thing again, this time making sure not only that the door was locked but that the alarm was on, too.

She scanned the street before heading toward the parking lot at the side of the building.

That was when she saw the clunker that was Daniel's.

She smiled but continued to watch her surroundings as she walked to her car. No errant SUVs pulling out to follow her, but she couldn't identify all the cars on the street.

As she got into her car, she looked toward Daniel.

There was a big smile on his face as he looked back at her.

A big sexy smile.

This man was doing strange things to her psyche. Turning her on just by looking at her.

Making her feel warm and fuzzy by his protectiveness, even though she knew why he was acting that way, and even though she had told him not to do so.

If she wasn't careful, she might even fall in love with him.

Love? No, not that, and certainly not with Daniel. Even if he were inclined to form some kind of relationship, which he clearly wasn't, she couldn't afford to care for anyone, especially not until she was sure her family was safe.

And then? Until all risks were dealt with and Preston Corcoris and any other involved members of his staff were convicted of their crimes, she would have to return to her new Beth Jones life in Washington State—while Daniel returned to his job in Washington, D.C., where he would be sent undercover again on other assignments.

Somewhere far from her, which would be just fine with him.

It was definitely foolish to allow her imagination to even take baby steps in that direction.

She was inside her car now, its doors locked and its engine on.

She gave a quick, friendly but remote wave toward Daniel and headed toward the Corcoris office.

Chapter 14

Despite some contemplation of things she wanted to accomplish that day, Beth's mind remained mostly on Daniel for the entire drive to the Corcoris campus. Not surprising. He was always there, either directly following her or a car or two behind.

She realized she was rehashing some of the things that had gone through her mind during her frequent sleeplessness the night before. The pros and cons of what she wanted to suggest to him had nearly driven her crazy. But she'd concluded that as long as she kept all emotion out of it—as he would—it was a good idea.

That was why, after pulling into a parking space and waiting a minute for Daniel to find a spot, too, she called him.

"We need to talk," she said. "And what I say will give us a good reason to meet up right here, in the parking lot, before we both head to our jobs."

* * *

How could a woman look so gorgeous and hot in a Corcoris Cleaning Staff T-shirt and jeans, her dark hair deliberately too short to be sexy, and her eyes continuously downcast to fulfill the role she played here?

Daniel didn't know, but he suspected that the knowledge he had about what was inside—both her clothes and her sharp mind—were factors.

Only...was whatever she had to say worth the risk of their being seen together here? She obviously thought so, and that intrigued him.

He hoped she was right.

He knew where she had parked, but she hadn't seen exactly where he had driven, so they had arranged for him to walk back to her car and join her.

Since it was the beginning of a regular workday, he passed a lot of cars in the lot on both sides of the garage and many still entering.

There were quite a few other people around, too. He was new enough there that he doubted he'd be recognized by many. The same was probably true for Beth.

But those who did recognize either of them, and saw them together outside the rooms where they might just coincidentally run into each other because of their jobs, could be a problem.

She stood beside her driver's door now as he joined her. "Hello, Beth," he said, not sure whether to sound jovial or angry or completely casual. That depended on what she had in mind.

"Hi, Daniel." She, on the other hand, obviously knew how she wanted to play this—as her usual persona, a shy member of the cleaning staff. She moved her bent head to look up at him with her eyes, then back down. "I gave this a lot of thought last night, and I now believe we're going about part of this wrong. Want to know how?"

Her voice sounded normal now, although very quiet. Interesting. But her body maintained her usual uneasy quality, with her shoulders bent, head down.

"Of course," he replied, concerned that she was going to tell him to get lost, that she didn't need his input, let alone his concern about her.

If so, he would have to convince her otherwise.

"Okay, then," she said. "We don't know who stole that SUV and followed me, but we can assume it's someone who works here or was given instructions by someone who works here. They started following me from your apartment. That means there's some knowledge—and maybe curiosity—about how well we know each other."

"Right…" He drew the word out as if urging her to continue, which she did.

"That means it could be someone who saw us together in the lab. Or when we've eaten together in public. Or even Preston Corcoris seeing me apparently try to slip into the lab where you were working—and speaking loudly enough to warn you that you were about to have company that wasn't me. So instead of trying to hide what might be clear to anyone watching, that we know each other, let's use it to our advantage."

"We should somehow flaunt it?" He wasn't thrilled about the idea, yet maybe she had a good point.

"I know I thought otherwise before," she acknowledged. "But why not act like we have some kind of romantic relationship that we know isn't necessarily applauded between a tech guy and cleaning-crew member? If we do that, whoever may be checking us out might accept that we're not looking for anything around the offices and labs but each other. Unless the worst has happened and they know exactly who one or both of us is, they could be less suspicious of us that way. And if that worst is true, then we can watch each other's backs more easily."

"Interesting proposition." Daniel knew he'd have to ponder this even more before accepting it. But it did sound feasible. And it was a whole lot better than her telling him to buzz off.

Would it hurt either of them, and their efforts to dig up evidence, to try to pull this off?

Unlikely. And the way Beth had presented it, it might even help them.

And…well, hell, even just appearing to be attracted to Beth, whichever persona she happened to be using at the moment, wouldn't be hard at all. The difficult thing was pretending otherwise.

"Your opinion?" she pushed.

"All right," he said, bending down and smiling as if whispering sweet nothings into this cleaning-staff member's ear. "Let's give it a try. As far as anyone here can see, we're just a horny couple who're hiding their mutual sexual interest from the world while at work."

Beth grinned, then looked down again. "Great. But now I want to really challenge you."

He stepped back and looked at her quizzically. "What do you mean?"

"I've been considering how we need to check out the other building on this campus. There've got to be things there that could help us. And I suspect you have the better shot at grabbing something helpful."

"I've been there a few times since I started working here," Daniel said. "It's just a big manufacturing and packaging facility, and they don't let people who aren't involved in either of those activities onto the floor. I've only been able to observe from an area above."

She looked disappointed. "That's all I was ever able to do there when I...you know. But I thought now that you, as a lab guy, could at least find a way onto the floor to grab some samples to compare with what's sent over for the quality-control tests."

"Not that I've been able to figure out so far."

"Well," she said, turning her head to smile grimly at him. "That's the challenge. It's for both of us. I'm going to find a way to get into that building today and see what I can do, and maybe you can, too."

When Beth had signed in and gone downstairs for her day's cleaning assignment, she made her mind focus not on how Daniel and she might be interacting here from now on—or how, possibly, it was a bad idea after all. Instead, she considered how she was going to get into the manufacturing building.

When she entered the long room filled with cleaning carts, she had to wait to get Mary Cantrera's attention. But as soon as she did, she smiled briefly at the scowling older woman, kept her gaze downward toward the bottom of Mary's Corcoris Cleaning Staff T-shirt and asked, "I know this may be wrong, and I know they have their own specially trained people there, but is it ever possible for one of us to get assigned to clean in the manufacturing plant?"

"Why do you want to do that?" Mary demanded. "Isn't the work here enough for you?"

"Oh, yes, of course it is. But, well...I've always heard of Corcoris and what a wonderful company it is, and I've just been so curious about how it works to make and package the medicines. I'd just like to see it sometime."

"Well…tell you what…" It wasn't an absolute no, and that almost made Beth smile for real. "I won't be able to get you any overtime pay if you don't finish your regular assignment today—and I have you scheduled to do some deep cleaning in the cafeteria—but I got a call earlier and the cleaning staff in the manufacturing building is low on sanitizing solution. You can take a few containers over there and get a look at the place—as long as you hurry back. Okay?"

"Oh, yes," Beth said. "Thank you."

Of course, she knew that popping over there with heavy containers of liquids wouldn't allow her to delve into what she really wanted—like a chance to collect samples of CorcoTrim from where the diet pills were manufactured and packaged or even the unlikely scenario of finding one of the handwritten log books and sneaking it out—but at least she would be able to see the place.

And she'd be able to tell Daniel later that she'd succeeded in getting in, even if she didn't actually meet the challenge she had told him about.

Later, when they were pretending to be involved in a secret relationship.

At first when he started to work in the lab that day, Daniel could think of little besides Beth.

He was worried about her attempting to find a way into the other building and getting into trouble. It would be a lot better for him to go there first and report to her any further ideas he got about obtaining evidence there, though he didn't think he'd be particularly successful. He really believed that what he had already started here, in this building, was the way to go.

But his thoughts focused even more on how to engage in Beth's latest approach to their joining forces for the same goal.

Donning his white jacket like the other half-dozen geeks present in the lab, he'd exchanged hellos with them while wondering what they would think about one of their members hobnobbing with a member of the cleaning staff.

If they knew what Beth was really like, outside her assumed nonentity personality, all the guys would be envious—and that was about half of the staff there.

But he soon gave himself a mental butt-kick. In addition to figuring out how to check out the manufacturing facility just to tell Beth he'd succeeded, he had work to do that day—and that work included not only the lab assignment handed to him here but also the task of figuring out what he could do next to further his real purpose at the company.

As a lab rat, he was scheduled to review some reports that morning—not do any new quality-control testing or analysis of ingredients or formulations. In other words, nothing that could lead to concrete evidence.

At least his month of working here and getting to know people, gaining a little bit of trust, was starting to pay off. Instead of being assigned to work with only the older, tried-and-true Corcoris products, he had begun to receive some reports on newer pharmaceuticals to double-check their contents along with other technicians.

At the moment, Daniel sat at the cubicle designated as his in one of the lab areas on the second floor. Since no password was necessary to access the reports he'd been assigned, the results must be perfect, in favor of Corcoris.

Unlike what he'd hoped to see after using Georgine's password—which he didn't want to do here and now, surrounded by other lab geeks.

Today the guy who'd been here the longest, Manny Busbey, was holding court with two of the female lab rats at his cubicle just a couple away from Daniel's. They were loudly discussing how proud they all were over the latest reports about to be sent to the FDA.

The ones supposedly confirming the purity of Corco-Trim.

Manny was theoretically a level above Daniel only because of his seniority here, but he liked to tell everyone around him what to do.

Daniel had an idea. He pasted a geeky smile on his face, rose and joined his three ostensible coworkers. "I couldn't help overhearing," he said, looking at Manny.

The guy was shorter than the women, dark haired, with a swarthy complexion and an ego bigger than the huge manufacturing building across the property. He just gave Daniel a condescending stare.

"I'm just so glad to hear about the good results," Daniel continued. "But for me to be able to completely get what I'm reading, I need to understand the whole process. Which I kind of do, but do you know if it's okay for me just to peek in at the manufacturing building again?" When none of the others responded immediately, he shrugged and grinned even more. "Okay, I admit it. I just love to stand right there on the observation deck and watch and listen from a distance to all those machines chugging along making, then packaging, those pills."

"We're not really encouraged to do that," said one of the women, whose name was Ilana. She was tall enough that her lab jacket reached just to her waist, and her concerned smile revealed uneven teeth. "At least not by ourselves. You haven't been here long enough to know, but we're invited to go there every few months as a group to check it out. Otherwise, we're supposed to stay away."

"So you've gone there before on your own anyway?" Manny glared at him as if he had committed some major crime.

"Well, yeah. Maybe it's not the best thing, but…well, I've got a few minutes right now to do it again. Anyone care to join me?"

Manny just snorted and shook his head. The women, too, just stood there. Would Manny complain? Report him?

Heck, he had to sign in there anyway, so it wouldn't be a big secret that he'd gone inside. He'd only mentioned it since his absence, even though he'd keep it brief, would probably be noted. The other times had been just as he had been leaving the campus to return to his apartment.

Now, though, it was late morning. He left the lab, signed out downstairs, and crossed the area between the two buildings that was landscaped with well-tended grass and rows of hedges and palm trees.

He could hear the equipment even before he opened the door. There was an entry area staffed by a woman who wore all white, including a sanitary cap on her head.

"Can I help you?" she asked. She was middle-aged, and she stared at him harshly as if he was an intruder. Which, of course, he was.

Daniel explained that he was a Corcoris lab employee and only wanted to take a peek at the facility.

Too bad he couldn't tell her that what he really wanted was to be given free rein to inspect every inch of the place, including the areas containing all the pharmaceuticals' ingredients. Not to mention the log books for each brand, the assembly lines where each type of medication was mass-produced and packaged, everything.

But that wasn't going to happen.

"Okay if I go to the viewing area?" Daniel asked the

greeter. That was a raised walkway where visitors could look down on what was happening below. Some of the functioning areas were glassed in for sanitation and it wasn't possible to see much of what happened inside them, but the observation area at least gave a global view of what was going on.

"All right," the woman said. "Go ahead." But before he reached the door that led from the reception area to the hallway and stairs to the observation area, it opened.

Beth came through it. She met his eyes for only a second before lowering her gaze.

"I've dropped the sanitizers off with the plant cleaning manager," she said softly to the lady behind the desk.

"Good. Thanks for bringing them over."

Her sideways glance at Daniel as he moved forward was triumphant.

They would have lots to talk about later.

Especially if the clever woman, who'd found an acceptable way of visiting here, had also figured out a way to check out the plant even more.

Despite having gotten into the other building and walked around on the main level, Beth recognized that she had accomplished little that day.

She'd found no way to gather samples. She hadn't entered the areas where pharmaceuticals were manufactured and packaged. She hadn't even figured out how to reprise her entry into the building.

The cleaning manager wasn't going to run out of sanitizing solution often—if ever again.

Beth thought about her limited success all day, and especially now as she finished her last cleaning assignment before her designated time to leave—a hallway on the first floor outside the elevators and the unimportant administrative offices located on that level.

People walked by, usually in pairs or groups. They all ignored her, which was fine with her.

She was dressed like a janitress. She smelled sweet and tangy, like the cleaning brews she utilized.

She supposed she should feel grateful that no one seemed to recognize her at work—or at least no one had confronted her. Nor had anyone made catty remarks about the time she'd spent talking to that nerdy tech guy in the parking lot.

But she wished she had done more that day than simply enter the manufacturing plant.

Although…maybe it had been enough. She'd seen what it was about and realized how unlikely it was that she, at least, would be able to study it enough and grab stuff up that could be used as evidence.

For now, she pushed her filled cart around and cleaned the areas designated by her boss, Mary—including the cafeteria, as she'd been told, and also some storage areas.

That meant she didn't run into Daniel again, which might be a good thing.

Their ruse would involve their pretending to be seeing each other outside work. While here, they would need to act cordial but remote, as if they'd seen one another before but that was all.

Would anyone buy that? Probably at least those people with no agenda regarding them.

But how about the person who had followed her, or whoever had told him to do it?

And Beth was convinced that, whoever it was, Preston Corcoris had to be involved.

As she finished dusting the top of a door frame and dismounted from the small footstool that she carried around on the cart, she saw Daniel approach from the main entry door.

Her heart stopped, then started again at an elevated pace.

Dumb reaction.

As he reached her, she heard him mutter, "Six o'clock." He didn't slow down or stop but continued to a door to a stairway.

Six o'clock? That was half an hour from now.

She had to interpret what he'd meant. Well, after their apparent agreement that morning, she would assume he wanted to meet her at her car at that time so they could continue their pretense of being a couple hiding their relationship.

That would also be a good time to briefly recap what they had learned that day.

Should she exaggerate her success in getting into the manufacturing facility to show that she, at least, had met the challenge she had given them?

Heck, he'd met it, too. She had even seen him there.

Had he, unlike her, learned anything helpful?

Their efforts here weren't really a contest. If either of them succeeded in finding the needed evidence, they both would succeed.

Then, eventually, she would believe that both her family and she would finally be safe.

Okay, Daniel, she thought. *Tell me what you found.*

She hoped it was exactly what they both had been looking for.

Chapter 15

It was no accident that at six o'clock Daniel followed Beth out the employees' exit with a few other people between them. He had planned it that way, finding a place to hang out, ostensibly talking on his cell phone, pushing his geeky glasses up to the bridge of his nose, as he waited for her to leave.

He wouldn't tell her why, since she'd seemed so intent on taking care of herself, even when she was clearly rattled by what was going on around her. And even though, like it or not, she knew why he felt compelled to ensure her safety.

But that was before. He'd been concerned about her when he saw her gloat inside the production building, and he remained concerned for her now.

The SUV that had followed her yesterday late in the day remained squarely on his mind as they prepared to leave the quasi safety of the Corcoris campus.

At least with the new game they were beginning to play about being a secret couple, presumably no one who paid any attention to them would see anything off about his nearness to her, now or any other time.

Would that change the approach of anyone trying to harm her—or him, for that matter? Unlikely, but Daniel did like that Beth was now including him in her planning.

And her challenges.

The crowd surged pretty much in the direction they were both heading: toward the company's parking garage, at the edge of the property behind both buildings.

"Hi, Daniel." The feminine voice beside him startled him. He turned to see one of the other lab rats who helped in random quality-control tests walking beside him.

"Hi, Samantha," he returned, giving her a friendly grin. "Good day today?" Like, did any of your QC tests on some of the newer, less established and more lucrative drugs show any problems? If so, did those problems appear in any reports? But he couldn't ask her that.

"Good enough," the tall plain woman answered, but a troubled expression marred her pale face.

Before Beth's arrival here, Daniel had tried to get to know Samantha and some other female lab rats like Ilana better, hoping that if he acted interested in them they would share secrets.

But whether it was warnings—explicit or tacit—that floated between the walls of the company headquarters or just his unsexy demeanor here, that angle hadn't succeeded.

"How about you?" Samantha continued, giving him a smile.

Interesting. Maybe his earlier efforts were now paying off after all. If he hadn't already had plans—like meeting up with Beth and ensuring her safety—he would have invited Samantha to join him for a drink.

Not now, though. Not while he was following Beth.

Even so, he drew a little closer, trying to make it appear as if the press of others heading toward the garage was crowding him. Maybe he could suggest some more businesslike reason to meet up with her.

He bent toward Samantha and said softly, "As you know, I'm fairly new here, and I have some questions. Do any of you ever get together to talk about inconsistencies in any tests?"

"Inconsistencies?" Her voice, though still low, squeaked. "I've never seen any. And, no, I've never heard anyone else talk about any, either."

Which meant, Daniel surmised, that she'd seen something troubling, and so had others working in the labs, but they didn't dare to discuss it. Interesting—but he doubted that following up with Samantha would yield anything.

Especially now, when he was Beth's new guy.

Samantha probably had no idea about that, but she had started walking faster, evidently wanting to get away from him.

He didn't step up his own pace, since he was walking about the same speed as Beth, who remained ahead of him among a bunch of other people.

She soon reached her car and headed toward the driver's side. She rooted in her purse for her key, and he figured she took her time finding it since the time was almost exactly six o'clock and she would expect him to meet her there.

Which he did, maneuvering his way between her car and the one nearest it.

"Hello, Beth." He stuck his dweebiest smile on his face in case anyone was watching. "How was your day?"

That was a nice, friendly question he could ask everyone he met, not just Samantha and Beth.

"Okay." She looked down toward her car door in her shyness mode. "And yours?"

"Okay." He spoke loudly enough so the people behind them could probably hear. He followed it up, though, by moving only his lips: *See you at your place.*

She blinked before looking shyly down again.

She got it.

Even knowing that Daniel had her back again, Beth drove carefully to her apartment, keeping watch behind her and even off to the sides.

Her apparently being followed last evening had freaked her out, and since the vehicle had been stolen, she didn't even try to convince herself it was a coincidence. Sure, she had already been observing her surroundings, but now she was even more cautious.

She wanted to talk to Daniel again. Not that she had much to report about what she'd accomplished that day, but having someone to bounce thoughts and concerns off of—well, that was worth a lot.

She didn't intend to cook, though. If he wanted to stay, she would order out. Pizza, probably.

She finally reached her building and pulled into her spot.

By the time she had turned off her engine and gotten out of the car, Daniel was at her side.

"Hi, Daniel," she said in her janitress's soft voice. "Nice to see you again."

"Ditto, Beth." He still wore his glasses and sent her a toothy smile.

Ah, yes, they were both still in their roles.

But after she had carefully turned off the alarm and

used her key to get inside the building's door, he didn't wait till they were upstairs to plant that sexy body of his right in front of her. "Hello, Beth," he said in what she now knew was his normal, enticing voice.

"Ditto, Daniel," she said, much louder than she had spoken for hours.

In moments, right there in the entry, which fortunately was opaque with no glass that anyone could see through, he took her into his arms. His searing kiss left her almost breathless.

But she managed to stop and back away.

"Let's not go there," she said. "Things become too difficult." She looked into his face, ignoring the heat and need in his blue eyes. "Agreed?"

"You're right—this time," he responded in a teasing tone.

"I'm always right." She checked in the room where the building's mail boxes lined the walls, unlocked hers with a key and pulled out the contents—all advertising flyers.

As it had been since her arrival. No one who might send her anything with meaning other than utility bills knew where she was.

She led Daniel upstairs and unlocked her apartment door. Her first glance inside ended at her convertible sofa. Tonight it would stay a sofa until Daniel left again.

"Come in," she invited him. "Learn anything interesting today—like at the manufacturing building?"

"Just more suspicions."

"You need to tell me. Okay if I order in a pizza?"

It was fine, and they negotiated what to order on it. She liked veggies and cheese; he liked pepperoni and sausage. They decided on half-and-half.

She laid her purse down on the floor near the entry

to the kitchen and walked inside. "Beer, wine, soda or water?"

"Beer sounds good."

She got two bottles out of the fridge and opened them, then walked into the main room of the small apartment and handed Daniel his beer. Placing hers on the small oblong table against the wall, she pulled out one of the two chairs and sat, waiting for him to do the same.

When she looked at him again, she blinked. He had taken off those geeky glasses and stuck them in the pocket of his shirt—a black knit one that hugged his muscles now that he wasn't bent over in lab-tech mode again.

Sexy? Oh, yeah. No matter what she had told him downstairs, she ached to be in those muscular arms again. Maybe without that shirt. No, definitely without it, or his dark trousers. Not that she would let on what she was feeling. She took a long swig of beer.

"So tell me what you learned today," she said, all business.

Now, if only she could stay that way.

Daniel was glad she'd asked him that. It gave him better perspective on why he was here—in case he needed the reminder. Which he didn't.

Being in her apartment again with Beth was just another convenient way for them to coordinate what they were doing and to continue playing their new roles as coworkers who were attracted to one another.

"For one thing, I didn't get much out of my visit to the production building—but at least I got inside. Did you see anything helpful?"

By the sad expression that passed over her face, the answer he expected was confirmed. "Not really. And I doubt that I'd be able to find anything we can use even if I get back there. Too much going on, and a cleaning-staff member not assigned to work there wouldn't be able to snoop around much. How about you?"

"Same goes for a lab guy who's working in the admin building—and I was advised today that there are occasional group meetings for us over there but that otherwise we're supposed to stay away."

"It shouldn't matter," Beth said. "I really think we can find what we need in the building where we spend most of our time."

"Agreed. In fact, I had a very short talk with another lab tech as I followed you out to your car that gave me even more optimism about that."

He started to describe what had—and hadn't—been said as he'd spoken so briefly with Samantha, but his phone rang.

He pulled it out of his pocket and checked the caller ID.

"Got to take this," he told Beth. "It's Judge Treena." He saw worry flood Beth's face and smiled reassuringly. "Hi, Judge."

"Hello, Daniel," she responded. "How are things in Moravo Beach?"

"Good, but not as productive as I'd like."

"Well, we're going to step things up. First of all, we've gotten some information from those two physicians that Beth Jones heard talking. They're not completely cooperative, but they've told us enough to get us started looking specifically into the diet medication they mentioned."

"No kidding." He put his hand over the phone and told Beth what the judge had said.

She smiled and gave a thumbs-up.

"In fact," the judge continued, "I've convinced the

FDA to send the additional inspectors I'd requested. They're arriving there tomorrow to go over the official records again."

Daniel snorted. "I'll bet they won't get into the un-official records any more than they did last time." He glanced at Beth. "You'll be interested to know that the cavalry arrives tomorrow," he said softly. At her questioning look he chuckled and added, "The FDA again."

"Who are you talking to?" Judge Treena barked sharply into his ear.

"Beth Jones. She looks glad about the news about those doctors. She and I are collaborating now even more on our search for what can be used as evidence."

"Still? It's a good idea, but…" The judge paused and asked, "Where are you now? Are you somewhere you can talk?"

"We're fine. We're at Beth's place."

Another pause. "How closely are you working to-gether?" She sounded suspicious.

He didn't need to explain their new ruse to the judge. Instead, he told her what she already knew. "We're both after the same thing and we're collaborating on the best ways to get it, not just comparing notes."

But he knew what the judge really wanted to learn.

Was it just a business relationship, as it should be?

"And have you made any additional progress by planning that way?"

"It's still a work in progress."

"I'll bet."

His discussion with the judge continued for another few minutes, and then she asked to speak with Beth, whom she said she had intended to call later.

Taking the phone, Beth listened for a moment, then said, "No, I don't think I've been followed again. And

Daniel has been really great in keeping watch on my behalf. Any word yet on who stole that SUV?" Beth listened for a moment and her eyes grew wide. "You're kidding. No, I know you're not. That street is only a few blocks from my parents' house. Did he say—?"

As Daniel watched, he grew angrier, although he wouldn't let it show. What was going on? And why hadn't the judge told him?

Beth listened some more, then handed the phone back to him.

"What—?" he began, but Judge Treena interrupted.

"That was next on my list to tell you. The SUV's been found and impounded. The thief happened to be in it, too, a guy with a lot of car thefts on his record. Name of Billings. He's not talking, but his happening to have followed Beth in the stolen vehicle, then getting caught in the neighborhood she used to live in... Well, the local cops are still working on it and so are we. Plus, we've gotten them to step up their patrols in the neighborhood where the car was found. We'll let you know if we find anything else."

"Please do that." His tone was more irritable than he'd intended, but the judge's response was in her normal brisk tone.

"Stay in touch, Daniel. I will, with anything I learn, but I especially want to know how things work out with the FDA. And also..."

"Also what, Judge?"

"Be careful about your...collaboration. Got it?"

He did.

"No problem," he responded. And just in case she needed more, he added, "All is cool."

Beth was even more frightened now for her parents. At least the thief had been caught, but where he'd been found had surely been no coincidence. She was glad to hear that there was added security in the neighborhood, but was that enough?

This wasn't a good time, but she would call home soon—and urge her family even more to get out of town.

Beth was also concerned about Judge Treena and what she must be thinking now. At least so far she hadn't threatened Beth with any repercussions for her disobeying what Her Honor and her crew had ordered her to do for her own safety—stay away from Moravo Beach and particularly Corcoris Pharmaceuticals—and was even going beyond what she had promised to do to help Beth's family.

But she'd known for a while that Beth was also working with one of the judge's undercover agents. The CIU had wanted results. When they'd sent Daniel to achieve them, they hadn't known that anyone else—Beth—was working on them, too.

The judge had undoubtedly believed, at least at first, that Beth could mess things up. Or at least slow things down.

Well, she hadn't yet and never would. In fact, she needed to make sure progress occurred even faster now. For her family's sake.

Yet now, as she sat with Daniel at her tiny table eating pizza and trying not to meet his eyes, she couldn't help worrying about what would come next.

The FDA was sending inspectors again? That could be a good thing. But they all knew well that Corcoris had plans in place to deal with a visit from the regulatory agency.

Even if the examiners got into the reports once more regarding the weight-loss medication that the doctors had criticized when Beth was eavesdropping, what was undoubtedly maintained for federal scrutiny would show that the tests had all gone well and that nothing was wrong. Sure, the FDA's Office of Testing and Research could conduct its limited inquiry into safety and quality, but would they? Even if they did, what they were given to check could be modified.

And if Corcoris ever learned the reason for the feds' new visit… Beth shuddered inside. So far, even with the incident with the SUV, her family had only been threatened.

After the FDA conducted its next unscheduled inspection, might her family actually be harmed?

"What are you thinking?"

Beth jumped, startled by Daniel's voice. "I'm just worrying about my family. I know they're okay for now, but— Do you think this second visit by the FDA will finally resolve everything?"

"Count on it." He smiled at her over a half-eaten slice of pizza.

He looked so certain—and so cute as he boyishly dug into his meal again—that she couldn't help smiling back.

Which might not have been the best idea. Not when, notwithstanding the impression they might give to the world, they had vowed to keep their hands off one another tonight and forever.

Yet what if Daniel was right? What if this time, after what they had learned during their last visit, the FDA inspectors were wise enough to uncover whatever hidden information existed…especially with a little help?

From the man who had discovered some of the records that might not have been available before but were this time, thanks to the "borrowed" password.

Daniel.

And if he was right, and everything was finally resolved starting tomorrow by actual evidence uncovered by the FDA that could even—she hoped—result in arrests, then tonight might be one of the last times Daniel and she would see each other alone for a coordination meeting or anything else.

Would this be the last opportunity she might have to engage in unforgettable sex with Daniel? Could be, for there was no doubt that he would exit her life immediately when his undercover services here were no longer necessary.

She looked away and took another bite of pizza. Those thoughts needed to be squelched. Especially since she realized they could just be an excuse to herself in case she tried to seduce him this night.

And yet when she did move her gaze back to Daniel, she found him regarding her with a heated stare that suggested his mind was heading in the same direction.

Interesting that their thoughts—and bodies—seemed to be in sync. Or was she just hoping…?

"Beth," Daniel said softly, placing his slice of pizza back on the paper plate on the table in front of him. He stood and held out his arms.

Almost as if mesmerized, Beth did the same thing: food down, body standing, and suddenly she pressed herself tightly against him.

She inhaled slowly at the incredible feel of his hard body, its angles fitting so enticingly against her curves. She tried once more to remember what a bad idea this was. And failed as his head bent toward hers, causing her to raise her lips for the searching and stimulating kiss she anticipated.

She wasn't disappointed. Nor did she passively accept his embrace. She tried to let her mouth outtease, out-search his. Her tongue kicked off a game with a rhythm that mimicked what their lower bodies could do.

Would do. Had to. She felt Daniel's arousal pressed tightly against her center, and her body responded with growing desire.

Her knees weakened, or was that just an instinctive reaction? She yearned to slide to the floor with him while pulling off their clothes.

Daniel put one of his hands between them, caressed her aching breasts. Instead of lowering them where they stood, he began undressing her even as he moved them in a dance of passion toward her small and narrow couch.

Would he convert it? Should she?

He let go of her. Oh, yes, she felt bereft, but she determined the time wouldn't go to waste. She stripped off the rest of her clothes.

The bed immediately emerged from the sofa under Daniel's strong and relentless tug. Beth smiled as he turned back and saw that she was naked.

"Beautiful," he breathed and stepped toward her.

"You need to share the view," she said softly, and also drew closer, unbuttoning his shirt as he bent and slid off his pants.

Oh, yes. He did share the view. His toned, muscular body was every bit as gorgeous as she recalled. And the way his shaft stretched toward her...

She couldn't help it. She knelt and took him into her mouth, sucking gently, then releasing his erection just enough to lick its length before he bent and pulled her toward the bed.

It was his turn to touch, then taste her. She moaned as his lips reached her breasts and almost cried out when he licked first one hard nipple, then the other, even as his clever hands played with the lower part of her body, teasing her, then gently pushing one, then two fingers inside in the way she wanted not his hand but his hardness to go.

Instead, he moved off the bed again. She almost cried out until she realized where he was headed: toward the pile of his clothes on the floor.

He had come prepared, and when he tore open the condom and returned to her, she held out her hand.

"Let me," she whispered.

He did. Moments after he was sheathed, he was inside her, loving her, bringing her to the highest crescendo of need.

When she bucked and cried out in her raging orgasm, he, too, moaned and stilled.

His body soon straightened on top of her. He was heavy, but the weight remained fraught with passion and suggestion.

Which meant that after a short time to rest, they began their lovemaking all over again.

Chapter 16

Daniel stayed the night. Good idea? Maybe not. But it felt so good to wake up now and then and draw Beth's nude form close to him again.

It led to more lovemaking. And more.

He woke up before her and hit the shower. He'd need to go to his place to change clothes before heading to work. He didn't want to have to explain wearing the same outfit twice, even though his geek personality there could suggest that he simply forgot what he'd had on yesterday.

Although if someone really was making assumptions about Beth and him…maybe to maintain their cover, wearing yesterday's clothes again might be a good thing.

In fact, when a grinning Beth joined him in the shower and their subsequent activities took up a lot of the time he'd have needed to go home, he decided that a change of clothes was unnecessary after all.

* * *

Beth drove separately to work when her bed was once more a sofa and they'd left her apartment.

She refused to let her mind dwell on the reasons that what they had done all night had been a series of mistakes.

Instead, she convinced herself—maybe—that it had been a good diversion, an enjoyable interlude that would be the last time they'd have the opportunity to engage in sex.

They both had to return to reality.

That was exactly what she did after Daniel and she assumed their chosen roles at Corcoris once more in the parking lot and wished each other a good day.

She would wait until later to call her parents, when it wouldn't be so awkward to do so. Not that she'd have hesitated even in the middle of the night if she'd felt she had to warn them…again.

But even if the danger to them had been increased by the man who'd stolen the SUV and followed her, her family should be okay now—especially since not only had he been caught, but the security patrols in their neighborhood had also been stepped up.

Beth walked into the building, used her ID card at the entry and was met immediately by Mary Cantrera, who was giving assignments for the day to the entire group.

"Glad you're on time today," the older woman stated. "Busy day. Word is out there'll be some unscheduled government inspections conducted this afternoon, so we need to make sure all the lab areas where tests are conducted are spotless."

Not that Beth had doubted Judge Treena's warning, but now it appeared that the whole company was aware of the impending FDA visit.

How had that happened? And was it a good thing?

Usually, the feds were concerned with records and reports. This could be overkill to help make the best possible impression.

Unless the cleaning was somehow also designed to obscure something that could otherwise be used as evidence. Beth would keep her eyes open for that.

But shouldn't the FDA just have shown up completely unannounced? Beth had only a vague idea about how those things were usually handled. She had sometimes been aware of inspections when she had worked here before, but the only time she had heard much about them was when they went well and she was ordered, in her public relations capacity, to come up with releases to announce that to the world.

Less favorable results had been handled delicately by her bosses. Like her missing friend, Milt Ranich.

When all this was over, would she finally know where he was?

In a short while, she and the other cleaning-staff members gathered their equipment and started off with their carts down the hall toward the service elevator.

She had to wait for several carloads but eventually got into the same ride as Gabrielle Maroni. The young cleaning-staff member seemed giddy about being so important that day. "It all depends on us," she said, grinning broadly as she held on to the long handle of one of the mops extending from the top of her cart. "If we don't sanitize something right, our company could fail the inspection and get into big trouble." She did a fist pump. "It's about time they recognize that the cleaning crew rocks."

Beth couldn't help smiling, even as she maintained her shy personality—and realized that this young woman didn't catch the irony in what she said. Too much cleaning in areas of the FDA's focus might be the exact wrong thing to do, in the agency's estimation. It could appear that they were attempting to mask a problem. And maybe they were.

"I just hope I do everything okay," was all she said.

"You will." Gabrielle gave Beth's arm a squeeze. "But if you're worried, you can always tell Mama Mary to double-check what you've done."

Beth would as soon drink some of the cleansing soap as ask their boss to inspect her work. But she said, "Good idea. Are you going to do that?"

"No way," Gabrielle said. "I may be pretty new at this, but I know I'm handling it just fine."

It wouldn't be long until the elevator stopped on the second floor. Beth hadn't been alone with Gabrielle since the major lab cleanup to which she'd been assigned.

"You've been here longer than me," Beth said. "I've been wondering since the other day—have there been any other…accidents…like the one we had to clean up? I mean, where so much stuff was trashed and all over the floor."

Gabrielle's vivacious expression suddenly turned blank. "We've been told not to talk about that."

"Then there have been others," Beth speculated. "How many since you've started working here? And do you know how—?"

She really meant *who* rather than *how,* but it didn't matter. Their elevator arrived and the door opened. Gabrielle shot her a glance that looked both scared and relieved. But before she got out, she said very softly, "What I heard was that it happens sometimes when a report shows stuff it shouldn't."

In other words, where the results were bad, Beth figured. But it was too late to get anything else from Gabrielle. She was already out the door, shoving her equipment ahead of her.

Beth pushed her cart out of the elevator, too. She watched Gabrielle's back for a few seconds, then started making her way down the hall to the lab area where she was assigned to clean.

It was, she recalled, the same one where she had met Daniel—was it only a few days ago? It was Friday now. That had been Monday, not even a week.

As she entered the outer room of the lab, she went through the same procedure as she had then: changing into sanitary clothing, pulling on a vinyl cap and sanitary gloves. And, yes, she exchanged her cart for the cleaner one that waited for her.

Then she opened the inner door and went inside.

And stopped. Her being assigned here was a mistake. This lab was occupied now by several technicians who appeared busy. Conducting regular tests—or some kind of preparations for the inspection? That, Beth couldn't tell.

But Daniel was there among the half a dozen other men and women dressed in white lab jackets and also wearing gloves who clustered around the laboratory tables and computers.

With all the organized chaos, she considered leaving and reporting the apparent mistake to Mary.

On the other hand…could she somehow use this? Maybe she could find a way to clean corners without getting in anyone's way.

While eavesdropping.

Still, Daniel, with whatever he was doing, was much

more likely to extract something that could turn into evidence against Corcoris.

Especially if any of these lab worker bees had been instructed, officially or not, to change results or reports to make the company look better to their inspectors.

Was that possible, especially here, where there were so many of them? She would have to ask Daniel later.

Daniel appeared to be doing something with a formula, pouring stuff from one flask into another. She would ask him about that later, too.

Meantime, for now, she found an area at one corner of the room where no one was working. She said nothing to anyone, not even Daniel, and everyone seemed to ignore her.

The chaos gave the impression of fear. Or was it supposed to look efficient?

She was glad that her mother's long-term medication was now generic. Beth felt sure now that if she were ill and needed a prescription, Beth would ask her mother's doctor to give her something not manufactured by Corcoris.

Manufactured. Did all this furor in the labs today carry over to the other building across the campus where she'd been so briefly yesterday? Were the people involved in making the pills and liquids that the company sold also stressed-out while preparing for another possible inspection?

"Hey, why are you in here now?"

Beth had been using a disinfectant on the outside of some wall cabinets while listening to the people closest to her. They'd all been grumbling in terms that made them sound as if they were afraid for their jobs if they didn't get whatever they were doing right.

Now she turned to see who was talking. It was Ivan Rissinger, the deputy CEO, who worked closely with Preston Corcoris. He was all dressed in sanitary gear, too, but it was definitely him.

He had been there when Andrea had gotten into trouble at the company and with Preston Corcoris.

She had pretty much avoided Rissinger since her return, as she had the other top executives.

But now he was looking at her.

She made sure she was in character as a lowly staff member, glancing down at the floor before regarding him again. "Are you talking to me, sir?"

"Yes. There's work being done here. We don't need the cleaning crew getting in the way."

"I'm sorry, sir," she responded, not quite looking at him. Was her disguise good enough? "My boss said I should come here and I did, but I'll leave now."

She quickly collected the paper towels and bottles she had been using and reorganized them on her cart, then pushed it toward the door. Fortunately, Rissinger didn't seem to look at her again, as if she was way beneath his regard.

She did catch Daniel's quizzical glance and nodded slightly as she continued out the door. He didn't have to worry. She didn't need protection. She just needed to leave.

But Beth was concerned now. Whatever these people were doing seemed disorganized and inappropriate. Were the underlings being set up to take the fall in the event the feds agreed that something was amiss here at Corcoris?

That wasn't what she had been after.

She wanted the real people at fault—starting with Preston Corcoris—to pay for what they had done. Especially since her fears about at least some of the drugs they manufactured here might be coming true, judging by what she had overheard those doctors say.

People's lives might hang in the balance.

Daniel wasn't sure what that was about, but he wanted to make certain Beth got out of the lab all right.

He found it somewhat amusing that all these lab techs were trying to outmaneuver each other, all wanting to show that they knew exactly what they were doing.

"How are those tests going?" Ivan Rissinger had come up to Daniel where he worked with some samples of one of the long-term Corcoris antibiotics, CorcoBiotica.

"Perfect," Daniel said with a grin. "Every sample I've checked seems spot-on." He decided to ride the executive to see if he could learn anything. "But should I do something different to prove it? I mean, I've been preparing the same kinds of records as I was told to, but I heard that the testing and reports are going to be checked out by the FDA. I've never directly interacted with them before. Is there any way I can show them what I'm doing or whatever so I can prove everything here is fine?"

"We'll see." The look on Rissinger's long well-lined face appeared speculative.

Why? Daniel had expected him to shove a negative response to him immediately.

Was the company looking for scapegoats in case things didn't go right?

"Thanks," Daniel gushed. "Can I show you what I've been doing?"

Manny Busbey came over to them, looking miffed. Had he wanted to show off to Rissinger, too? Daniel hadn't worked directly with Manny before but, from his pompous know-it-all attitude, had the impression that the guy had been here since the start of time. Or at least the start of his career after college, which had to have been a couple of decades back.

"But I don't mean to steal Manny's thunder," Daniel said, using his hands to gesture toward Manny in a way that a model on a TV game show pointed out something valuable.

Rissinger turned toward Manny and started questioning him, too—about his tests on the new diet drug, CorcoTrim.

That gave Daniel exactly what he needed: a lack of attention.

Time for a restroom break…and, he hoped, an opportunity to check in with Beth.

Beth didn't really want to return to the basement and Mary Cantrera's disapproving glare. And criticism. She had no doubt that Mary would tell her that Beth was the one who was wrong, that she had given her a different room number for her cleaning assignment.

Maybe she should just head for the lab where Gabrielle had been assigned to work at the end of this hallway. But then all she would be able to do was clean, not learn anything helpful. Gabrielle had already mentioned more than she'd appeared comfortable saying.

Not that Beth had heard anything before that would assist her much while in Daniel's lab. She hadn't been able to interact with or learn anything from him—or from anyone. No one she'd been near had said anything worth her eavesdropping.

Grumbles and concerns, yes. Admission of fooling with the formulations or hiding anything from the FDA, no.

That didn't mean that none of them were doing any

of that. But if they were, they simply weren't talking about it.

Well, she couldn't just stand here. The hall was empty, but with what was anticipated for later in the day, there would undoubtedly be a lot of foot traffic here soon.

And Ivan Rissinger wouldn't hang out in the lab forever.

She pressed the button for the elevator, then heard a door open from the direction from which she had just come.

Assuming it would be someone she wouldn't want to communicate with, she studied the damp equipment on her cart as if searching for something.

"Are you done cleaning?" asked a wonderfully familiar voice. Daniel's.

She reminded herself to stay in character despite how glad she was to see him. Seeing no one nearby didn't mean they were definitely alone. "I need to find out my next assignment," she said softly, daring to look at him.

He remained in his dorky character, smiling broadly beneath his glasses. Somehow even that was a turn-on for her, but thinking about his hard, hot body now seemed completely out of place.

"I wondered why you were in my lab," he said. "We were given a lot of instructions when I got here about preparing for the inspection later." A fleeting rise to his brows told her that he'd heard things that might be interesting.

She would be eager to get a recap from him, but that wouldn't happen until later. After the workday.

Over the weekend? Today was Friday, and like it or not, she had the next two days off. Shouldn't the janitorial crew be required to clean when fewer other people would be around?

It would surely be easier to snoop then.

If she were given the opportunity by Mary Cantrera, she would volunteer. Because she needed the overtime pay, she would tell the woman, not for the first time. That should sound realistic.

Of course, she would need to be careful. The FDA didn't work only on weekdays, so they might still be around conducting their inspection.

That could be a good thing if she found a way to make some suggestions about what they should look for and on which computer accounts they should check for it. They most likely had—or could get by subpoena— unlimited authority.

"I was told to clean in there," she responded to Daniel's voiced words, not their unspoken conversation. "I need to find out where to go next." She wished she could just leave her cart here rather than rolling the heavy thing with her, but that was against policy—and she didn't want to call any more attention to herself than she had to.

Like now, when the door to the lab opened again and Ivan Rissinger strode into the hall. He glanced at them. Beth looked toward the elevator, which remained one floor below, according to the digital readout above it.

"I'm taking a bathroom break," Daniel said to the other man. "But after, would you like me to show you more of what I was working on?"

"No, I'm taking a break, too, then going back upstairs," Rissinger said. Beth wished she could glance at the expression on the executive's face, try to determine what he was thinking, but that would be a bad idea. "I understand from Manny, though, that the preparations going on in that lab are progressing well. You agree?"

The elevator arrived and the door opened. The last

thing Beth heard before rolling her cart inside was Daniel's voice. "Couldn't be better," he said.

Daniel felt frustrated.

First because he had seen Beth and couldn't really talk to her. He wanted to warn her.

While working in the lab, he had seen and heard some things that could mean the company was busy not only fudging reports in a way that could be undetectable by the FDA but also making threats against those who might disclose anything. Tacit threats, where reports about them also would not amount to usable evidence—sort of the way Beth had experienced. But threats just the same.

His fellow techies were busy covering their tails, even as they grumbled.

"Do you know why the FDA is coming a second time on such short notice?" he asked Rissinger as they both still stood in the hall. The enthusiastic lab rat who was him might as well take advantage of the opportunity to question Rissinger. "I heard they were here not long ago and thought they only made unannounced inspections if they've heard about some kind of problem with a product or something." He looked expectantly at his current companion after pasting an interested but nonaccusatory expression on his face.

"Nothing I've heard about." The gaze the older man shot toward Daniel clearly expressed an order to shut up.

Daniel wanted to keep pushing, but his cover persona wouldn't do such a thing. He took a few quick steps and reached the restroom door first, then held it open for the other guy, his ostensible superior.

"Thanks," Rissinger said.

They weren't alone inside, and Daniel had nothing else to say. He soon hurried back out.

Time to return to the lab, perform more quality-control tests that could be shown to the FDA as coming out perfectly—whether they were based on actual ingredients or not—and record voices of his fellow workers if they were still in complaint mode.

Daniel discovered, interestingly enough, that at least one of his coworkers, Samantha, was freaked-out by what was going on.

Her cubicle was around the corner from his. When he returned to the lab, he started to pass her—and saw that she was simply staring at her computer screen. Her hands were on her keyboard but she wasn't typing.

And when he looked a little closer, he saw how frozen her expression appeared beneath her wire-rimmed glasses.

The tall woman was sitting up straight in her chair. Her light brown hair was tied behind her head with a yellow band.

Maybe he should just leave her alone. He already had taken on the responsibility of making sure one person stayed safe: Beth. And yet...

Even though he couldn't protect everyone, this woman had worked here long enough to possibly have some answers for him.

He approached her, and she aimed a startled glance in his direction.

"You look as tired as I feel," he lied. Scared, yes. Tired, no. "I need some caffeine. How about you? Want to join me in the cafeteria for some coffee?"

She appeared ready to tell him to get lost, but instead she said simply, "Okay."

Since they were in the lab offices area, they neither had to sign out nor change clothes. Soon they had filled disposable cups with coffee upstairs in the cafeteria. Daniel also bought a large chocolate chip cookie for them to share.

The room filled with tables was nearly empty at this hour of the late morning. That was good. They'd be able to talk.

Daniel looked around, though. Beth might come here at any time to clean. Or maybe one of the other cleaning staff would. But at the moment, there were only a few other workers—low-level executives, since they wore dark trousers and button shirts that would have gone well with a suit jacket and tie—and the two women cashiers in view.

"How long have you worked here?" Daniel began their conversation.

"About a year and a half," she said. As she sipped her coffee, Daniel was able to see her white teeth that he'd noticed before.

She seemed more relaxed now, and he led her into a nice benign conversation—until he broached the first subject he'd intended to ask about: different levels of passwords for access to reports. He phrased it as if he were just so fascinated by the company's products that he wanted to learn all about them.

But she didn't answer. Looked as if she was going to dash off, so he changed the subject—to their work in the labs. Including… "Did you see the mess in the primary QC lab the other morning? Broken glass all over the place, and—"

"I saw it," she said. "It happens now and then, when some of the reports are bad. So mostly, they're never bad."

"Then someone does that intentionally? Who?"

"Don't know. We don't talk about it." She seemed even

more uncomfortable now than when he had suggested possible inconsistencies in tests. "Now, you'd better excuse me. I need to get back to work." And with that, her coffee cup in hand, she fled.

Chapter 17

Much later that day, Beth wheeled her cart out of the service elevator downstairs, ready to store it and head home.

As always, she would be glad to rid herself of the heavy and sweet-smelling load she'd had to push around from place to place, scrubbing and mopping and dusting when she wasn't moving the burdensome equipment.

At least she had managed to get Mary Cantrera to assign her to the entry area for a while, under strict orders to disappear when anyone looking official arrived.

Around two that afternoon, three people—two men, one woman, all in suits—had stridden through the glass doors and up to the welcome desk, where they had been greeted in a friendly manner, told to sign in and met by some of the executives from the top floor.

Beth hadn't confirmed where they'd gone after that, but she'd figured they would be taken upstairs, treated cordially as if they were really welcome, then shown to where they could dig into the computers and lab samples.

Would they find anything helpful, anything this time that could actually be used as the evidence against Corcoris?

Maybe she was growing too cynical, but she doubted it. Too bad this visit hadn't been a complete surprise. There would have been more possibilities that way.

Which made her wonder even more: How had the people here at Corcoris learned of the impending inspection?

Judge Treena wouldn't have called the executives here to warn them. Would someone from the FDA?

If so, did that mean that someone was being bribed for information—and perhaps also to make sure that whatever harmful data was found, it would disappear before anything bad could rain down on Corcoris?

She finally rolled her cart up to Mary, who scanned it, then said, "Looks fine. Everything accounted for?"

"Yes, I brought everything back except for the bottles I emptied. And I put them in the designated trash bins." Beth had been here long enough to know the basic rules.

Mary returned to her place behind the counter and looked at the computer screen there. "Okay, then. See you on Monday."

It was time to make her plea for the weekend. "Ms. Cantrera, would it be possible for me to work a few hours tomorrow? Sunday, too?" She looked down as if embarrassed. "I need the money."

Mary didn't answer right away. She seemed to be scanning something else on the computer. "Well…I suppose so. I have only a skeleton staff scheduled to come in, and with the inspection possibly ongoing… Why don't you come in tomorrow at 9:00 a.m. and stay till 2:00 p.m.? That would be helpful, and it'll earn you some overtime."

Did that mean this woman had a heart after all? Beth wasn't sure. It was more likely to indicate that she actually did believe that more grunt work like cleaning hallways or labs would impress the FDA inspectors—and thereby make her look better in the eyes of the Corcoris executives, too.

"That sounds perfect," Beth said, making her voice ring in apparent delight. "And Sunday?"

"You can talk about it tomorrow with whoever's in charge here then."

When Daniel left for the day, he made sure to walk past the area of the campus garage where Beth had left her car that morning.

The space where she'd parked was empty. Not a surprise. He had stayed a bit late, trying to look busy in the areas where the FDA inspectors were starting their work.

He'd overheard them say they were going to spend time in the manufacturing building the next morning. He would have no good reason to hang out there to eavesdrop, so that wouldn't do him any good. But they would be back in his building in the afternoon, so he made sure he had some quality-control tests of his own to run then.

Right now he really wanted to talk to Beth. He felt pleased and confident about what he believed the results of this inspection would be.

And he'd had the opportunity to plant some ideas of where to look in the mind of one of the feds—once again finding the men's room a handy place.

He reached his old clunker, unlocked the driver's door and slipped behind the steering wheel.

Then he pulled his phone from his pocket and called Beth.

"Can you talk now?" he asked, unsure if she was driving or someplace else too awkward to conduct a conversation.

"Yes, but you'd better hurry home."

His heart began racing. Was something wrong? "Why? Is everything okay?"

"Yes, but the take-out Italian food I bought us for dinner is going to get cold."

Daniel had hurried to his place. He'd scolded Beth for going there without talking to him first.

Even if the suspect who'd followed her the other day was in custody, the guy was unlikely to have chosen her coincidentally. And that meant someone else could be stalking outside his apartment building, watching for her.

He pulled into his designated spot in the building's underground garage and jumped out of his car, rushing to the street in front.

Beth was parked right where he had anticipated. Anxiously, he scanned the street for any other occupied vehicles.

She rolled down her window. "It's okay. I've been watching for anyone who didn't look like they belonged here. Just in case, I was ready to drive somewhere where there'd be lots of other people around."

He shook his head. "It's not that easy. What if—?"

"I get it. It wasn't the smartest thing, but I didn't think you'd get here this much later than me. Anyway, can we go inside now?"

He nodded, and she picked up a bag from the passenger's seat along with her purse. He opened her door, still keeping his attention on everywhere but her—for now.

"Everything seem okay to you?"

He made himself relax a little since her voice now sounded anxious.

She might as well save that anxiety until sometime when it was justified.

He was incredibly glad to see her here. So they could discuss what they had learned today, he told himself, then almost laughed aloud.

No, it wasn't just that. He was delighted to view her gorgeous, slim butt as she walked up the stairs ahead of him. His imagination tore her clothes off her as he anticipated her staying the night. In his bed.

Sharing another bout of unforgettable sex?

Maybe.

At the top of the stairs, he moved around Beth and unlocked his door. After opening it, he walked inside first.

His apartment was empty, as it should be. He took the bag from Beth and took it into the kitchen, placing it on the table.

When he came back out, she was in his living room. She had pulled her phone from her purse, but before she could call anyone he drew close and pulled her into his arms.

She responded immediately, embracing him as her mouth rose invitingly for his kiss.

He was glad to oblige.

Beth hadn't intended to kiss Daniel now. Despite what she had told him, she had been a little worried sitting out there in her car, so she hadn't wanted to take on any distractions.

But now that she was with Daniel and everything was okay, she wanted to turn on her burner phone and at last give a call to check on her parents. She knew they were okay despite that vehicle showing up in their neighborhood, with the extra security Judge Treena had arranged for. Her calling them, showing her concern, might only frighten them more, and that was one reason she'd delayed getting in touch for now. But Beth couldn't help but worry.

Yet having Daniel so near, alone in his apartment... She reacted instinctively.

Her tongue darted into his mouth to taste his, an appetizer far more enjoyable than their pending dinner. His taste was hot and enticing, his tongue suggesting coffee and mint and the rhythm of sex.

And his arms around her, the feel of his tight, toned body pressed against hers and his erection straining against her... Definitely, she now hoped, a preview of things to come.

To encourage him, and herself, she held him all the tighter. Was he as aware of her body as she was of his?

Eventually, as they both became breathless, Daniel was the one to end their kiss.

"Wow," he said, his mouth now a frustrating few inches from hers.

"Yes, wow," she said as clearly as she could muster considering the unevenness of her respiration.

"Let's eat and then talk," he continued, his businesslike tone spoiling the mood for her, as if their kiss hadn't happened at all. It clearly hadn't stirred his senses as heatedly as it had hers. His backing away more didn't help, either.

"Okay," she said, trying to sound cool and businesslike. If that was the way he wanted it, fine. She wanted it, too. They needed to discuss what they had learned that day. That was the whole reason they had gotten together. Their newly created cover of two coworkers having the hots for one another was irrelevant after hours unless they were out together for dinner. And surely they'd already overdone their restaurant meet-ups.

Well, she was the one who would benefit from their upcoming conversation. Her day had been useless, and she had little information to contribute. But what he had to say would be of interest.

"Would you mind putting the stuff out on the table?" she asked. "There's something I need to take care of."

"Sure."

Beth watched Daniel's still-enticing body move out of the living room toward the kitchen. Like it or not, that was where her hunger of the evening lay, not gobbling down a gourmet dinner of veal scaloppine and pasta that she had bought at a nearby Italian restaurant for them.

But when he was gone, she pulled her burner phone from her pocket. She'd felt it there as they kissed but she'd definitely been distracted from making any calls.

Now, when she pushed the button to turn it on, it immediately beeped, signifying a message.

That was odd.

She had given the number to her folks but made it clear that she virtually never turned the thing on. Trying to reach her, even in an emergency, wouldn't work.

Had that car thief gotten to them after all? Harmed them despite all the security Judge Treena had arranged for?

Why hadn't they left on that trip yet?

Beth pressed the button to retrieve the message.

And gasped when she heard her mother's voice say, "Andrea? It's Friday morning, and we've gotten another threat. We called the police and those other people like you said, and they've stepped up the security they're doing for us. And we really are going to take a trip, start-

ing in a couple of days. That's all fine, and we appreciate it, but the message we got said that you're in more
danger now, not us. Oh, Andrea, we're so worried about
you. Please be careful."

"What was that?" Daniel demanded about two minutes later.

Beth sat there fighting back tears of anger and frustration. She glanced at Daniel, who had rejoined her in the
living room. "My parents. They…they didn't say anything about the car thief or anything like that—but they
left a message warning me that there have been more
threats." She didn't want to mention that any threats had
been aimed at her. "They've been in touch with Judge
Treena and her staff, of course, so I'm hoping…"

"Don't lie to me, Beth. I heard part of the message.
They called because some threats were leveled at you.
It's time for you to go back to Seattle—as long as Judge
Treena has local staff to make sure you're still okay
there—and let the professionals here do their job. If
you're hurt, it won't help your family or anyone else."

His glare as he stood looking down at her was furious. As if she had caused this latest problem.

She wanted to shout at him. Sure, she was an ama-
teur, but so what? The sooner they both were successful—him as well as her—the sooner she and her family
would finally be safe.

But accusing him of ineptitude, or at least being too
slow, wouldn't solve anything. It would just underscore
and broaden their conflict.

And he wasn't inept. He was doing all he could without giving himself and her away. That took time. She
knew that.

As much as she craved immediacy.

She needed somehow to get past her own emotionalism and talk and act so rationally that Daniel would feel comfortable that working with her right here, right now, remained their best course of action.

"You're right," she told him as he sat down at the far end of the sofa from her, emphasizing how far apart their positions were. "And I don't want my family to be hurt, or me, either. But I have to assume that Preston is feeling under a lot of pressure right now, thanks to the latest FDA unscheduled investigation. He's probably lashing out in all the ways he can think of to try to get everyone to back off, and since I was involved with the last FDA inspection, maybe he assumes I'm somehow remotely involved with this one, too. But the additional threat doesn't make me want to leave. It makes me want to act all the faster, if I could."

There. He could read into it what he wanted, including her need for him to hurry, too.

"But don't you get it? Your being followed the other day, even by that perp who's a stranger, means that someone, probably Corcoris, knows who you are. Maybe they believe that scaring your family and threatening you more will somehow turn off the menace to the company that you've unleashed."

"They're smarter than that." Beth looked Daniel straight in the eye without wincing under his fury. Instead, she kept her expression neutral. "I suspect Preston's not only trying to send a message. He wants revenge. And even if he knows I'm here, it won't be easy for me to just disappear again anyway with no further repercussions. So I have to stay in my undercover role but be even more cautious. And try to help this all play out as it should. We need to bring Corcoris to justice and stop the company from endangering patients who take its drugs."

She also needed to keep her family safe, of course. And to find out once and for all what had happened to her friend and mentor, Milt Ranich.

But at least her family's safety should follow if the other results came to fruition and all the bad guys were caught and prosecuted. Her safety, too. And Milt's...?

Daniel stood. His fists were clenched at his side as if he was considering punching something.

"Look, Daniel," she said gently, fighting her inappropriate urge to rise and hug him in gratitude for his protectiveness. "Let's just keep things as they are for now. I'm aware of the risks, and I'll be careful." And make sure her family's security remained at a high level, too. "If this latest inspection finally yields what we hope it does, the situation here could be over without either of us having to get more involved."

"And if it doesn't?" He pivoted toward her. "There wasn't anything conclusive gathered today—or at least there've been no rumors that I've heard. Or— Here. Tell you what. Let's call Judge Treena again. She'll know where things stand." He whipped his phone from his pocket and pushed a button. He put the phone to his ear. In a few seconds, he said, "Hi, Judge. I— Yes. I know, but—" Daniel's expression grew steamed again. Obviously he wasn't in control of this conversation, and he wasn't happy about it.

Beth thought about trying to take over the conversation, but reminding the judge that they were acting as a team might not be the best idea—not that Her Honor was likely to have forgotten it. Instead, she gave Daniel a smile she intended to look smug but also to toss a grain of sympathy his way.

"Just tell me if the FDA team had any success at all today," Daniel finally insisted. He listened a moment longer, then closed his eyes and shook his head. "I get it. Okay, I'll be there tomorrow despite the usual smaller staff over the weekend. Just tell them how to contact me, and we'll figure out a way for me to give them what I've got to help them dig further."

And then the conversation was over. It sounded fruitless. Exasperating to Daniel, rather than as informative as he had hoped.

Beth empathized. She felt sorry to see his rigid pose that underscored how taut his muscles were, the scowl that did nothing to disguise how great-looking he was.

She worried all the more. Sure, the inspectors had been there for only an afternoon so far, but they must be feeling particularly discouraged for them to have apparently asked for help from the person who'd most likely set them officially on Corcoris.

The latest efforts that had been used by the Corcoris staff to hide whatever dirt was close enough to the surface to be uncovered by the feds must have been as successful as the last ones.

And that made Beth want to cry with frustration all over again.

Chapter 18

Daniel had already known that Judge Treena hadn't been completely satisfied with his accomplishments so far. But at least they had resulted in her success in getting another official FDA inspection for cause started.

He felt sure that something useful would occur this weekend. The end of their search? He hoped so.

Now, after hanging up with the judge, he went about setting his table, getting the delicious-looking Italian dinner Beth had brought in ready to be served. Unimportant but necessary stuff to get him to calm down.

He tried even harder to avoid taking Beth into his arms again, no matter how much his body ached to do so—and how much her curves snuggled against him would help to boost his sagging mood. But her sadness and frustration, or whatever she was feeling, had made her stay remote from him since the call, both physically and emotionally.

It was better that way. And he needed to back off, too. Both ways.

Rather than joining him, helping him get their dinner ready, she had turned his TV on and now watched a stupid sitcom. She pretended to be captivated by it.

He could pretend, too, to want to watch while sitting next to her. Close by her side.

But that wasn't going to happen. Not now.

Lord, how he wanted to reassure her. To tell her that the message she had received from her parents meant nothing. She would be fine. They would be fine.

But even if he said that in all sincerity, she would undoubtedly claim to believe it, but she wouldn't. And neither did he.

He would keep her safe, though. He had to.

But the ups and downs—the SUV that had followed her, the driver's capture and then the message from her parents—it was no wonder that she was upset. Even distraught.

She was a strong person, but it was too much.

He had to make sure this situation was finally resolved—fast. At least he appeared to be gaining some credibility as a lab technician. He'd been told that day that his responsibilities would be increased a bit more, with less supervision.

And that should help him achieve his ultimate goal.

He glanced at where Beth sat on his sofa, the remote control for the TV gripped in her slender fingers so tightly that it appeared she might want to try to use it to control not only what channel she was watching but the entire world.

Or at least her part of it.

Okay, he stopped resisting. He crossed the room and sat beside her.

She glanced at him. Her body language suggested she didn't want him any closer. That didn't mean he had to obey it.

"Here," he said. "Let's raise the volume a little." He planted his butt beside hers, ostensibly to reach the remote in her hand more easily. He was near enough to feel the heat of her stiff and slender body when he increased the sound level and handed her back the remote. He stayed right where he was.

"You like this show?" She sounded dubious.

"Not one of my faves. Believe it or not, I like some of the crime-scene types of shows. They teach me things."

She snorted. "Yeah, like how forensics and investigations don't really work."

"How do you know that?" He smiled, and as she glanced at him, he saw her try hard not to return the look. Fortunately, she lost that struggle, and her face lit up in a grin.

She was beautiful even when frowning, but now he wanted badly to take her into his arms again and kiss that beaming mouth.

"I watch those forensics shows sometimes, sure, but I also listen to the critics and read about them online. I did it even more when I was trying hard to figure out how to protect myself before I fled from this place." She sighed, and that lovely, tempting smile disappeared.

He put his arm around her shoulder and felt her stiffen even more. He had an urge to kiss her anyway until she melted into his embrace again, then almost snorted in derision at himself. Yeah, as if manhandling her now would make her fall into his arms…and back into his bed.

That gave him another thought. He didn't want her to be alone that night, not when they didn't know who was doing what around here. It could be even more dangerous to her.

So, reluctantly, yet knowing he had no choice if he wanted the chance to watch over her, he rose and headed toward the kitchen. "Let's grab our dinner. I put it in the oven. It should be warm enough by now. I want a beer with it. You?"

"Sure." She followed him into the kitchen. "I never asked if you were okay with what I brought."

"How could anyone say no to a free meal—gourmet Italian, no less. Or are you going to extract payment from me?" He hoped that the banter would get her mind off whatever she was thinking right now. Cheer her up again.

"No, no payback. Unless you consider my expecting you to leave me alone some kind of fee."

He felt almost as if she had sucker punched him. Especially when she regarded him coolly with those violet eyes, waiting for his answer.

"Nope. I get it. In fact, that's what I want, too." And he did. He needed to back off in all ways—except keeping her safe. And fulfilling his mission, of course, which now required her participation. But no emotional involvement. That was a given. "We're working toward the same goal, and we need to look like more than acquaintances if anyone sees us together on the job, but we don't actually need to be best buddies—or more—to achieve what we need to."

Though she nodded, he saw a slight twinge of something pass over her face. Regret? Or was he just hoping for some sign that she'd enjoyed their sex together, too?

He didn't even want to think about the possibility of anything more between them. She kept putting herself in danger, and he despised that.

He might protect her with his life, but when this was

all over, and she remained alive and safe and out of his life, he'd have gotten all he wanted.

As she reached the stove and looked in to check on how their dinner was heating, he headed for the refrigerator. He extracted two bottles of his favorite dark amber beer. He could always go back for more. Or even something stronger.

He had a feeling he would need something to boost his own spirits that evening, even as he remained in full control of his faculties while sparring verbally with this difficult—yet utterly hot—and completely frustrating woman.

Beth wanted to go home to her apartment that night. She yearned to be alone.

Only, if she were by herself, she might overthink the situation even more. They were at a point where something was likely to happen. The FDA's presence would probably act as a catalyst, if nothing else.

Would it be something good? Or something bad?

And after that message from her parents, she could only assume the latter, potentially aimed at her.

Even so, when Daniel suggested that she stay at his place for the night for her own protection, she wanted to scorn the idea. Tell him she would be fine. Then drive home and go to bed. Alone.

Except for her thoughts, her concerns, her fears.

As a result, instead of being certain and firm, she waffled at first. "I don't know...."

"I do."

They were in the kitchen. She had insisted on helping to rinse the dishes and put them in the dishwasher. He had stayed there, too, and although his kitchen was significantly larger than hers, she'd had to be very careful not to bump into him.

Touching him, even inadvertently, would still give her mutinous body ideas, especially if she did give in and agree to stay the night.

Now she turned decisively away from the sink and faced him. "Daniel, I appreciate what you're doing. But your job with the CIU is to collect the evidence I didn't find, not to protect me."

"As it turns out," he said wryly, "I'm not happy about how effective I've been so far at my real assignment, so at least I can do something good for the cause."

So she was part of the cause. His efforts to help her were part of his job.

Their lovemaking, assuming he had enjoyed it even a fraction as much as she had—and he'd seemed to—was just a perk.

That thought made her want to flee even more. But practically, she needed to come up with a plan.

And the only plan she had at the moment was to march into the Corcoris facilities—well, slouch her way in, in her usual guise—and find a way to finally help unearth something that the FDA or Daniel could use. Especially now, after the additional threats.

Worrying all night about her safety—and her future—wouldn't help her achieve what she wanted that weekend.

"Okay, then, I'll help you start feeling better with yourself," she told him. She smiled as she said it, not wanting to add her own jab against his ability to do his job successfully.

Besides, she remained grateful to him for all he had been doing.

"Then you'll stay here?" His handsome face brightened so much that she almost laughed. And fought an urge to give him a big mind-blowing kiss.

"Yes, but I'll sleep on the couch," she said in a tone intended to brook no contradiction.

But he did contradict it. "No need. And neither will I. My bed is big enough for us both to sleep there. And I do mean sleep. I'll keep my hands off you, as long as you keep yours off me."

Daniel felt damned proud of himself as he settled into his bed that night.

He had put on a loose T-shirt and sweatpants that were probably the most sexless things he owned—except for the similar clothes that he'd given Beth to put on.

A couple of indifferent people in unattractive garb, that was what they were.

Even so, when he got into bed after Beth was already lying down and staying as stiff as a statue on her side, he said, "Want me to roll a sheet to put between us as a barrier?"

The look she aimed at him was incredulous at first, and then she smiled.

That was when he noticed that her eyes were actually hazel. As he had suspected, the violet color must have been contact lenses, donned as part of her identity change. She hadn't taken them out before when he was around, as if she wanted to constantly keep up the ruse of who she had become, even with someone who knew who she was.

When they had engaged in that phenomenal sex together, her Beth persona was far from the shy character who mopped floors and scrubbed sinks.

But now she might be retreating into her Andrea Martinez self. For tonight, at least. And who knew how sexy

Andrea was, even though they shared the same body and undoubtedly more?

"Nope. I've got plenty of self-control." She crossed her arms over her gorgeous breasts, which were hidden beneath that large ugly green T-shirt yet clearly loose—and tempting. It looked like a challenge. She confirmed that by adding, "How about you?"

"Yep. Besides, I think we both need a good night's sleep tonight, not sex." He lay down as close to the edge of the bed as was practical without falling off, but he didn't cross his arms. Instead, he just lay on his back, arms at his sides.

Yes, his body was definitely aware of hers. That was evident, thanks to the ache he felt below. His physical interest was bound to be clear to her, too, because of the obvious bulge beneath his gray sweatpants.

"Okay to turn out the lights?" he asked. He turned slightly toward her.

Oh, yeah, she had noticed his arousal. That was clear from the way she quickly glanced away from him up at the ceiling. "Yes, fine. Good night, Daniel."

"Good night, Beth." He let his voice rumble a little, teasingly, seductively.

Let her think about that as she tried to fall asleep.

Beth lay for a while in the darkness, listening to Daniel's breathing shift from shallow to much deeper as he fell asleep.

Damn the man. She knew he'd been teasing her, but even so, her body had responded, tightening and even moistening from her attraction to him.

But eventually, she felt herself start to relax until she finally drifted into sleep.

Which was interrupted—what time was it? She

glanced toward the window across the room. A little bit of light slid in around the closed curtain. Was it dawn already?

What was that buzzer?

"Who the hell is here this early?" grumbled Daniel from beside her.

"Is that someone at the door?" Beth suddenly felt petrified. Could a person from Corcoris be here after Daniel? After her?

"Yeah. Don't worry." He looked at her in the dimness, and she saw the grim set to his strong chin, the way his hands clenched into fists at his side. "There's a good security system. I'd have to buzz whoever it is inside, and I'm not inclined to do that at this hour, whoever it is."

Even so, fully awake now, Beth padded after him in her bare feet as he exited the bedroom and went to the intercom in the wall beside the apartment's door. He pushed the button and grumbled, "Yeah? Who is it?"

"It's Judge Treena Avalon, Daniel. Let me in."

Chapter 19

Judge Treena smiled grimly as she walked up the stairs toward Daniel McManus's ID Department–funded apartment here in Moravo Beach. It was almost six-thirty in the morning, and she saw no one else in the halls or on the stairs.

She had a pretty good idea what—who—she would find at Daniel's place. She had stopped first at the building in a small nearby town where her operatives had located an apartment rented recently by "Beth Jones." No one had been home.

Daniel and Beth had confirmed to her that they were working together now to bring Corcoris down. But she also felt sure that wasn't all they were doing together.

She didn't care what her operatives did on their own time. She did care, though, what those whose identities she had helped to change did afterward.

Putting themselves back in danger, in the same situation that had led to their need for an identity change? That was definitely one of her biggest taboos.

When she reached the unit with the number she'd sought, she didn't have to knock. Daniel stood there with the door open.

"Hello, Judge," he said. "Come in. What—?"

"What am I doing here?" she interrupted. "Checking out the operation that I helped to set up. And—"

She stopped and crossed her arms as she glared into the living room of the compact apartment and saw exactly whom she'd expected sitting there watching the door while chewing on her bottom lip.

"—coming to check on one of my Transformation Unit ID-change subjects." She strode into the living room and stopped by the couch, looking down angrily at Beth. "I understand about the threats and all. And I'm doing something about that. But would you care to tell me, Ms. Jones, exactly why you're not only ignoring my most ironclad rule for TU subjects who receive new identities, but you're also ignoring my after-the-fact insistence that you go back home and let the CIU do its job?"

Beth felt embarrassed and uncomfortable. But she wouldn't let it show. She couldn't.

She looked at the woman who had helped to save her life, who had gone all out to make sure that the man who had threatened her life and tried to sexually assault her had no idea where—or who—she was.

The woman she admired so much. Whom she trusted and…well, yes, even loved like a caring aunt.

"I'm sorry, Your Honor. I understand that your rules are designed to keep me safe." As well as to keep the Covert Investigations Unit part of the Identity Division as undercover as its operatives, but mentioning that now would buy Beth nothing. "But…well, with my family still being threatened and no answers found yet, I just had to come back."

Judge Treena appeared to be in her early fifties. She was tall and slender and had a lovely face that, had she decided to take another route when younger, could have led her into a career as a model or actress.

But she had made it clear when they'd first met that she had chosen to take on very different kinds of roles—first in courtrooms as a litigating attorney and then presiding over those courtrooms as a federal judge.

She had specialized in criminal cases and had seen the injustices of what happened to people in danger because they happened to know bad things about potential felons who couldn't be prosecuted because of lack of evidence.

That was why, she'd told Andrea, she had found the right people within the U.S. Marshals office to allow her to help create the Identity Division as a nonwitness protection program so she could change the identities of those who were threatened—and conduct investigations to find the evidence that those in danger lacked.

Judge Treena's pretty face was aging, with lines that suggested myriad frowns at the wrong people over the years. Her hair was a soft shade of blond, a wavy nest about her face that she didn't seem to care much about styling.

Beth had mostly seen her in dark business suits like she wore now.

The judge stood over Beth and looked down assessingly. "Maybe," she said. "Even so, you could have left here again when I told you to. But I have a feeling there's more involved than your hanging out to try to help your family." She turned her head to look tellingly toward Daniel.

"It's nothing like that, Judge," he said. "Since Beth was followed by that car thief, she's received a message from her family that there have been more threats against them—and her. I'm just helping to keep her safe."

What he said was entirely correct, but it still pierced Beth. They had no relationship, just occasional bouts of sex to relieve tension.

And she herself had made it clear it could go no further.

But she had been—and still was—so attracted to Daniel that his acknowledging the reality aloud about their nonrelationship hurt.

"Maybe," the judge said. "If so, I commend you, Daniel, on continuing to go further than the crux of your assignment. But even so, you shouldn't have had to protect Beth. She's not your confidential informant. Her contact with you didn't put her into the danger she faces."

Beth hated to see Daniel wince, but the judge had struck a nerve.

She had reminded him of the woman whose life he'd failed to save—and the reason he felt obligated to protect Beth…while not getting emotionally involved with her.

Well, that was fine. She didn't want or need more from him. And she could take care of herself.

Beth tuned back in to what the judge, who hadn't stopped talking, was saying. "Had Beth gone home or, better yet, stayed away altogether, she would have been much safer." Her glare was leveled on Beth again.

Beth rose, wanting to feel more equal while debating with Judge Treena. "I understand what you're saying, and I'm not arguing with it—not exactly. But just staying away and hearing after the fact about what did or didn't happen—I just couldn't do that. I apologize for not following your rules. But…well, tell me. Tell us both. Did the FDA investigators find anything today to lead them to the evidence we've missed to bring Corcoris down?"

"They're still working on it," the judge said. "We need to let them do their job." She stepped forward and took Beth's hands into hers. "I really understand your frustration, Beth. You know, from our working together before, how much I want things to come together fast, for my protégés to get the justice they deserve. But it doesn't always work that way."

"You're right, Judge," Beth acknowledged, watching as Daniel drew closer to both of them behind the judge's back. His expression now looked so sympathetic that she wanted to clasp his hands, too, the way the judge still held hers. "And if something happens to me, it's all my own fault." She hoped Daniel heard that, too. She wasn't his responsibility. "But it's so important to me to get results. To save my family. And…well, you know from before that I was concerned about my friend and mentor, Milt Ranich. Around here, it's as though he never even existed. I really need to find out what happened to him, too."

"Let's get the evidence to finally prosecute Preston Corcoris and whoever's helping him commit the fraud he's been committing that endangers consumers," Daniel said, moving to a spot across the coffee table from Beth and Judge Treena. "Once we bring him down, we'll be able to stop the threats against you and your family. And if he has conspirators working with him—which he apparently does within the company and beyond—we'll find them and prosecute them, too."

That was what Beth had hoped all along. But so far… how had Corcoris been able to hide things so well? And how could she be certain that all his allies would be caught and brought down, too, to save her family? And her.

And Milt—if he was still alive.

The judge must have read her thoughts. "We don't know if your friend Milt has been placed into some kind of protection, but we doubt it. He's not one of mine, and he'd have had the evidence you lacked. Witness protection would have worked well for him if he'd been able to testify. They may have killed him, Beth," she said gently. "You still need to be prepared for that."

"On some level I am," Beth said, blinking back the tears that had flowed into her eyes. "I just need to know."

From his position near the two women, Daniel listened to their conversation and watched Beth's reactions.

He had worked with Judge Treena closely over the past couple of years, planning strategies with her for going undercover, then implementing them, several times. They'd gotten along well together. Daniel respected the head of the organization where he worked.

But he wasn't pleased about the judge's attitude right now. It was almost as if she wanted to scold him, rub his face in his past failures by mentioning his confidential informant, reminding him that Edie hadn't had to die—especially on his watch. At least partly thanks to their romantic relationship and his focus on her and little else, he'd gotten careless, and she'd been murdered by the people he had been investigating. He'd succeeded in bringing them down, but Edie was gone.

That wouldn't happen to anyone else he was working with, confidential informant or not.

He wasn't about to let his emotions get in the way as he had before. Sex? Yes. But he wasn't getting any closer to Beth than that.

But the judge also seemed to be scolding Beth, paying her back for disobedience, encouraging her to hurt all the more.

Even as she held Beth's hands in sympathy.

"I know we all hope that everything gets resolved this weekend," he said, managing not to grit his teeth. "I'll be around the labs since I'm finally trusted enough there to be working on one of the newer meds. Although I still have to run some of it by more experienced technicians, I've just been given the assignment of updating one of the quality-control tests Corcoris has been running on the weight-loss medication."

"Which should look good to the FDA," Judge Treena observed. "Although if the company's old system was really bad, that'll count against them." She released Beth's hands and turned toward Daniel.

"Their position is that it was good to begin with, but they're being proactive in keeping it as effective as possible." Daniel lifted his brows as he gave that tidbit to Judge Treena. "Meanwhile, I only saw a hint of how they were playing games. I've gotten no confirmation yet since apparently only certain execs can access the background data. But I still believe that the reports turned over to the FDA are based on fraudulent data."

"Don't they use data from the handwritten log notes that are kept during the manufacturing process?"

"Partly." Daniel exchanged glances with Beth.

They'd each hoped to get access to the actual logs when they'd visited the production center but had given up hope of that. What they really needed was to find proof of their suspicions—ones they had discussed briefly over dinner the other night.

"Since those notes I've seen scanned into the computer look perfect," he continued, "I suspect they've been doctored somehow but so far I haven't gotten hold of sufficient passwords to check out whether all the scanned-in information is identical or not. I hinted about that to the inspectors when no one else was around yesterday. I should be able to find a way to talk to them a little more, since today is Saturday. But I haven't had time alone on the computer to do any further checking of that myself with the passwords I borrowed."

"That's one reason the decision was made to have them come back here fast, unannounced, on a Friday afternoon—but I understand there was some notice after all. I'll look into that next week."

"Good." Daniel sat down in one of the armchairs facing the two women, now seated on the sofa. "Are you heading for the Corcoris facility today?" he asked the judge. If so, he wasn't sure how she would represent herself—as a federal judge? As some kind of support for the FDA inspection?

She wouldn't mention that she was even part of the CIU, let alone in charge of it. He was sure of that, even though hardly anyone had heard of the Identity Division of the U.S. Marshals Service, let alone its units, and even fewer knew what they were about. Which was a good thing, since the division's mission required that it stay as covert as possible.

"For now I plan to stay in the background. I'll let the FDA guys know I'm here and can lend a hand if needed."

He wanted to be blunt and ask why she had come at all. To check out how well he was doing?

To see if she could catch him and Beth in bed together?

In a way, she had—in the most innocent of ways. Just as well? Yes. But if she was going to make the hottest assumptions, too bad they hadn't been real that night.

"And you, Beth. I know it's Saturday, but cleaning crews sometimes can do their best work on weekends. Will you be at the Corcoris HQ today?"

"She already got a full workweek in," Daniel said. He didn't want her to be present today, since things could in fact come to a head and she would be safer somewhere else. In fact, before he headed to Corcoris, he intended to see her back to her apartment and make sure no one lay in wait for her.

"But I wanted to see if I could do anything with the FDA around," Beth said. "I've already arranged to be there. I begged for overtime for the extra wages." Her smile looked pleased, but he felt anything but.

"I don't—" he began, but he was interrupted by Judge Treena.

"Great. I'll have not only the FDA there checking things out but also my own mini CIU team—you two. I'll be eager to hear how things go."

Beth saw the irritation on Daniel's face. It wasn't hard to spot. He looked royally peeved.

Too bad. And if the judge hadn't been here, she might have teasingly kissed him to wipe his scowl away. Or not. They'd already started backing away from one another.

On the other hand, she liked the idea of trying to discombobulate him.

But instead, she had to get her day started to appear as eager to work this weekend as she'd claimed. "Gotta go," she said. "I need to head back to my place first for a change of clothes." A quick shower, too.

"I'll come with you," Daniel said. "To check things out."

"No need," she said. "I'll be careful."

But Judge Treena overrode her, too. "Won't hurt to

have a second pair of eyes." And the way she nodded at Daniel, Beth figured the judge also thought an extra pair of arms—strong muscular ones like Daniel's—wouldn't hurt, either.

"Okay," she conceded. "But let's hurry."

They got ready to leave Daniel's quickly. He accompanied her to her car and told her to stay parked till he drove around the building.

She took the opportunity to send a quick text to her family, one she probably should have sent last night, reassuring them that she was okay. She of course used the burner phone with its limited minutes and difficult-to-trace location.

When they reached her place, she obediently listened to Daniel's instructions. He checked things out, and all seemed safe. He even waited till she had showered and changed in the bathroom, the only place in her little unit where she could get some privacy, and then they left once more.

Knowing Daniel was behind her—for now—she drove back to the Corcoris campus, wondering what today would bring.

Because it was Saturday, Daniel was able to pull his car into a space directly beside Beth's. He got out and did what they'd previously decided on as their usual thing in case anyone was observing them—talking briefly, as if the nerdy lab guy had a crush on the shy cleaning-crew member.

"You sure I can't convince you to go home?" he asked softly, with those stupid glasses on and as geeky a smile as he could manage when he felt so mad.

"Of course not." She ducked her head in her pseudo shyness as if he had instead paid her a compliment.

"Then keep your phone on. Stay in touch. And I'll check on you as often as I can."

"Thanks, but no need." She pushed the button to lock her car and walked off.

He had to let her go to maintain their routine. Slowly, watching the sway of her slender form from behind as she headed out of the garage and toward the main building, he began to follow, his jaw clamped in frustration.

What he'd wanted to do, instead of pretending to flirt with the woman whose beauty was hidden beneath her pretense at being no one, was to shake her. Insist once and for all that she get out of there and leave the investigation—and potential danger—to someone who knew how to deal with it.

Now, he would not only have to do his job today and carefully assist the FDA in its inspection—and in finding anything useful hidden in the Corcoris labs and computer system—but he would also have to keep watch on Beth to make sure she didn't put herself in any further danger.

He might not have said a whole lot to her about her missing friend here, but that particularly worried him. He had apparently been even more of a threat to the company than Andrea—before—and he had disappeared. Another thing they'd continue to look into.

This was going to be an interesting day.

Daniel just hoped they both got out of it with their joint mission accomplished—and with both of them alive, healthy and safe.

As usual, Beth headed down to the basement after using her security card to get into the building. She hadn't expected to see Mary Cantrera there, since the woman had been around giving her orders for the past ten days. Her comment about Beth talking to someone else in charge about coming in on Sunday had also indicated she wouldn't be here. She should have the weekend off, shouldn't she?

But there she was, standing at the far end of a longer row of carts than Beth had seen here before. As expected, there were apparently fewer cleaners on duty today despite the need to primp labs and halls for the FDA inspectors.

Beth edged toward Mary, head bent, a subservient smile on her face. "Hi," she said. "You're working some extra time, too." She didn't inquire whether Mary needed the money, as Beth herself had claimed to.

Mary responded to her unasked question. "I'm here because I was asked to work this weekend to make sure things are done right."

Asked by whom, Beth wondered. Probably her boss. Beth knew Mary reported to the head of the Support Team, and he in turn reported to someone in Operations. She didn't know names, nor did she need to.

Her targets were several rungs above the top of that group.

"I'll do whatever I can to help. Where would you like me to clean today?"

She expected Mary to designate someplace on one of the laboratory floors, where the building staff could appear to be busily engaged in doing their jobs to impress their visitors.

Or maybe another stint cleaning the cafeteria or someplace like that.

But she intended to head upstairs to the executive floor sometime today. There would be fewer people around, so she could do some of the snooping she'd planned to do from the moment she'd arrived. That was where she might find some evidence.

And it was where she might find some answers… about Milt.

Since she had given the impression of being diligent but not overly intelligent, she should be able to get away with feigning confusion if she was caught.

She was shocked, therefore, when Mary said, "Our usual elite crew isn't here today, but Mr. Rissinger came down here himself a short while ago. The executives will be having some meetings with the inspectors later in the conference room a floor below their offices. They'll probably give the inspectors a tour of the executive floor, so they need someone there now to make sure everything is spotless. That's where I'm sending you today."

Chapter 20

Beth felt her eyes widen in surprise, and she quickly looked down at the floor.

This could be the perfect chance to finally achieve what she had come here to do.

It could also be a perfect fiasco.

She looked up at her ostensible boss with a tentative smile on her face. "Oh, this is such a wonderful opportunity to prove myself. I can do it. I know I can."

"I hope so." Mary sighed. "I just wish I had asked one of our usual staff who cleans on that floor to come in this weekend just in case." She stared hard at Beth. "You'd better do a good job. And let me know if you have any questions. Now, get up there right away."

But Beth said she needed to head to the ladies' room first.

"Hurry up," Mary cautioned her. "You know the bosses. They always want everything done yesterday."

"Oh, yes, I'll be quick."

Beth dashed down the hall. It wasn't that she needed to use the facilities—except for the mirror.

She had to look at herself, make sure she bore no resemblance to Andrea Martinez—who months ago had had an office on the executive floor.

A tiny office tucked way back in the public relations area, to be sure. But she had interfaced with a lot of the executives. Beth had no idea who would be around today, but because some Corcoris administrators were to meet with the FDA inspectors, she anticipated that Rissinger, who had demanded the cleaning, and his direct boss, Preston Corcoris, could be present.

If one of them knew who she was—and that was why that guy had been hired or whatever to follow her in that stolen vehicle—then both of them knew. But if so, why hadn't they confronted her before this?

More likely, it wasn't them but someone else who was curious about why a cleaning-staff member was hobnobbing with a lab tech—and that could be anyone in the chain of command, most likely someone fairly far down who had felt like checking it out. Either way, she would remain cautious.

Fortunately, there was no one else in the ladies' room. Beth squared her shoulders and stared into the mirror.

Who was she looking at?

The eyes, at least, belonged not to Andrea Martinez but to Beth Jones. She'd liked their bright violet shade when Beth had lived in Seattle and done proofreading for those online newspapers and magazines for a company headquartered in the area. She could be a quasi-normal person, a bit introverted, sure, since weren't all people who wanted to deal more with words than people introverted? She'd rarely had to appear in person at the office, so her appearance wasn't particularly important.

But here that eye color had probably made her stand out. Which was another good reason to assume a shy personality and watch the floor.

Her makeup was a lot different from public relations– staff member Andrea's, her hair shorter, blacker, less attractive than Andrea's longer, highlighted brown locks. Her body was more toned than Andrea's, even though she hadn't had an opportunity or a place to work out since arriving here the way she'd had in her Seattle home.

She supposed if someone looked only at her facial structure beneath the makeup and recognized her high cheekbones... Well, she could just keep her head bent as always here.

And if she found herself alone in an office with the computer on? Well, she knew one password now, thanks to Daniel's having "borrowed" Georgine Droman's and, at her urging, passing it along to her. Not that she'd ever had an opportunity to sit down at a computer here before.

Daniel. What would he have thought about her if she'd still looked like herself? Like Andrea?

It didn't matter. But she hoped she could impress him—and Judge Treena—by actually accomplishing something here.

Maybe she could even find more passwords. In their own offices, executives might post reminder notes on their monitors or in their desk drawers.

She would see.

In a few minutes, she would definitely see.

Daniel had been in the lab at his assigned cubicle for half an hour, wearing his white jacket and geek glasses as always. There were more people there than usual on a weekend—not surprising, given the flurry around the inspection.

He had an urge to drop something on the floor so he'd have an excuse to call the cleaning staff and have them send someone to take care of it. He couldn't specifically request Beth, but considering the likelihood of a reduced staff that day, he could hope he would get her.

But with the other lab techs there, all hanging over their assigned microscopes and computers, adding to the chaos there wouldn't be such a good idea.

He had to find another way to check up on Beth.

Just wandering the building wouldn't work, though. Nor would going to the cleaning storage area and asking whoever was in charge today what Beth's assignment was.

He decided to risk something else. After all, Beth wouldn't have to respond to a text if it put her in an awkward position. He headed into the hallway.

The FDA inspectors appeared to be just arriving. Weren't they supposed to be checking out the manufacturing building that morning?

They were alone, at least. This appeared like a good time to say hi…and more.

"Hello," he said, pasting on a nice geeky smile in case anyone was watching. He didn't remind the men that he'd had a brief interface with them yesterday. They'd remember it. "I so admire people like you who really care about the people who use our medicines. Of course, Corcoris works so hard on quality control, and we conduct tests all the time. I'm sure you've been told where to find the results and the reports, right?" The ones the execs wanted to be found, sure. But the rest?

The three officious-looking people, all in suits rather

than lab garb—for now, at least—maintained their cool expressions. Good. They helped to maintain his cover.

He edged closer and said softly, "Weren't you supposed to start out in the other building today?"

The only woman among them, Neva, said loudly, "It's so nice to meet a member of the staff who really gives a damn." More quietly, the young woman, without looking at him, said, "Change of plans. We've got a meeting later this morning with some of the executives. We'll check out manufacturing and packaging this afternoon."

"Got it," Daniel assured her in a whisper. He didn't dare talk to them any more, since Manny, the lab tech with whom he'd clashed now and then, emerged from the elevator. Daniel continued on his way to the restroom, figuring that Manny must think he had a bladder problem since he spent so much time there.

But so what? He headed for a stall and locked the door. He then pulled his cell phone from his pocket and texted Beth: Where are u 2day?

Her response was quick, which suggested there was no one near her—a good thing.

But when he read it, he stared, and his heart began hammering.

He had to figure out the best way to get to her. To keep an eye on her.

To protect her.

For her response was: Exec floor. All fine.

Because Ivan Rissinger had been the one to ask for someone to clean on this floor, Beth headed for his office first.

Not directly, though. Just because Andrea Martinez had known her way around this area didn't mean that lowly Beth Jones, who had never before cleaned around here, could easily figure it out.

Would it look best if she called Mary and asked directions? No, the less she remained in contact with the crew chief the better.

Fortunately, there wasn't anyone else visible to ask, either. The hallway was empty, and all office doors were shut.

They were labeled, though. And supposedly figuring out where Rissinger's lair was would allow her to walk the hall, try to see which offices were occupied… and even pop in one or two to learn anything she could up here.

Like whose computer might be on but in sleep mode.

Better yet, who had posted their password somewhere accessible, as she had already hoped she would find.

She—Andrea—knew that Rissinger's office was the next to last on the right. The farthest one, the corner office, belonged to Preston Corcoris.

She would be working next door to the hangout of the man she wanted least to see…and most to find something damning on.

Was he there right now?

Possibly. If there were to be meetings with the FDA folks as Mary had said, he would at least be coming in today.

Beth slowly wheeled her heavy cleaning cart along the carpeted hall of this floor.

Something was going to happen today. She could feel it.

She only hoped it would lead to the results she craved—and that she would come out of it okay.

And even more important, that Daniel would, too.

Her mind again focused on Daniel—as if he ever com-

pletely left her thoughts. He was in the same building.
He had already checked up on her. Should she have lied
to him about where she was? He would worry about her
being here—because she could mess things up for him
if she screwed up. Or make him look bad if she was
somehow harmed.

Not that it would hurt him the way the loss of his confidential informant had, of course. She knew that had to
be the main reason he wanted to protect her. And the only
reason he sometimes acted as if he cared about her was
their charade around here. No matter how attracted she'd
been to him, it was one-sided and nearly over.

Beth made herself push the cart forward. Time to get
to work.

Daniel was furious. He knew he should just let Beth
do as she pleased, allow her to get caught by Corcoris
or someone else.

Maybe they'd assume she was the person she appeared
to be.

Maybe they had known all along who she really was.

And he wasn't fooling himself. He would protect her
no matter what nonsense she tried. He would go look
for her shortly.

"What time is it?" he heard a voice say from outside
the bathroom stall.

"Nearly time for us to go upstairs to meet the execs."

Daniel smiled to himself as he flushed the toilet and
pushed open the door. Sure enough, the two FDA men
stood there.

"Hey, guys," he said in his dorky lab rat voice. "Don't
you think you could use a techie employee's presence
at the meeting to let you know all the wonderful things

Corcoris Pharmaceuticals is doing to ensure quality control?"

They got it. The one named Alan raised his eyebrows, and the one he knew as Doug just smiled. They understood that for whatever reason he wanted to accompany them upstairs.

"Sounds like a good idea to me," Doug said.

"Me, too," said Alan.

Beth still saw no one as she pushed the heavy cart down the hall lined not only with doors but also with oil paintings that were probably worth a fortune—unlike downstairs, where the only things resembling artwork were pictures of the Corcoris drugs on the hallway walls and posters encouraging people to work harder.

Were the silence and emptiness a good thing? Sure. She could go wherever she wanted and act totally oblivious if someone showed up and kicked her out.

She found herself heading to the executive office she had once been most familiar with—Milt Ranich's. Could her former boss and mentor have left something useful behind to point to evidence of the company's fraudulent quality control—and what had happened to him?

When she arrived there, she saw that the office was no longer designated for the head of PR but for Bert Jackson, the new VP of products, whom she'd heard dubbed the "manufacturing mogul" of Corcoris. He was in charge of all that went on inside the other building on the campus, where the products were mixed and packaged.

If anyone knew about quality control—or lack thereof—it would be Jackson.

Maybe she still could find something useful there.

She knocked on the door first, loudly enough to be

heard inside but not so loud that anyone besides someone inside that office was likely to hear it.

No answer. She carefully opened the door, which was, fortunately, unlocked. The good thing was that she could get in, but the accessibility also suggested that the guy whose office this currently was had nothing to hide.

This visit was likely to be useless.

Just in case he was there but hadn't heard her, she said, "Housekeeping." Still no response, so she pushed the door open.

This compact and completely neat office area was where his secretary would sit during working hours, so despite its being empty, Beth again remained careful since Jackson could still be in his own inner lair without knowing she had come in.

Luckily it, too, had no one inside. Beth shoved her cart in front of her, then pulled out the rags and other equipment she would use here if she were, in fact, cleaning. Instead, she looked around.

Previously, the places on this floor where she had hung out hadn't included those occupied by people in charge of manufacturing the products but by those who shouted their existence and superiority to the world. Or at least to the world of physicians and consumers.

Those people worth lying to.

Beth relaxed just a little. She thought of Daniel. Should she text him again and gloat that all was well?

No. No need to tempt fate—or to take up precious time she needed here to do some searching.

Too bad Daniel wasn't here, though. She could use an extra pair of eyes and hands to get through here as quickly as possible.

And his presence would help keep her calm and directed, as far from the shy, inept woman she had to pretend to be around other people here as Beth was from Andrea.

The office gave the impression that Jackson was proud of what he did. Awards from organizations she hadn't even heard of hung on the wall; giant and colorful plastic representations of pills sat on shelves in a cabinet that also contained photos and books on the pharmaceuticals industry.

And, of course, there was a desk with a computer on it.

Beth would head there in a minute, but first she continued to scout to see what else might be of interest.

She smiled when she noticed, just under the desk, a covered wastebasket that was labeled For Shredding. Perfect—assuming the guy hadn't sent everything potentially iffy to be destroyed before in anticipation of the FDA visit. Wearing the rubber gloves that were supposed to prevent contamination but also succeeded in preventing her from leaving fingerprints, she knelt and pulled the container toward her.

It was heavy enough to suggest it wasn't empty.

Sure enough, when she managed to pull off the top, she found a bunch of printouts of the scanned-in manufacturing log pages as well as reports. Some also appeared to be forms addressed to the FDA.

Just because they were hard copies and were intended to be shredded didn't mean they contained anything harmful to Corcoris—like the truth about the quality and contents of some of its products. But they just might. Unfortunately, she didn't have time to check them out here. Besides, experts like the FDA guys would be better able to figure that out.

But if these described things the way she hoped they did, they might provide exactly the evidence she was looking for.

Wouldn't it be fun to be able to show Daniel that she'd accomplished what she had set out to do?

Daniel waited impatiently on the second floor with the FDA guys. They were to be met by Ivan Rissinger and accompanied upstairs to the conference room.

He wished he could keep up his guise but meet them up there later. Unfortunately, for now, he had to stick with them so no one's suspicions about this nerdy lab guy would be aroused.

But he'd break away as soon as he could. He needed to know what was going on with Beth.

Could she actually be latching on to something helpful? The FDA inspectors still hadn't so far. That was what the two men had quietly related to him as they had left the men's room together to meet up with their counterpart, Neva.

Of course, they hadn't had much time here today to look. They now intended to spend most of the afternoon in the other building getting a tour and checking out the manufacturing facilities, then return to the lab area for a while.

If necessary, they'd stay around tomorrow, too.

"Hey, all of you. Welcome." Rissinger was striding down the hall toward where the four of them stood. Where had he been? He hadn't just gotten out of the elevator. "Are you ready for our meeting upstairs?"

Alan seemed to be the inspector in charge. "We sure are. How many people will be there?"

"You know," said the executive, whose lined face suggested that working here had aged him significantly, "I'm not sure. But if anyone isn't there that you want to talk to, we'll make sure they come in here today, even if they're too late for the meeting." He seemed just to notice Daniel then and frowned. "Er...how are things working out in the lab today...Daniel?" He'd seemed to make an effort before coming up with Daniel's name. Daniel was surprised he had been correct.

Or was that just an act? Was he suspicious—or even aware—of what Daniel was actually doing here?

Daniel had to remain wary of everyone, of course. Imagine the worst of all of them. "They're fine," he answered, pasting his best geek smile on his face. "I hope it's okay, but these nice FDA folks asked me to join you in the meeting in case there's any translation of chemical jargon that needs to be made."

"Of course," Rissinger said, but his smile looked forced. "Shall we go?"

He led them to the elevator, and for the first time for at least the last half hour, Daniel felt a shred of relief.

He would at least be closer to the floor Beth was on. He could seek her out. Make sure she was all right.

And find out if the damned stubborn woman had actually done as she had intended here and finally found the evidence she needed.

Nothing. Beth found nothing else in Jackson's office that might be in the least useful.

No computer passwords stuck on Post-it Notes anywhere or even inside drawers. No samples of products gone bad with labels that said they'd been sold anyway.

And there certainly weren't any indications that Milt Ranich had been its prior occupant.

Her head shaking in disappointment, she began pushing her cleaning cart toward the door.

At least she was still on the executives' floor. And the bottom of her large trash receptacle was now lined with those reports that had been earmarked for shredding. That should give her a sense of triumph, she told herself. Surely something there contained evidence that could be used against Corcoris.

But before she reached the door, it opened.

Beth froze. Her mind groped for the best way to handle this. It had to be Bert Jackson coming into his office.

Instead, it was worse. Much worse.

Preston Corcoris stomped in and glared at her.

"So here you are. I've been looking for you. You're supposed to come to my office to clean."

But the evil grin on his face told Beth that the man knew exactly who she was.

Chapter 21

Even so, Beth decided to play dumb. "Oh, sorry, sir, but I was told to start cleaning in here. I'll hurry and check with Ms. Cantrera, though, to see if it's okay for me to go to your office."

Better yet, she would check in with Daniel. She realized she was in over her head now.

She hated to admit it, but she needed Daniel's protection—and his presence to reassure her that all would work out.

She needed to leave here right away. But how could she get around Corcoris? He stood in the doorway, tall and unyielding. The pudginess of his face was exaggerated by the width of his ugly, snide smile.

"I'm the boss around here. I'm even Ms. Cantrera's boss. You'll come with me." He strode into the room toward her.

Beth quickly ducked behind her cart, then made a dash

for the open door. But he was faster. He returned to the door first and slammed it in front of her.

"You're coming with me," he repeated. "Bring your cart."

What should she do now? Going into the hallway with him seemed like the smartest move. Someone might be around, or there might be other distractions to help her get away from this evil man.

Head down, trying again to assume her cleaning-staff character, she got behind the cart and began pushing it, stopping long enough to open the door again.

"Don't even think about it," Corcoris whispered into her ear. He stood behind the cart with her, and he linked his arm in hers. She nearly shivered at the unwelcome touch. At least he still wore his suit jacket so she didn't have to feel his skin against her arm, which was bare beneath her T-shirt sleeves.

Together they pushed the heavy thing into the hall, which was empty. And there weren't any other people inside nearby offices, at least not within yelling distance. None that Beth could see.

The cart rumbled less and went slower on the carpeted floor than it did on many of the other levels where she had cleaned. The lab floor had a linoleum surface to keep it more easily cleanable, and even the cafeteria's tile was easier to push the cart along.

The extra effort delayed their progress. It gave Beth a little more time to think.

Maybe she could turn this into an opportunity. A way to finally get Preston Corcoris to admit his ongoing treachery, the way he endangered thousands of people's lives. And threatened hers and her family's.

And just maybe she could find a way to get him to say what had happened to Milt Ranich.

They reached the end of the hall. Corcoris kept hold of her arm, yanking her toward him as he pushed the door open to enter his office. He shoved her inside.

The outer area was, as with Jackson's, a secretarial office, clean and orderly and bland. But Corcoris propelled her through it and into the office beyond.

It was much as she remembered Preston Corcoris's personal domain, containing an elegant teak desk with matching chairs and tables, a leather sofa and shelves around the room's perimeter holding framed testimonials to Corcoris Pharmaceuticals products—all garnered when Preston's father had been at the company's helm. It smelled of the overly sweet shaving lotion that Corcoris favored. Beth remembered it too well.

"Wait here," Preston commanded. He went back out but was gone less than a minute before he pushed the cart through the door. "Time for you to get to work…Beth."

But she knew he didn't want her to do any cleaning. He just hadn't wanted to leave the cart in the hall to indicate where she was.

She nevertheless said, "Yes, sir," and eased her way toward the cart, her mind analyzing what she had on it that she could use as a weapon. Strong soap hurled into his eyes? A mop handle shoved into his gut? She would have to see what opportunities arose.

In the meantime, though, she'd managed, while Corcoris was so briefly in the hall, to push a button on the burner phone in her pants pocket—the button that should record their conversation.

Then there was the other phone, in the pocket on the other side. She had also pushed a button on it—to call Daniel. Assuming he had his own phone on him in the lab.

If so, he, too, would be able to hear everything. She

only hoped he would understand and get up here in time to help her.

She began going through the motions of getting ready to clean the office. "Is there someplace you'd like for me to start, sir?" She didn't look at him as she talked.

"Yes," he replied. "Right over here."

She had to look to see where he was designating. It was an inside corner of the elegantly appointed room where the wall was devoid of pictures.

But a door was suddenly opening into it. She saw that Corcoris was holding something that appeared to be a button. What was that all about?

She didn't want to find out.

"You know, sir," she said, emphasizing the word *sir* as if it were an insult, "I think I'd better leave now. I'll come back later."

"No, Andrea." All pretense was gone, and his voice sounded menacing. "You're coming with me."

All bets were off. Daniel, seeing the caller ID when he'd grabbed his muted phone after it began vibrating in his pocket, was frantic. And furious.

He had listened to what was being said.

The meeting with the FDA guys hadn't yet begun, but Corcoris executives were trickling into the conference room a floor below their offices.

Not Preston Corcoris, though.

He was with Beth. And now it was clear that Daniel's suspicions, and hers, were true. Preston knew who she really was.

Daniel had seated himself in the front row, right beside where the FDA inspectors had been told to sit by Ivan Rissinger. Georgine Droman now stood before them, chatting away with Alan Correy, Neva Therber and Doug Wrisken.

Daniel didn't bother to assume his geeky personality as he rose. "Sorry. I have to run."

Neva looked up. "Everything okay?"

Daniel didn't answer but headed toward the door, phone held tightly to his ear.

To his surprise, he was followed into the crowded hallway by the FDA gang. He shot them an irritated look. "I'll be back soon," he lied.

"Considering your suddenly dropping your undercover personality," Neva said, "I think Judge Treena would rather we go with you."

Daniel took an instant to assess them. "What do you mean?"

"We're CIU, too," Alan said.

"Andrea? Who's that?" Beth pretended to be confused even as she struggled to maintain her shy cleaner's personality. But she felt horrified.

And scared.

Daniel, are you listening? she cried out in her mind. She was in even more over her head than she'd thought.

"You, of course, my darling Andrea." Corcoris's tone was mocking, his eyes hard, as he leaned against a bookcase near the door, in effect challenging her to try to run. But she knew he'd grab her again if she tried. "I've been keeping an eye on you since you got here. Even tried to confirm who you are by having a guy I've occasionally hired to help me with some less savory activities steal a car and follow you, but that damned tech guy you've been pretending to care about got in the way. Then I sent him to break in at your parents', but he was too stupid and got caught." He glared at Beth. "Are you trying to get—what's his name? Daniel?—to file lab reports with contents you tell him to?"

Then he knew who she was, but not Daniel. She dropped some of the pretense without revealing the entire truth. "Yeah, but that Daniel's too honest, and they pretty much only have him working on some of the older stuff from your father's day that was actually safe and effective." She stood up straighter, squaring her shoulders. "It's only your more recent meds where you're filing official reports that contain fraudulent quality-control test results, right?"

"What does it matter? Our clinical trials are nothing short of perfect."

"Only because the highest-level ingredients are used for the drugs that are provided for those tests, the stuff that's used in the labs in this building. The stuff you sell to the public, with the ingredients shipped to the manufacturing building—that's another story."

"No one's proven that," Corcoris spat. "And once you're gone, no one will even try to."

That wasn't true. The wheels had already been set in motion to investigate and prosecute everyone here who was involved—him especially. But to inform him of that would only be more dangerous.

He motioned to her. "Here. Let's go." He was pointing toward the door that formed a hole in his office wall.

"What's that door?" Beth said, partly for Daniel's benefit. He had to be listening. Otherwise, she would undoubtedly die.

Like Milt?

"I'm going to show you." Corcoris's leer suggested that to go there would be dangerous. Potentially lethal.

"I don't think so."

"I do."

Beth gasped as Corcoris darted around to the front of his desk, opened a drawer and extracted a small but lethal-looking gun, which he cocked and aimed toward her.

"Are you going to shoot me if I don't?" Again, that was for Daniel's benefit. Beth hated how her voice squeaked in fear.

Too late for her to grab something from the cleaning car to protect herself. None of it would do any good against a gun anyway.

"Of course. Let's go."

She didn't move, though. To go there would certainly be foolish. If she had any chance at all to survive, she had to stay here.

Instead, she tried to keep talking. If nothing else, there would be a record of this conversation to make it easier to prosecute Corcoris…even if she was no longer around. "Is that what you did with Milt Ranich? You know, even though he seemed thoroughly disgusted by the way this company was being run, he didn't betray you."

"Really? Well, if he hadn't yet, it was only a matter of time. The guy was a wimp. He kept telling me how to run my business *for the good of our customers.*" He said the last in a high-pitched, mocking tone. "But I'd have lost millions if I'd done things his way."

Which would have been the right way, but to keep him talking Beth didn't remind him of that.

"So where is Milt now?" she asked.

"He's down there." He motioned again toward the doorway. "Come on. I'll show you."

"I don't think so." The only thing Beth could do now was to stay as stubborn as possible. If he shot her here, it'd be pretty clear who did it, another crime to add to his already huge list. "He's down there?" she asked. "Or is it his remains?"

"Whatever." He pulled the gun up and held it the way Beth saw cops aim on TV shows—stiffened and ready to shoot. "Let's go."

"No." Beth closed her eyes, bracing for the pain she knew would come—assuming she was alive long enough to feel anything.

"No!" That was another voice from outside the office door, which suddenly burst open. A beloved male voice that she had longed to hear for so many reasons. "U.S. Marshal," Daniel shouted. "Drop your weapon." He held a gun that looked even more lethal than Corcoris's, and it was aimed right at the horrible man.

Daniel got right beside Beth. She had never been happier to see anyone. He no longer looked like the lab geek he had portrayed here. He was all tough-and-muscular lawman, even wearing a protective vest over his shirt that said U.S. Marshals Service. "Drop it, Corcoris."

"You? Then you're not—" Instead of dropping his gun, the man fired.

Daniel had used his body to shove Beth out of the line of fire, but she screamed, "Daniel!" Surely he hadn't been hurt.

Apparently not, since he shot back, several rounds.

Preston Corcoris crumpled to the floor.

Daniel hurried past Beth, grabbed Corcoris's gun and checked his neck for a pulse.

"He's still alive. Call the paramedics."

"Already done," said a female voice from near the door. Only then did Beth glance that way. The three FDA inspectors were there—also wearing U.S. Marshals vests.

Really? What was going on here?

It didn't matter. Beth stood and ran over to Daniel. "Are you okay?" she asked.

"I should be asking you the same thing. It was a damned fool stunt you pulled to come up here and face him alone. You should have told me that was what you were up to."

"You'd have tried to stop me."

"You bet I would. In fact—"

Beth reached up, planted her arms around his neck and drew him down for a hard, determined kiss.

Chapter 22

It was over.

Beth let Daniel tell her what to do as EMTs came and checked over the still-alive Preston.

Their opinion was that he would survive. Good. The jerk would pay for all he had done.

They went downstairs to the conference room once Preston had been whisked away in an ambulance. The two of them intended to talk with the executives who had planned to hold a meeting with the FDA at Preston's orders. Instead, the execs were told only the minimum amount of information, but it was clear that investigations of the company would continue, and all of its executives would be interrogated to learn what they did or didn't know.

Law enforcement officials, both local and federal, began to arrive to conduct their investigation.

And Beth called her parents outright. "It'll be over

soon, Mom and Dad," she told them. "I'll be able to stay in closer touch anyway. It still would be a good idea for you to take that vacation until things are all straightened out, but I think we're all safe."

Thanks to Daniel McManus, but she didn't tell them that.

Eventually, after her information had been taken and local Moravo Beach detectives had interrogated her briefly, Beth was permitted to leave.

Daniel was waiting for her in the Corcoris main building's lobby. "Are you okay?" he asked her. "You look tired."

"Nothing that a nice dinner and a glass of wine won't cure," she told him. "I'm jazzed. That jerk is going to get his comeuppance at last. Not to mention have some nice scars where you shot him."

Daniel laughed, then grew grim. "He could have killed you and stashed your body where he said he put Milt's."

"But he didn't." She paused. "Care to celebrate with me?"

"Oh, yeah." His sexy smile made it very clear how he intended to celebrate, and that only made Beth want it all the more.

Later that night, Daniel lay awake in his bed long into the night.

Beth was breathing softly beside him, sound asleep.

Lovely, sexy, naked Beth. Their lovemaking had been extraordinary, topping even the memorable times they had engaged in sex before.

He wanted more. In fact, he wanted her beside him like this for the rest of his life.

But that wasn't going to happen. They had discussed their futures a bit over dinner. She'd talked to Judge

Treena about the possibility of taking back her former persona. It would still take a while to ensure she was safe from repercussions from any of Corcoris's coconspirators, but maybe eventually, she could come back to Moravo Beach forever.

And Daniel? He felt utterly relieved that Beth was okay. Maybe it hadn't been his job to protect her, but he had. At last he could put his sense of failure over Edie behind him. The situation had been different. He could never bring Edie back. But now he had to look forward.

With Beth? Unlikely. He enjoyed working for the CIU. He didn't see how he could be headquartered here.

They might be around this town for another few days as things settled down. Maybe as much as a week.

But then Beth Jones would return to Seattle, at least temporarily.

And undercover agent Daniel McManus would go back to the Covert Investigations Unit of the Identity Division, U.S. Marshals Service, in Washington, D.C.

He sighed and took Beth into his arms again. For now. Since it couldn't be forever.

Sitting back in her narrow seat in the government plane and sipping a glass of wine, Judge Treena Avalon was pleased.

A week had passed, and she was finally returning home.

Oh, things hadn't gone down exactly as she had planned. She had intended for Beth, formerly Andrea, to stay safely in Seattle while the first CIU undercover operative she'd sent, Daniel, gathered the evidence needed to bring that brazen jerk Preston Corcoris and his cronies down.

But things had grown more complicated with Beth's arrival. It had been time to modify her strategy.

Now she was on her way back to D.C. on a government plane. So were her three operatives who'd also gone undercover and helped to precipitate a happy ending to this operation: Neva, Alan and Doug.

They had left Preston Corcoris in federal custody in California. Yeah, the guy had survived. He might be sorry.

For now CIU had a lot of physical evidence, not to mention eyewitness testimony, that could be used against him and some of his top-ranking coconspirators in court—not just the hearsay that was all Beth had had before.

The reports Beth had rescued from the to-be-shredded pile in executive Bert Jackson's office had contained some pretty damning stuff. Preston's threats against her were pretty damning, too, and they were all recorded on her phone and Daniel McManus's.

There were indications that someone in the FDA had been accepting bribes—and warning Corcoris of pending raids. Whoever it was still hadn't been identified, but that would come.

And that person hadn't been Corcoris's sole coconspirator. Several people within Corcoris Pharmaceuticals were now suspects, and evidence was being collected to use against them. That included his assistant Ivan Rissinger, manufacturing mogul Bert Jackson and more.

And there were even indications that Preston Corcoris, if he didn't get the results in lab tests that he wanted, would sneak in at night and throw samples on the floor in a rage, although no one had ever proven—yet—that it was him.

But worst of all for him, and best for them? That some-

what secret door he had opened from his office and tried
to get Beth to go through led down into the bowels of
the headquarters building, someplace no one ever went.
Except for Corcoris.

And on one of his trips months earlier he had apparently brought along Milt Ranich, ostensibly to show the
guy some records that would exonerate not only Corcoris
but his whole company. Or that had been the implication,
at least, before Corcoris lawyered up and stopped talking.

Poor Ranich had instead been shown a gun, possibly
the same one Corcoris had leveled at Beth. Remains believed to be Ranich's were found buried down there. Forensics results and a coroner's report were still pending.

Treena knew what they would show. She lifted her
wineglass in a silent toast to Beth and Daniel and the
three musketeers behind her.

"Hey, Judge, are you okay up here alone?" That was
Neva, who'd taken off her seat belt and wended her way
up the aisle of the small, noisy but fortunately smooth
plane.

"Just fine, thanks. So, you think you might want to
quit CIU and join the FDA instead?"

"Not unless you intend to fire me." But Neva's wide
grin appeared confident that wasn't in the cards. And
she was right.

Treena unbuckled her own seat belt and went back to
chat with Neva and the rest of her team, Alan and Doug.
She thanked them again, yelling a bit over the engine
growl of their compact jet.

But her mind had been percolating on a plan. She had
two other people to stay in touch with and thank.

Soon she returned to her seat. An idea had come to
her, and she made notes about it on her laptop.

She smiled when she was done. "Let's see what happens with this," she said aloud.

A month had passed since Preston Corcoris had been shot and subsequently arrested.

Beth was on a commercial jet heading from Seattle to Washington, D.C. Judge Treena had asked her to come. There were some things about the case against Corcoris that she wanted to discuss.

Beth thumbed through the magazine on her lap, not really noticing the pages. She looked forward to seeing the judge who had helped to save her life.

Even more, she hoped she would see Daniel, who had been right there beside her. Who had definitely saved her life, and more. Had celebrated with her and made sure she was okay as she gave her initial testimony to the investigators on the case.

And then left her after several more nights of incredibly hot and wonderful sex that she would never, ever forget.

She had finally remembered to check the lottery ticket she had bought all those weeks ago. Unsurprisingly, it hadn't been a winner.

Beth hadn't cared. She had been a winner in the ways that counted—saving her life and her family's.

Her parents, her brother and his family—they were all fine now. They'd taken that planned trip while things were still being worked out. Since then, she had even been able to visit them briefly. And consider moving home.

But now…well, it would take more than luck to get her through the meetings to come, but she knew she could handle it.

Couldn't she?

She sighed now as one of the flight attendants asked if she would like a glass of water. She said yes. But what she really wanted was something to help her deal with the next couple of days.

Would it be better if she saw Daniel to officially say goodbye?

Or would it be better if she never saw him again?

"You're kidding me, aren't you?" Beth was in Judge Treena's office at the U.S. Marshals Service in the building occupied by the Department of Justice.

"Not hardly." Judge Treena glared at her from across her standard-issue metal government desk with its pristine top bare except for her computer and two stacks of files. As always when Beth had seen her, Judge Treena wore a dark suit that contrasted nicely with her unkempt blond hair. "I don't want an answer immediately unless it's positive. But your working for us makes a hell of a lot of sense, Beth."

Her voice had softened just a little. Startled, Beth looked at her. She was smiling with what appeared to be sympathy.

"What if I like proofreading online newspapers and magazines? When this is all finally over, I can move back to Moravo Beach and do that from my home, with my family around."

But Beth's mind was circulating around the job offer the judge had just presented: join the Identity Division, not as an investigator for the Covert Investigations Unit but as one of the people within the Transformation Unit who helped to create new identities for deserving victims who'd been menaced by awful, crooked people but hadn't been able to collect a shred of usable evidence to get the crooks prosecuted and in prison where they belonged.

Just as she had been not so long ago.

She wouldn't admit it to the judge, but she was extremely tempted. Helping people the way she had been helped. Having her life changed from hopeless to full of promise for actually having a future. She would be away from her family, but she could visit often.

But if she took the job, she would be headquartered in D.C.

And so was Daniel.

That was the crux of her problem. She had heard from him during the past weeks, sure. Now and then, when he'd had a few minutes to talk, not to see her.

He was on another undercover assignment. That made it a case of "don't call me, I'll call you." He could get in touch with her whenever he felt like it, but she didn't dare call or even text him. He had told her not to. Email messages? Sure. And he even responded to them occasionally.

How could she live in this area knowing that the man she loved was here but not here and not really interested in her—for, yes, she had admitted to herself, though not to him, that she had fallen for Daniel McManus. Hard. And she needed time to get over him…if she ever did.

"Well, it's ultimately up to you," Judge Treena said. "But I do have a little help on my side." A huge smile lit her gracefully aging face, surprising Beth.

But only for an instant. When Her Honor looked over Beth's shoulder to the door behind her, Beth knew who she'd see if she turned around.

Which she did.

Daniel stood there grinning sexily at her. Hungrily. Oh, heavens, why was he doing that in front of Judge Treena?

And what were the two of them still doing there, instead of rushing to the nearest hotel?

Okay. Time to get ahold of herself. But she stood quickly anyway and found herself running into Daniel's arms.

His kiss was immediate and hot, and her insides, especially down below, simmered with need.

"I've missed you," he muttered against her mouth.

"All right, you two," the judge said from behind her. "I'll give you some alone time right here, but it's a good thing I don't have a bed in this office."

Feeling her face redden, Beth backed away from Daniel, but only a little.

"Save all that for when you're by yourselves tonight," Judge Treena ordered as she moved around them and out the door. "But I expect you to do your job, Daniel, and convince Beth to accept the position I offered her." Then the judge was gone, closing the door behind her.

Beth heard herself giggle—and she couldn't recall when she'd last giggled. "So are you going to try to convince me?"

"I sure am," he responded, looking down at her with blue eyes so tender that she almost melted and accepted the job right there. "But, honestly, it's up to you whether to take the job and move here. Although after all the evenings we spent together, I still owe you a home-cooked meal—and I'm a damned good chef. Right now, though, I have something else I need to convince you to do."

Beth's heart started pounding. Surely he wasn't—

But in moments, Daniel was on his knees on the floor in front of her. "Beth Jones, aka Andrea Martinez, will you marry me?" He pulled a jewelry box out of his pocket and opened it. A lovely engagement ring sat in it, and he pulled it out as he held her hand and stood. "Please? It's been hell since we've last been together. I have to warn you that I'm keeping my job here, and that means I'll be out in the field a lot, still doing undercover work. But if I have you to come home to…well, I'll work a lot faster. I promise. So…?"

"Yes," Beth exclaimed, and then she smiled. "Yes, I'll take Judge Treena's offer."

The hope that was on Daniel's face suddenly segued into worry. "But what about my offer?"

"Oh, yes, Daniel McManus. I will definitely marry you."

He grinned as he slipped the ring onto her finger. It was gorgeous and a perfect fit.

And as they kissed, Beth knew that this, Daniel's love and anticipating spending their lives together, made up for all she had gone through.

"I love you, Daniel," she whispered against him.

"And I love you, Beth."

* * * * *

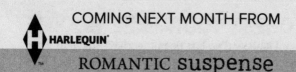

REQUEST YOUR FREE BOOKS!
2 FREE NOVELS PLUS 2 FREE GIFTS!

ⒽHARLEQUIN®

ROMANTIC suspense

Sparked by danger, fueled by passion

YES! Please send me 2 FREE Harlequin® Romantic Suspense novels and my 2 FREE gifts (gifts are worth about $10). After receiving them, if I don't wish to receive any more books, I can return the shipping statement marked "cancel." If I don't cancel, I will receive 4 brand-new novels every month and be billed just $4.74 per book in the U.S. or $5.24 per book in Canada. That's a savings of at least 14% off the cover price! It's quite a bargain! Shipping and handling is just 50¢ per book in the U.S. and 75¢ per book in Canada.* I understand that accepting the 2 free books and gifts places me under no obligation to buy anything. I can always return a shipment and cancel at any time. Even if I never buy another book, the two free books and gifts are mine to keep forever.

240/340 HDN F45N

Name _____ (PLEASE PRINT)

Address _____ Apt. #

City _____ State/Prov. _____ Zip/Postal Code

Signature (if under 18, a parent or guardian must sign)

Mail to the Harlequin® Reader Service:
IN U.S.A.: P.O. Box 1867, Buffalo, NY 14240-1867
IN CANADA: P.O. Box 609, Fort Erie, Ontario L2A 5X3

Want to try two free books from another line?
Call 1-800-873-8635 or visit www.ReaderService.com.

* Terms and prices subject to change without notice. Prices do not include applicable taxes. Sales tax applicable in N.Y. Canadian residents will be charged applicable taxes. Offer not valid in Quebec. This offer is limited to one order per household. Not valid for current subscribers to Harlequin Romantic Suspense books. All orders subject to credit approval. Credit or debit balances in a customer's account(s) may be offset by any other outstanding balance owed by or to the customer. Please allow 4 to 6 weeks for delivery. Offer available while quantities last.

Your Privacy—The Harlequin® Reader Service is committed to protecting your privacy. Our Privacy Policy is available online at www.ReaderService.com or upon request from the Harlequin Reader Service.

We make a portion of our mailing list available to reputable third parties that offer products we believe may interest you. If you prefer that we not exchange your name with third parties, or if you wish to clarify or modify your communication preferences, please visit us at www.ReaderService.com/consumerschoice or write to us at Harlequin Reader Service Preference Service, P.O. Box 9062, Buffalo, NY 14269. Include your complete name and address.

HRS13R

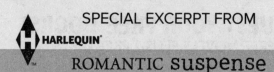
Connor Mansfield leaves witness protection to save
his daughter's life and reclaim the woman he loves,
but to have a future together, they must escape assassins
and rebuild lost trust.

Read on for a sneak peek of

THE RETURN OF CONNOR MANSFIELD

by Beth Cornelison, available January 2014 from
Harlequin® Romantic Suspense.

Darby's chin snapped up, her eyes widening. "That sounds
like a threat. What do you mean assure my silence? Connor,
what kind of thugs are you involved with?"

"Not thugs, ma'am," Jones said, pulling out his badge.
"U.S. Marshals. Connor Mansfield is under our protection as
part of WitSec, the Witness Security Program."

"U.S. Marshals?" Darby ignored Jones's badge and scowled
at him. "Since when is it okay for federal agents to kidnap
law-abiding citizens?"

Darby's stomach swirled sourly, and she held her breath,
wondering where she'd found the nerve to so openly challenge
these men. The bulges under their jackets were almost assuredly
guns. How far would these men go to *assure her silence?*

The man named Jones looked surprised. "You haven't been
kidnapped. You're free to go whenever you like."

HRSEXP1213

Darby scoffed. "Childproof locks ring a bell?"

Jones smiled and sent Connor a side glance. "Feisty."

"Just one of her many attributes," he replied.

"Marshal Raleigh," Jones said, still smiling, "would you be so kind as to unlock Ms. Kent's door for her?"

"Roger that." Raleigh pushed a button on the driver's door, and the rear door locks clicked off.

Darby blinked, startled by the turn of events. Was she really free to go, or would they shoot her in the back if she tried to leave? She glanced from the door to Jones, narrowing her eyes as she decided whether Jones was pulling a trick. She tested the door release, and it popped open. Then she paused. *Connor.*

She jerked her gaze back to Connor, the man she'd once loved and conceived a child with, and her heart staggered. This wasn't about a standoff between her and two U.S. Marshals. The important issue was Connor. Who was alive. In Witness Security. And who'd contacted Dr. Reed.

He could well be a tissue match for Savannah's bone marrow transplant. *Connor.*

She exhaled a ragged breath, shifting her gaze from one man to another. And closed the car door. "I… All right. You have my attention."

**Don't miss
THE RETURN OF CONNOR MANSFIELD
by Beth Cornelison, available January 2014 from
Harlequin® Romantic Suspense.**

HARLEQUIN®

ROMANTIC suspense

LETHAL LAWMAN
by Carla Cassidy

Trust your love...

Marlene Marcoli made the mistake of falling
in love, and almost lost her life. Hoping to
put her abusive marriage behind her,
Marlene moves to Wolf Creek, Pennsylvania.
When targeted by a madman bent on revenge,
Detective Frank Delaney vows to protect Marlene
while threatening to break down the walls that
shield her heart from love.

Look for the next title in Carla Cassidy's
Men of Wolf Creek miniseries next month.

HARLEQUIN®

ROMANTIC suspense

SECRET AGENT SECRETARY
by Melissa Cutler

No ordinary secretary

Catapulted into the middle of an international manhunt, secretary Avery has no one to rely on but herself...and Ryan, the mysterious spy with a secret connection to the enemy.

Look for the next title in Melissa Cutler's *ICE: Black Ops Defenders* miniseries next month, from Harlequin® Romantic Suspense!

Available wherever books and ebooks are sold.

Heart-racing romance, high-stakes suspense!

www.Harlequin.com

HRS278565

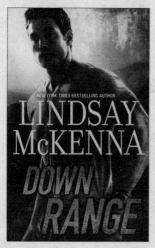